T0064152

LAHORE EXPRESS

LAHORE EXPRESS

Cyriac Thomas

PARTRIDGE
A Penguin Random House Company

To order additional copies of this book, contact
Partridge India
000 800 10062 62
orders.india@partridgepublishing.com

www.partridgepublishing.com/india

Acknowledgement

This novel tells the story of a daring love affair in the backdrop of the dirty politics of the Indian Subcontinent and of the shrewd political manipulations of global powers. The story depicts vividly the other side of politics in India and Pakistan and hints at a plausible way to solve the impasse in the love-hate relationship between the two countries.

The basic story was written as far back as 2004. Because the story is political, it had to be edited, reedited and redesigned during the past decade to fit to the political realities.

My students were the greatest supporters, who encouraged me to get this novel published without further delay. My friend, Dr. Anupama Kunal, gave me the last push to go ahead. I request my readers to enjoy reading this maiden novel, to encourage me and to criticize me.

Special thanks to Mr. Maveric Pana for the constant support and advice on all publishing matters, Ms. Gemma Ramos, for being my personal Publishing Services Assistant, and to Patridge India for agreeing to help publish this maiden novel.

Cyriac Thomas

Dedicated to

Narendra Modi

(Prime Minister of India)

a key player in global politics in the current decade
who can pull the right strings, strike the right chord
to bring about reconciliation and peace
between India and Pakistan

1

Abu Sabeer was taking his usual tour of the refugee camps. His four-wheel-drive Toyota Ranger was a familiar sight here. He was known as the saviour of the slums. He could walk into any alley and house. He was always welcome there. Everyone, especially the womenfolk, admired his 6'1" height and handsome features. They would say, 'Allah has blessed him with height and fervour. Blessed be the name of Allah.'

Abu Sabeer spotted the foursome of youths sitting on the rock and chatting. During his last visit too, he had seen them. He saw them clinging together. He was curious to know more about them. He called them to him. They came running.

'*Salaam alaikum*', they greeted him in unison.

'*Asalamu alaikum*', replied Abu Sabeer.

Turning to the young man with a thick black moustache, Sabeer asked, 'What is your name?'

'Mujeeb,' said the young man, proud that he was called out first. He had seen Sabeer several times, but always from a distance. He had heard his mother praising the selflessness of Sabeer, and his winning smile. 'These are my friends. Aslam, Anwar, and Azees,' he added in a breath. All of them were between sixteen and nineteen.

Sabeer knew they were the stuff he wanted.

1

'Why are you sitting idle and letting your bodies waste away doing nothing?' Abu Sabeer asked them.

'What can we do, sir? Who is there to help us or to give us a job? We are neither Afghans nor Pakistanis.'

'Don't call me sir. I am your brother. Every Muslim is my brother. I'll help you. Nay, I need your help. I should rather say, Allah needs you and he will help you.'

'*Allahu Akbar.* We are ready to do anything for the sake of Allah. You need just tell us what we have to do.'

'Allah needs you. With his blessing, you will get a job, dear brothers. Allahu Akbar. Allah needs all of us. But are you ready to give yourselves totally to Allah? And take up the job that he gives?'

'Whatever the job, we are ready. We trust you too.'

This was the assurance that Sabeer wanted.

'Well, then, children, my man will come this evening to pick you up. Talk to your parents and be ready by that time.'

The parents of the youngsters had come originally from Jagdalak some thirty kilometres east of Kabul, in Afghanistan. In the thick of the fights and bloodshed, they fled their village and landed here as refugees. They could take only the few dresses and some utensils. Everything else had to be left behind. Their little land, their little hut, their small farm, their relatives, friends, and the whole ambience in which they lived -- all of them were dear to them, but had to be left behind. They lived here in makeshift tents. No running water, no sewage system, no regular food supply, no proper market, no social worker, nothing which a human life needed. Living here was like hell on earth. They were left to themselves. They did not know anyone here; they were the only ones from Jagdalak. On the one hand, they regretted they had left Afghanistan, and on the other, they were happy that they were still alive. But the fact remained that they had peace neither here nor in their country, Afghanistan.

In their tents in the lonely moments of life they ruminated over the events of the past few years: the Russian invasion of Afghanistan and the imposition of the Najibullah regime, then the counter-activities of the United States with the effective support of the Taliban, the subversion of Najibullah regime, the total control of Afghanistan by Taliban, the rise of al-Qaeda, then the total turnaround of the sentiments, the birth of hatred towards the Americans, the rise of Osama Bin Laden, who became the symbol of Muslim resistance to the presence of 'infidels' in the Arab world, the invasion of Afghanistan as a result of al-Qaeda attack on the World Trade Center at New York, the final subjugation of Afghanistan by the Americans and the elevation of Hamid Karzai as the president of Afghanistan, the continued anti-American feelings and violence in the streets of Kabul and other cities.

These revolutionary events that took place in Afghanistan during the last decades did not contribute to peace. Even now blood flows on the streets and lanes of Kabul, of Kandahar, or of every other city and village of Afghanistan.

During the fight between Taliban and Dastur factions, the parents of these youngsters took refuge in the mountains and got settled at Kandhura in the North-West Frontier Province of Pakistan. They were classified as refugees and lived an ignominious life at the mercy of the Pakistan government.

Refugee camps are an excellent breeding ground of militants. Lack of work and food is a maddening problem especially for the children and youth. The youth are ready to do anything to feed themselves, their parents, and their younger brothers and sisters. Any job is welcome. And if that job fits into their religious belief, it is even better.

There are over three million Afghan refugees in Pakistan. Despite the establishment of the 'democratic' government, many of the refugees fear to go back to Afghanistan. They live still in shackles, they have no jobs, and the Pak government is unable to feed them all. Dirt is everywhere. Diarrhoea and typhoid eat into the life of the people; during the colder months, pneumonia and bronchitis are a regular feature. There is no medical facility in the camps; in urgent cases, they have to travel two kilometres to reach the next medical facility. Not even medical stores are there. Deaths due to pneumonia and typhoid are a regular event in the refugee camps. Pakistan is unable to handle the needs of its own citizens; how can it then take care of the millions of refugees who refuse to go back to Afghanistan, even after the end of al-Qaeda rule there?

———◆———

Abu Sabeer was the regional commander of the RRM (Right-wing Radical Mujahideen). He had good following in all the refugee camps. In fact, he was a specialist on such camps; he knew the location of each and every refugee camp like the back of his hand. His man came exactly at 5 p.m. that day to pick up the four new recruits.

The four youngsters were ready when the truck arrived. Altaf Hussain came out of his seat, went to the parents, and offered each of them a cover. The parents were curious to know what was in the cover. They tore open the cover and were thrilled when they saw the contents. One one-hundred dollar note! Each of the families got One hundred dollar each. 'One hundred dollar! My God, can I believe my eyes? Thank you. Thank you.' They showed the precious One hundred dollar notes to all those assembled there. They sang and danced for joy. Never had they seen so much money; that too in American dollars. They kissed the dollar notes in excitement.

The parents and relatives hugged the four children, and told them, 'Go in peace. Allah will guide and protect you. We hope you will come back soon, inshallah.' The four bade farewell to the other kith and kin, and boarded the truck, willingly and happily, with a sense of mission.

When Mujeeb came to his mother, he lost all control. He hugged her tight and wept profusely, like a small baby. Torrents of tears flowed down his cheeks and wetted the thick gown of his mother. She too was sobbing and crying. She did not know how to console him. She did not know how she would suffer his absence.

'Ma, I'll come back soon. Sooner than you think. Don't worry, Ma,' he said in one breath; he let go of her and ran to the truck with the little bundle of dress in his hands.

'We will come back soon, inshallah,' he said aloud to the crowd of relatives. He was starting to be their leader.

The new recruits were brought to a camp. They were told it was a training camp for the volunteers of Allah. The camp was situated near the border to India. They were taught that there were some enemy spots across the border, where infidels were doing things which Allah hated. So they had to cross over to the other side and put an end to those heinous crimes. That, in a nutshell, was their mission.

To cross over to enemy territory and come back safe is a difficult and risky task, but there are willing volunteers on both sides of the border; Mujeeb and friends were more than willing to take up this adventurous job. They did not have any qualm; they were not afraid of the possible consequences to their own life. In fact, they had no other choice. They had to obey. They obeyed.

The terrorists on the Pakistan side had the advantage of religion. Terrorist activities are labelled as part of jihad for them. It is the wish of Allah. You have to be part of that jihad. By sacrificing your life for Allah, you are attaining martyrdom and glory in heaven. You have to bring an end to the rule of Satan, wherever he rules. The wish of Allah is the rule of life for every Muslim.

The training camp at Saidu proved it. The four new recruits were simply happy that Allah had at last come to their rescue. God comes to the hungry in the form of bread!

They prayed five times every day. Every now and then, they murmured, '*La ilaha, illallah*'. Prayer steadied their minds. The hard military training hardened their bodies. The muscles had become firmer. The mind had become steely. They had only one thing in their mind now, to do the will of Allah. '*La ilaha, illallah*', they continued muttering every now and then.

They were convinced that Allah had called them for a particular mission; it was their duty to accomplish it, whatever it was and however difficult it might be.

During the military training, they were asked to live in the wilderness for a whole week without fire and utensils. They had to look out for their food in the wilderness. They had to eat whatever they could put their hands on. It could not be cooked by fire, because they had no matches or similar device with them. They ate whatever leaf or fruit they thought they could eat. Sometimes they got nothing; they starved. If they were lucky, they got some wild deer, or rabbits.

They could not cook the food; they ate everything raw. The first two days, it was a terrible feeling. On the one hand, they were hungry, and on the other, they could not eat things raw. Slowly the survival instinct forced them to adapt to the circumstance. They tried to dry the meat in the scorching sun and preserve it for the next day; they crushed the leaves of cactus to derive some sort of drink. They dug into the dry sand in search of water. They managed to be alive for the seven consecutive days.

Mujeeb's thoughts wandered to his home. He could see each of them vividly as in a film. His parents and sisters were eating tasty food, though the quantity was less. Their mother was a wonderful cook. Even when the food was rationed, she knew how to make the food taste great. While eating food at home, the children forgot the harsh realities outside.

After the class in the makeshift school, he would rush home to get a taste of what his mama had cooked for him. After a game in the evening, he wouldn't wait for the friends to disperse. In one mighty run, he would target home. At the door of his tent, he would shout aloud to make his presence register. 'Mama, I'm home,' he would declare. She would bring water for him to wash his dirty hands and feet, before taking him to the tiny kitchen to have his food. He would perch on the mat laid on the kitchen floor and look to Mama for food.

'Mama, can I have one more roti, please?' he cried aloud.

As the sound escaped his mouth, he knew he was in a wilderness cut off from home and all civilization; he did not even know if and when he would meet his sweet mother, nor whether he would ever meet her. He was on a mission! A mission for Allah!

On the eighth day, the trainers picked them up. After the gruelling wilderness test and the military training, they were ready for their mission and ready to face any wild situation.

During the military training, they were taught the techniques of handling rifles, using grenades, making bombs, laying mines, and handling handheld missiles. Commander Abu Sabeer saw to it that they learned all the details. He was happy that with a little bit of instruction, these illiterates could do such a wonderful job. Yes, they did learn within a week to fabricate crude but powerful country bombs. They were taught to dig holes in unsuspected places, hide the landmines, and camouflage them and wait for their explosion. Actually this exercise thrilled them.

'When I'm back home, I shall show these techniques to my peers, and they would be appalled at my technical capabilities,' so thought Aslam, while he was manufacturing his first bomb. 'I should be able to frighten and threaten the family of Mohammed Zaka, who used to threaten my father for nothing!' he thought.

Being young, they liked adventures; they liked the sound of a real explosion. When it exploded, they jumped for joy like small kids.

Then they started the training in shooting. At first they were given airguns, then crude rifles. Guns were more exciting. You shoot and see the results at once. You don't have to wait and watch. In four weeks of rigorous training, the youngsters from the refugee camp became excellent sharpshooters.

Finally, they were allowed to touch the formidable AK-47 and rocket launchers. They were seeing AK-47 for the first time in their life. They had only heard of them. How much did they long to see one! They touched it as if touching a holy relic; they took it in their hands, kissed it, held it close to their chests, and prayed to Allah. Then they placed it reverently on the ground, knelt beside it, then throwing their hands up into the holy air, they cried for joy and sang the praises of Allah. '*We are going to use it for Allah.*' They cleared their consciences and made their minds straight. They did not want to use it for any selfish motive. They had only the holy desire to use it for whatever purpose Allah's representatives told them.

Rocket launchers were real stuff to play with. They forgot how dreadful these weapons were. They were much happier about the fun these gadgets would give them. At first they were shown the stationary rocket launchers and how these functioned. Rockets were dismantled and reassembled. Then they were privileged to see and touch and carry the handheld rocket launchers, which was more fun. When they held the handheld rocket launchers, they became very important persons; they were special persons, one in a million, called for a special mission. They were no more the ordinary urchins they were at the refugee camp. They had been chosen and set apart for greater things for the glory of Allah. When they first operated it, they were thrilled at the enormous power such a small weapon wielded.

They had been in the training camp for over a year.

They could not go home to visit either parents or relatives. How much did they wish to brandish the AK-47s and the rocket launchers before them and tell them how wonderful it was to be an effective instrument in the hands of Almighty Allah?

After the training, they were packed off to an offloading station near the border. When they arrived there, they had no weapons with them. They were given pyjamas, kurtas (country shirts), headgear, and a woollen blanket. They had no weapons, not even knives.

They stayed in that offloading station for three days. Three days of expectation and suspense. They prayed to Allah; they discussed matters among themselves. Until now, they were not told what their job was and they were not supposed to ask what it was; they would just obey whatever they were told. They did their daily exercises to keep themselves fit. They did not know where they would be sent. Despite the heart-rending suspense, they never dared to ask questions. They would be told what to do.

On the fourth day at 2.30 a.m., shuffles of boots awakened them. They peeped through the window and found regular army personnel in full uniform. A military truck was stationed just near the door; its engine was running. They were perplexed. *'Are they friends or enemies? Have they come to take us and put us in prison, or simply to shoot us down mercilessly?'* Before they could think about speaking to each other about what to do, the boots were at the doorstep, and then came the commanding voice: 'Rush, rush, get ready. Out, into the truck, you four!' They had no other choice than to obey. They did not think of resisting. They got ready in no time and rushed out of the room, and off into the truck. They were huddled into the truck; there was no space in the truck for them to sit comfortably. Off went the truck to its unknown destination.

They were not sure of where they were heading to. If they were enemy soldiers, they would be executed in some dark corner of the countryside. But if they were their supporters and masters, then they were nearing the execution of their long-awaited mission. They were mentally preparing themselves for any eventuality. The better part of their minds told them that they were going to do some real task for Allah. It was their chosen time to do the wish of Allah.

There were a lot of new faces in the truck, none of whom had they seen before. When one of the soldiers showed a vaguely smiling face, they were pacified and got the assurance they sought. The heaviness of mind and uncertainty of destination had disappeared. They chatted with the soldiers and encouraged each other. A cool sense of mission engulfed their minds and bodies. Mujeeb was the leader of the group. He said at last, 'We are onto our real task, I presume.'

When Abu Sabeer recruited him, his father Mujibur Rafzanjani told him, 'Mujeeb, this is the will of Allah. Don't look back. Your life is in the hands of Allah. If you die while on this mission, you will be remembered as a martyr. But,

I am sure, you will come back safe, because Allah is kind towards his servants. Inshallah.'

Allahu Akbar. First they were taken to a camp on the outskirts of Nathia Gali. Thick bushes and pitch-darkness hid them from the world. There were about twelve warriors of Allah. None of them knew where they had to go or what they had to do. They would be told.

The next day at 11 p.m., the shuffles of boots were heard again. Commander Mohammed Ali entered the room and shouted, 'Rush, get ready, all of you,' he ordered. All the twelve recruits were ready within ten minutes.

The vehicle stopped some 200 meters away from the line of control (LOC).

Commander Mohammed told them to get out of the vehicle.

He started giving them instructions in a hushed conspiratorial voice: 'You see the fencing? Beyond that point, the Indian soldiers are active and watching. But you have to cross over to that side and have to come back within fifteen minutes. Understood?'

'Yes,' they replied.

'Are you ready to try?'

'Yes,' murmured all of them in one voice.

They did as they were told. The process was repeated three times at intervals.

'This is an exercise to make you familiar with the techniques of going over to the other side and coming back safe. Safety is the most important part of this exercise. Take as short a time as possible to do this exercise.'

The terrain was now clear for them.

They were brought back to the barrack. After several days of expectation, the mission area at least was clear to them. They had a very sound sleep that night.

———◆———

After seven days, by about midnight, Commander Mohammed Ali came back again. He picked the foursome Ali, Anwar, Azees, and Mujeeb.

Commander Mohammed Ali started to give instructions: 'You four are the specially chosen persons. You are the first ones to do some real task for Allah. Now it is the time to do or die,' he cried.

They were ready for anything, without any doubt. They were convinced of their mission and they had subjugated themselves to the wishes of Allah.

'Now see, boys, you will be given real weapons. You have to do a real mission.'

They were given four landmines, one AK-47, one country rifle, two .22-calibre pistols, four knives, and one small spade. Commander Mohammed Ali meticulously explained to them what they had to do and how they had to do it.

They were to deposit the landmines on the road between Uri and Punch before 1.45 a.m. They were shown the map of the area and Cmdr Mohammed pointed out the exact location where they had to deposit the mines. The task seemed simple for them.

They knew the way. They knew by now every inch of the border area. Doing the present job seemed very simple for them. Under the cover of pitch-darkness, they crossed over to the Indian side and camped in a lonely field away from the village of Bagt.

Bagt is a very small village. There lived not more than sixty people, in the not more than nine or ten thatched huts. All of them must be farmers. They worked hard during the day. By evening they would be dead tired and they used to sleep soundly despite the unkind weather.

The foursome reached Bagt a little after midnight. They sat in the field for fifteen minutes to watch the situation. There was no movement of human beings, not even of animals. At about 12.45 a.m., they set out again. Their target was the road from Uri to Punch.

It was a terrible night. They have never experienced such pitch-darkness in their life.

'Can night be so dark and dreadful?' they asked themselves.

But the faith in Allah, the command of the leader, and a sense of mission pushed them forward. They reached the road at 1.15 a.m., and at the curve of the road at the exact location indicated by the commander, they dug the hole, placed the mine, camouflaged it well with leaves and grass, ran to the fields, and travelled back to the Bagt area. They were just happy that they could accomplish their mission so easily and without any hitch. They enjoyed the peace and tranquillity that resulted from the accomplishment of a mission.

Physically they were exhausted, and decided to take rest for a few minutes before crossing over to Pakistan area. All of them fell asleep quickly.

The Indian military truck with twelve soldiers was coming from the Punch military barracks. They started at

2.30 a.m. and were heading for Uri, which lies some 25 km north of Punch. After 12 km, the truck ran over the mine. The grenade exploded with a deafening bang.

At Bagt, the foursome was awakened by the sound of the explosion. They jumped for joy. They sang in subdued voices, '*Allahu Akbar.*' The mission was a success. Thank God. *Allahu Akbar.* God is great. They could not contain their joy. They wept for joy. They hugged each other and murmured, '*This is our first mission and it is a grand success; Allahu Akbar.*'

Because of the extraordinary impact, the truck was thrown some thirty metres away. Eight of the ten soldiers met with sudden death; the bodies of two soldiers were shattered to pieces. The body parts and pieces of human flesh were scattered all over the place. The two survivors lay seriously injured. The smell of burning flesh was everywhere.

Because of the automatic information system built into the military trucks and into the communication system of the unit, the alarm went off at the nearby military posts at Punch and Uri. The Punch military commander in charge, Mr Narain Rao, rushed with emergency personnel and medical support to the spot. They arrived in three armoured vehicles within thirty minutes. The bloody scene shook them. They were taken aback by the brutality of the deed.

The totally damaged truck, mutilated bodies, the call for help by the survivors were all a maddening experience. One of the soldiers had lost a hand, and one of them could not be easily recognized because of severe deformation of the face. The medical personnel took charge of the two injured soldiers and carefully carried them over to the ambulance; others gathered the remains of the bodies of the ten martyrs, and packed them into ten different body bags. While carrying the body bags to the van, the emergency personnel muttered in their hearts, 'You, young men, you died for the country; we will never forget you.' Tears flowed down their cheeks. They thought about the possible reaction and emotions of their parents and relatives; this made them cry even more. They cried profusely.'

The dead soldiers were from five different states of India: Punjab, Andhra Pradesh, Uttar Pradesh, Madhya Pradesh, and Orissa. The commander took stock of the situation, studied the remains of the mines. They were manufactured in 1989 in the USA, definitely left over from the Afghan War.

The dead bodies were taken to Punch; from there, they Would be flown to New Delhi via Jammu. They would be kept in the military morgue at New Delhi till the relatives were informed and burial ceremonies were planned by them. When the relatives were ready, the bodies of the soldiers would be flown to their respective places in military planes. Military officials accompanied the bodies, to honour the dead martyrs and to console and comfort the relatives.

Very strong military patrolling of the nearby areas was immediately ordered; a combing operation was in full swing within an hour. Border areas west of Punch and Uri were carefully checked. All the fields and village clusters along the Punch–Uri road were thoroughly combed.

One of the military pickets spotted some movement in a field near Bagt. There was an exchange of fire. All stopped within fifteen minutes. Then there was deadly silence. The casualties were one soldier and four militants dead. On the dead bodies of the militants, their identity cards revealed their names: Mujeeb, Aslam, Anwar, and Azees. The bodies of the militants were recovered and sent to Red Cross in Baramula to be handed over to Pakistan, if they cared to claim the bodies. No one claimed the bodies.

———— ⋈ ————

The event at Uri was received with shock and dismay by the political leadership of India. They condemned the cross-border terrorism in the usual strong terms.

There was heated discussion in the Parliament the next day about the event. All the Members of Parliament (MPs), whether they belonged to the ruling party or to the opposition, were unanimous in their condemnation of Pakistan. They strongly criticized Pakistan's tacit support to the terrorists and wanted the country to shun any and every contact with Pakistan.

All discussion with Pakistan regarding opening up further road links to Pakistan and the resumption of rail and air service also should be kept in cold storage. It was a setback to the process of normalization.

In the aftermath of the terrorist attack at Punch, the sports ministry denied permission to the BCCI (Board of Cricket Control of India) to play cricket in Pakistan.

BCCI had been planning to have a test series in Pakistan. It would have been played in the four cities of Karachi, Lahore, Islamabad, and Rawalpindi.

'Let the relationship between the two countries improve to a satisfactory level; only then can we have matches between the two countries. That is the official stand,' the minister declared pompously.

Any occasion to show a cold shoulder to the BCCI was welcome to Sports Minister Rita Choudhari. She hated the present bosses of BCCI. When the Indian cricket team was going last August to England for a one-day international match, the sports minister had just one small request:

'Include two players from my constituency in the list of players.'

The so-called players of the minister were naturally her relatives, near or distant, who wanted a free foreign trip at the cost of BCCI!

The BCCI flatly refused, saying that there was a selection process for finalizing the list of players, and it could not arbitrarily include any outsider in the list. It was not right; the players would resent it, and it would create bad precedence, they argued.

The sports minister did not take it lightly. The relationship of the sports minister with the BCCI was not in the best of form since then. She looked for every occasion to dig at the BCCI.

Whenever the BCCI wanted some permission from her, she stuck to the letter of the law. Her first reaction was to deny permission. Then after prolonged negotiations, things would be straightened out.

This time when the BCCI asked for permission to play in Pakistan, she had an added reason to deny—the recent incident at the border!

It was a lucrative business for BCCI to play matches inside or outside India. BCCI makes millions of rupees from such matches. Also, the players earn handsomely. Many of the political bigwigs are unhappy that they cannot have a piece of the cake, like any other undertaking in the country!

She declared, 'India has played with Pakistan in the past, but in the present circumstances, we cannot allow any matches with Pakistan till further orders.'

But the common man was wondering why permission should be obtained from the sports ministry at all to organize sports events.

Pakistan's cricket board strongly criticized India for that. They said India was mixing politics with sports. This would affect all the future games, including the several tournaments scheduled for the coming years. Little did they know that this was really an internal war between the BCCI and the sports minister!

'Will this acrimony between our two nations ever end?' asked Anwar.

'It should end. The sooner the better,' replied Anand. 'I have decided to work for it. I look for the day when our two countries will be friends, like the two of us.'

Anand happened to be the only son of Indian Defence Minister Charles Almeida Rodriguez. And Anwar was the son of Mohammed Siddiqui, the Pakistan high commissioner at New Delhi. They met during an iftar function at the Rashtrapati Bhavan, the official residence of the president of India at Delhi. Since that evening, Anand became thick with Anwar, despite the official enmity between the two countries.

2

Despite the skirmishes along the Indo-Pak border, the bus service between New Delhi and Lahore continued unabated. The bus service from Delhi to Lahore was inaugurated by the former Indian prime minister; he travelled in the first bus to Lahore. Since then, there was always rush for a seat in that bus; in both directions, the bus was always full. Many Indians travel to Lahore; many Pakistanis come to India too for various purposes, like visiting relatives, tourism, medical treatment, etc.

'Anand, do you mind coming to Lahore for a change?' asked Anwar over the phone.

Anand was excited. Without thinking about the pros and cons of it, he said, 'Yes. I'd like very much to do that.'

Anand is a businessman. He is in the hospitality industry. He owns one five-star hotel in Delhi, the famous New Delhi International Hotel, and another one, Hotel New Malabar Hills, at Mumbai beach.

Anand could not resist the invitation of his friend Anwar to visit Pakistan. His hectic business schedules kept Anand from going to Pakistan. But Anwar continued inviting Anand.

When he booked a seat on the Lahore bus, he did not want to reveal his identity. So he travelled under a different name, Abdul Hameed.

He came to the bus station and looked around to make sure no one he knew was there. Then quickly he rushed into the bus. He was the last man to take a seat in the bus going to Lahore.

As usual, the Lahore Express, as it is popularly called, crossed the Indian border at Wagah Post and proceeded to Lahore. The relatives were informed well in advance, and they waited for their people at the bus station of Lahore to give them a warm reception.

Despite the sporadic outburst along the border and the confrontations of the army with the militants and the expressions of desperation by political leaders, the Lahore Express continued to ply between New Delhi and Lahore. It was the only live bridge between the two countries.

Anand thoroughly enjoyed the journey, though it was long and tedious. He was not used to such long bus rides. At Lahore, he alighted from the bus, took a taxi, and checked into Lahore Marriott International.

After shower and change of dress, he dialled room service, ordered a coffee with toast bread and scrambled egg. Then he dialled his friend, Anwar Siddiqui.

'Hi, Anwar, this is Anand, sorry, Abdul Hameed.'

'Hi, Anand, sorry, Abdul. How was the trip?'

'Excellent. Tiring, but interesting. I could see a lot of the countryside on both sides of the border. It was a pleasure watching the countryside. Can you come over?'

'Of course. I was expecting your call. I will be there in thirty minutes. I live a bit far away from the Marriott.'

Lahore had become a favourite tourist spot for Indians ever since the inauguration of the Delhi–Lahore bus service a few years ago. All major international newspapers and

TV channels covered the event. It was an event similar to the one initiated by Willy Brandt, the then-chancellor of West Germany, while the two Germanys were still divided. After that historic visit of Willy Brandt to East Germany, there was a stream of West Germans wishing to visit East Germany.

Despite the big publicity, the establishment of the bus link did not cut much ice in the relationship between the two nations.

One bus of the Road Transport Corporation of Lahore travelled every day from Lahore to New Delhi, and one of the Delhi Transport Corporation from New Delhi to Lahore. Relatives could visit relatives and businessmen could meet businessmen. The apathy and strangeness were slowly giving way to ordinariness and everyday routine. More and more people ventured to travel to the other side. There was more warmth and friendliness in the relationships on both sides of the border. This was on a very private level, though.

The bus link and all the travels and encounters on the personal plane did not change the rigid political attitudes on either side. India continued to allege that Pakistan's government, or rather its secret service, ISI, was encouraging insurgency activities in Kashmir and that all necessary protection was given to the terrorists (the Pakistan side called them freedom fighters) who would cross to the Indian side over the line of control. It was alleged that not only in Kashmir but also in the whole of India, the ISI agents were very active; the Indian intelligence department believed that the ISI was doing everything possible to destabilize and subvert the Indian government.

The Pakistan side believed that the Indian side was on the lookout for any occasion to create troubles and instability in Pakistan. Any confrontation between the Shiites and Sunnis was a welcome occasion for the Indian intelligence sleuths to create trouble in the enemy territory, they said. In short, the relationship between the two nations was, even to this date, one of enmity and distrust; it was alleged that subversive activities were practiced by both the nations, through their respective secret service agencies.

Anwar was punctual. He arrived as promised. It took him only twenty-five minutes to reach the hotel.

Anand ordered a coffee for his friend. 'Anwar, what can I see here in Lahore during the next two days? After two days, I wish to go to Islamabad; then I will come back to Lahore to take the bus back to India.'

'Tonight, Anand, there is a performance of the Pakistani pop idol Hasina, who happens to be the daughter of Abdul Lateef, the current president of our country. She is giving her gala music performance in the Lahore cricket stadium. If you like good music, you should be there.'

'Why not? I am not a musician, but I enjoy music, especially the fast ones. Let's go.'

'I shall arrange tickets for you and me. I will be back here at 6.30 p.m. to pick you up. In the meantime take a nap and refresh yourself.'

'OK, bye.'

'Till then, bye.'

The music performance was excellent. The crowd in the stadium was hysterical. Anand too enjoyed it thoroughly. He never believed that Pakistanis had such wonderful musical talent.

At the end of the show, Anwar took Anand to the green room. Although Anwar and Hasina were good friends, it was not easy to get near Hasina because of the high-level security accorded to her. Anwar's political connections helped. Hasina was a charming personality.

'Anwar, how is your sister, Razila, doing?' asked Hasina in her sweet heavenly voice. 'Give her my regards,' she said.

'This is my friend Abdul from India.' Anand was thrilled at the beauty of Hasina, but tried to hide his admiration. He was not introduced as the son of Charles Almeida Rodriguez, the defence minister of India!

'How nice. It is very rare that I meet an Indian here in Pakistan,' Hasina said with an air of surprise.

'It's rare, I know. The relationship between our two countries is such that there is very little or no communication between the ordinary people on either side of the border,' Anand philosophized. After each phrase, he was gasping for air; the pristine beauty of Hasina, so to say, suffocated him. He looked at her in wonderment and enjoyed every bit of her beauty.

'The New Delhi–Lahore bus is giving us the occasion to meet each other. It is a small step.'

'It is a big step.' She did not want to politicize but was very frank in her opinions. 'It would be easier for the political leadership if the two people met each other and exchanged views, and became friends. If the people become friends, the political leadership need only to ratify it.' She was happy that she could make such a political statement with such ease.

'We have to go a long way,' Anand said.

The conversation went on for a few minutes. Hasina expressed her wish to come one day to India to perform.

'Is that far away?' asked Anand.

'Need not be, Mr Abdul Hameed,' answered Hasina. 'Let's all make small steps towards that big goal.'

'Let us hope for the best,' said he.

For the sake of formality, she gave him her visiting card. Anand fumbled and excused himself, saying, 'Sorry, I did not bring my visiting card. I did not think I would meet anybody in this stadium. You can get my details from Anwar, your friend. And I will definitely keep in touch with you.'

'That's fine. Goodnight.'

'Goodnight!'

They said goodbye.

Anand wished to prolong the conversation; he wanted to immerse himself in her melodious voice. He wanted to enjoy her enchanting presence, the enticing smile, the attractive figure, the mesmerizing words. The soft skin, how he longed to touch it, at least once—why didn't she shake hands with him? How sad!

On his way back to the hotel, Anand was restless. He rebuked himself for not shaking hands with her; he should have tried to touch her heavenly hand at least once! What a radiant face she had!

Could people be so beautiful, he wondered. He was all adoration and admiration. The person of Hasina was haunting him ever since.

She used only the perfumes of Yves Saint Laurent, but it was not what attracted him. He was taken up by the fragrance of her personal beauty and brilliance. 'Will I ever be able to forget her inebriating fragrance?' The fashionable dress she wore spoke volumes about her exquisite taste in fashion and decorum, but that did not move him at all; he was carried away by the innate splendour and natural rhythm of her words. The mellifluous voice of her conversation captured his attention much more. 'Can women be so beautiful and intelligent at the same time?' he asked himself. Her perfectly lined teeth shone like Hyderabadi pearls. Before her beautifully chiselled nose, Cleopatra would be a silly shadow. Her perfectly sculptured body curves reminded one of Michelangelo's aesthetic greatness. Well, God's hands were much more creative and his creations much more lavish and unfathomable.

All along his taxi ride to Hotel Marriott, he was seeing her talking to him. It was like a trance! He wanted just to listen to her for hours!

'Sir, we are there!' said the taxi driver.

He was awoken from his daydreaming.

'Of course!' he said. He jumped out of the taxi, paid the taxi man, and proceeded to his room. He did not see anything in the lounge; he did not bother to look at anyone. In a swift pace, he walked to his room and quickly closed the door shut. He had lost all appetite. He wanted to sit quiet for some time in order to digest the experience he had this evening.

On my way back from Islamabad I shall try to visit her again. Maybe Anwar will be helpful, he mused. But how?

The next day, Anand wound up his visit at Islamabad and came back to Lahore and took the bus back to India.

———◆———

Every morning after a shower, Hasina went to her MacBook Pro laptop and checked her email. There would be hundreds of them every day, from her fans, friends, relatives, music companies, composers. She was prompt in writing appropriate replies to each one of them. She spent almost an hour in the morning at her computer.

Today she noticed an email from India. It was absolutely unexpected. She had no friends in India; she could not have one. And no one ever dared to send her one. But today . . . It read:

Dear Hasina,

I do not know if you remember me. We met at Lahore. After your stunning performance at the Lahore cricket stadium last Saturday, Anwar and I met you in the green room. Your voice is marvellous. I am not flattering you. It's real good. Do you perform also outside Pakistan? If yes, please let me know. I may not be able to travel often to Pakistan. Not this year anyway. Next time I visit a music store, I shall look for your CDs.

I would like to make a correction. Anwar introduced me as Abdul Hameed. In my travel documents, I was that name. Otherwise, I would not have had the chance to visit your country. My real name is Anand. I hope you won't take it amiss. I am sorry. I was not supposed to reveal my identity at that moment, because of the hordes of security people around you.

I shall be writing to you again. Keep in touch.

With warm regards,
Anand

She was actually thrilled by the flattery. She read it again. Again. And again. But she did not know what to write in the reply.

Will it be prudent to send an email to India? I am a Pakistani and he an Indian. I am not just any Pakistani. My father is the president of Pakistan. It would not be prudent to write emails to an unknown Indian. It could create problems, at least later on . . .

She decided to ignore his email.

After a cursory surfing through the other emails, she went to the dining room. Breakfast was ready. With the breakfast, she got the surface mail.

At the other end of the world, Anand was checking his emails almost every hour, to find out whether there was any response from Hasina.

She must be angry that he met her under another name. She must be thinking that this was a ploy of the Indian secret service organizations. *Maybe she thinks I could be a spy trying to get near her.*

Anand continued to send Hasina emails day after day. He wished that Hasina would change her mind someday and send him an email.

Hasina did read all the emails of Anand, but refused to send a reply. This one-way traffic went on for quite some time.

Dear Hasina,

I have been to Germany last week. It was very cold there. Snow was falling. I had difficulty adjusting to the extreme cold climate there. When

I visited the Berliner Symphonie orchestra the other day, I thought about your performance at Lahore. Your voice is superb and there is no one who can beat you in the matter. Your voice is fantastic. Your melodious songs are still ringing in my ears.

Sincerely,
Anand

No reply. But Anand did not give up.

When he went for the music show of Sonu Nigam and Kavita Krishnamurthy in Mumbai, he remembered Hasina again. He sent another email:

Dear Hasina,

This evening, I had the privilege to attend the music concert of Sonu Nigam and Kavita Krishnamurthy. Every time I hear a female singer, automatically I go back to Lahore Stadium. I would imagine that I am hearing your fast numbers. And I would see you on the screen of my memory. One day I am sure, you will perform here in Mumbai and enthral the music lovers of this megacity.

You may not be able to send me a reply. But I am sure you will take time to read my emails.

Yours sincerely,
Anand

Anand met Anwar Siddiqui during an iftar party in Delhi during the month of Ramzan. Iftar parties are held all over India, especially in Delhi. It is the function of ending the fast for the day. Both Hindus and Muslims organize iftar parties.

Dear Hasina,

During the iftar reception of the Minister of Human Resource Development I met your friend, Anwar Siddiqui. We chatted for a long time over the biriyani. During the conversation, Siddiqui mentioned about your performance at Kathmandu the other day. I did not know about it, otherwise I would have tried my level best to be there. Next time, be sure I will be at Kathmandu if you are performing there. I wish to hear your melodious voice once more. Will you inform me, if you are going to perform at Kathmandu again?

Sincerely,
Anand

After some fifty emails from Anand and six months, Hasina sent him a reply.

Anand had almost given up his hope, when he received the following email. When he saw it, he was exuberant.

She wrote:

Dear Mr Anand,

Thank you for your emails. You must have noticed that I have been ignoring your mails in the hope that you will finally give up. It is better so. I don't think that I can carry on an email correspondence with you. There are a lot of security reasons, personal as well. If it comes to light, it can be very damaging and embarrassing for my father.

I respect your sentiments. But let us stop here.

Hasina

This is fine with me, mulled Anand. *At least she has been receiving my emails and reading them too. Well, this is a good sign!* He read it over and over again.

———◆———

The noted film producer Jayaprakash Dutta was planning to produce his new Hindi film *Deevani Deevani*. Nazeer Khan was the hero and Mishma Rana the heroine. Nazeer Khan had the cut of the famous Amitabh Bachchan and the liveliness of Shah Rukh Khan.

Now Jayaprakash Dutta had to make a decision regarding the songs. He called his assistant Devan Arora and asked him, 'Dev, whom shall we fix for the song of Mishma? I want something special.'

'Shall we go for Asha Bhosle or Kavita Krishnamurthy? Or shall we go for someone like Shreya Ghoshal or Alka Yagnik?" asked Arora.

'None of these.' After a pause, he asked, 'Have you heard of the Pakistani singer Hasina?'

'No.'

'You should try to get some of her CDs. She has a superb voice. Her melodious voice will be a sensation in this part of the world,' said Dutta.

Arora called in the production executive and asked him to get all possible CDs of Hasina.

Wishes of Dutta were commands for Arora. He went to his room with CDs of Hasina and heard all of them at one sitting. He was impressed by the songs.

He went to the room of Dutta and exclaimed, 'She is superb, sir, absolutely superb.'

'Well then, shall we fix her? But remember you are going to have a lot of news. Also a lot of criticism,' said Dutta.

'Why criticism? If she sings well, we are going to have her. No one can stop us.' Arora was businesslike.

'Because she is Pakistani,' said Dutta. 'A lot of encouragement and support will come too, because she is Pakistani.'

'Criticism and opposition will give more publicity for our film,' said the businessman in Arora.

'Do you know exactly who Hasina is?' asked Dutta.

'No, no. How can we Indians know about Pakistani singers? Actually we should have some means to meet them too. At any rate, her voice is marvellous, that is enough for us. The rest of it is not our concern.'

'You should know who she is,' said Dutta.

'Of course, who is she? Tell me, who is she?'

'She is the daughter of Abdul Lateef, the president of Pakistan,' disclosed Dutta.

This was totally new to Arora. He was mumbling for words. Though he heard all of her music, he did not bother to find out who she was.

'I did not know that. In that case, I do not know if we will be able to get her. Even if we get her for our film, the criticisms will be tougher, but the publicity is assured.'

'But remember there will be a lot of opposition and violence from the part of the Brahma Sena and similar fanatic outfits,' cautioned Dutta.

'But that will ensure even more publicity for the film' was the answer of Arora.

Dutta knew how to get the required clearance from the foreign ministry, and from the ministry of information and broadcasting.

Mohan Dixit would do the music, and the sound recording would be done in Kathmandu at the famous Himalaya Studios. Hasina could go there without any problem. Mishma would take care of all the arrangements for the star singer. Mishma was the daughter of the Nepal prime minister.

The voice of Hasina was superb. Jayaprakash Dutta and his colleagues were all praise for her. Mishma could not hide her admiration for Hasina. She ran to the voice room as soon as the recording was over, and hugged Hasina and would not let her go for quite some time. 'You are fantastic, you are simply marvellous,' Mishma kept on repeating.

What was considered as a stunt for publicity turned out to be the biggest selling point, the USP for the film. It also turned out to be a big leap forward in the direction of India-Pakistan reconciliation.

Of late, hill resorts had been a success. Tucked away in the white snowy mountains and glaciers, the resorts would offer the visitors the bliss of silence and exuberance of cold thin air. The magical geological shapes, the landscape marked by soft whitish colour and bluish shadows at 5,000-metre height were views you see nowhere in the world. The rugged mountains offered a spectacular view for the visitors who wished to enjoy nature in its pristine beauty. The atmosphere was soothing and friendly.

Anand did not want to miss an opportunity to strengthen his hospitality business. He decided to put up a five-star resort at 5,000-metre-high Manali under the name Manali International Hill Resort.

The road trek from Shimla to Bilaspur, through Dehar, Sundernagar, Malther, Mandi, Pandoh, Aut was exhilarating; pure nature confronted the soft air. From Aut, you really start the upward climb. The first 60 kilometres to Kullu via Bajaura and Bhuntar takes more than two hours. Then the real climb starts from Kullu. The 40-kilometre climb from Kullu through Kukri Ser, Raison, Katrain, Patlikuhl, Jagatsuch to Manali is an exhilarating and refreshing adventure trip which normally takes two more hours.

A 5-kilometre ride to Palchan will show you the extraordinary area for skiing. Manali is the ideal resort location if you look for customers who wish to enjoy the soothing touch of snow. There was no doubt that the resort would be a success. It would also attract ski lovers from all over the world.

The work on the Manali International Hill Resort was going on smoothly. The Mahesh and Mahesh Company were the main contractors. They were famous for their timing. If they took up a job, they would finish one day earlier than agreed. And the work would have an M&M touch to it. So Anand was sure the resort could be opened within fifteen months.

Precisely as agreed upon, the work of the Manali International Hill Resort was ready. The 5th of October was the date fixed for its official opening. The prime minister of Nepal, Manickchand Rana, had agreed to inaugurate the Manali International Hill Resort. It was going to be the best hotel in this part of the world. The inauguration would be followed by a fantastic colourful cultural event, with a lot of film stars, and world-renowned musicians and models would arrive from all over the world on the occasion.

Anand wanted to have also Hasina on the occasion. But he did not dare to invite her. Instead he requested Mishma Rana to invite Hasina for the function, because he said all the top artistes of film and fashion were coming. He knew that Hasina had sung for Mishma and that she was by now thick with Mishma, so Hasina would not reject her request. Mishma readily agreed to oblige, and phoned up Hasina. Hasina was giving her big show at Beijing on the third of October and so she agreed to arrive at Kathmandu from Beijing on her way back.

And the big day arrived. Hasina landed at Kathmandu on the previous day and stayed at Kathmandu Royal Retreat. When she arrived for the function, Mishma ran to her, hugged her tight, and took her directly to her father, Manickchand Rana, Prime Minister of Nepal. Then she introduced her to Mr. Anand who was standing next to the Prime Minister. But Mishma was surprised to learn that they knew each other. But Hasina was matter-of-fact, and maybe even a bit aloof. After pleasantries, each of them went their separate ways.

The big function of inauguration was really colourful. Hasina went to the green room to meet the famous Indian singers and composers. She was thrilled to have such an opportunity to meet the leading singers of India.

Mishma Rana had invited Hasina for lunch at their home the next day. Anand naturally was invited too.

Nepal PM Manickchand Rana was surprised to see the children of two known enemies at his banquet.

Pakistani ISI and Indian RAW were activated. They were watching. Reports were flying to both the capitals.

The very next day early morning, Hasina flew back to Pakistan. Her father was not home. He was on an official visit to Karachi.

The next morning, Hasina was going through her emails when her father, Abdul Lateef, approached her. He was visibly shaken. He was furious when he heard of her rendezvous with Anand.

'You are meeting the son of the guy who points his gun at me!' These words were trying to escape the prison of his gnashing teeth. But he did control himself.

'How dare you go to a function organized by Anand? Don't you know that he is the son of Mr Charles Almeida Rodriguez, the defence minister of India?' he blurted out.

Hasina was silent. She knew her father. She knew his likes and dislikes, his tempers and sensibilities. She knew it would come. She expected this outburst of anger and frustration. She was silent. She cast her eyes to the floor and stood like a culprit.

'It is he who is behind all the machinations against Pakistan. He is a Christian who wishes to lead a modern crusade against our Muslim country. He wants to humiliate us and, if possible, to destroy us. If we did not have the nuclear device, they would have fought the Kargil war on our soil, rather than on the mountains of Kargil.'

Hasina was still silent. She was wondering why these statesmen could not talk to each other, just like she and Anand did. She had nothing against Anand, and Anand had nothing against her. They even liked each other, though on the unconscious level. Then who was fighting for whom? Given the occasion and atmosphere, the people of India and Pakistan could live like real neighbours, like friends. Simple friends without the heavy baggage of history, without the weight of painful memories.

'Let this be a warning. You should not meet him again. You should consider this as a closed chapter.'

'Yes, Dad, as you wish.'

But Hasina was restless the rest of the day. At night, she could hardly sleep. She tossed herself from side to side. But sleep was eluding her. Her mind started reviewing her visit at Kathmandu, each of the faces she met there. Anand's stood out as the best. He was good-looking, energetic. Although he was a businessman, he was very humble in his manners and sweet in his responses. Except for the fact that he was an Indian, there was nothing you'd find fault with him. When he laughed, he was the most handsome; she even kept looking at him for more time than she should. One or two times she sort of stared at him. During the dinner, she misplaced some dishes just because she was inattentive, was preoccupied with the handsome images of the young man sitting across. He liked jokes, he was fond of films; he knew almost all the songs of the Hindi movies. He even remembered the lyrics of her own song, which she sang for the movie *Deevani, Deevani* of Jayaprakash Dutta. The more she tried to get rid of his memories, the more strongly his handsome face popped up again and again.

'Can I forget this handsome gentleman, ever?'

Charles Almeida was equally furious.

'How dare you ever meet the daughter of the enemy no. 1 of India?

'What will the people of our country think if they come to know that the children of arch-enemies are having secret meets in the Himalayas? I will lose my credibility and the respectable position in the government. The fanatic Hindus, and their fellow travellers like the Bharat Kranti Dal, Brahma Sena, etc., will clamour for my blood.'

Anand was silent. What he said was right. If this thing became public, Charles Almeida's image would be tarnished, especially in the present season of coalition governments.

Still, so reasoned Anand, why couldn't the responsible people in the government try to meet their counterparts, and hold some talks privately, secretly? Like what we youngsters do! That might solve all the problems. That might make the enormous military expenses superfluous, unnecessary. The money so saved could be used for something creative—for example, to create jobs for the millions of poor on both sides of the border.

'Anyway, Anand, take this matter in all seriousness. The media will come to know of it, sometime or the other. Our intelligence wing, or right-wing radicals in that organization, may leak this news to the media. That will open the floodgate of speculations and unnecessary investigations. So stop it, once and for all.'

Anand was not convinced. He could not convince himself, but he agreed that the arguments were valid, seen from the side of the defence minister, seen from the side of the coalition politics, seen through the mirrors of Indian politics at large. But he was not sure whether the people of India could be kept in bondage like this for long. People as such do not have anything against Pakistan. If the politicians could forget it, it would be over in a week's time.

Further, Anand was not sure, if he could ever forget Hasina just like that. At any rate, he did say, 'OK, Dad. I do not want to bring you into any controversy. India needs an honest politician like you. People like you are a rare specimen in India. I am proud of you.'

He wanted to say, *But, dear Dad, think of the enormous wastage of money and manpower for the sake of historical blunders committed by the separation of states on the basis of religion.*

Dr Akshay Manohar Tiwari (54), the architect of the indigenously built Ashoka atomic reactor and the chief designer of micro-nuclear warheads, was appointed as the chairman of the Atomic Energy Commission and secretary of the Atomic Energy Department.

Though the Department of Atomic Energy is directly under the prime minister, Charles Almeida had a say in everything atomic, because he was the defence minister. So Charles Almeida was consulted and his concurrence was given for this appointment.

In the light of the recent skirmishes along the border, India wanted to demonstrate that it was very serious about its nuclear options.

Pakistan media reacted strongly to this appointment by saying that India has made this appointment with a view to further develop the atomic weapons and to carry on escalation on the strategic front.

3

Anand flew to Kathmandu to visit his Manali International Hill Resort and to assess its progress. He had a sitting with General Manager Norbert MacFarland and his staff. They congratulated him for his business acumen and assured him that within the short span of a few months, the resort would begin to make satisfactory returns.

Anand was not miserly in praising the efficiency of his staff.

Before boarding the plane back to New Delhi, he did pay a short visit to Chief Minister Manickchand Rana. Rana was happy to receive Anand and thanked him for investing in his country.

He reached the airport just in time, just a few minutes before the security check area was closed. Being well known to the security and immigration people, he was rushed through all the formalities. He phoned up home and told his mom that he was going to board the plane and that he would be home at New Delhi within two hours.

He always travelled in the executive class. Stewards and air hostesses were very considerate to him. The Indian Airlines officials were considerate not only to the ministers and the bureaucrats, but also to all their kith and kin. Keeping them in good humour would be rewarded with some benefits in the future, they knew. It might be difficult to meet the minister, but in the Indian political economy, the son of a minister is as important as the minister himself. A son of a minister can make or break somebody. He can help or destroy. And the ministers are good fathers, and fulfil the wishes, good and bad, of their progeny. The bureaucrats and officers were aware of that. Connection is all that matters in this part of the world! Connection to a VVIP is then very, very important.

In other countries, the term VIP is enough, but in a vast country like ours, we need to add one more V. Those who are now VIP do not give up the title and its benefits even after they quit the office. They hang on to the rights of a VIP. They hang on, for example, to the residence which was allotted to them, when they became minister or officer. They do not give up these posh residences, even if the government issues them eviction notices. They hold on shamelessly to whatever benefits they enjoyed. They hang on to the bodyguards allotted to them while they were in office. To withdraw these benefits a lot of correspondences have to be done between departments. It may take years before the proper orders are passed and executed. The former ministers and officers know this labyrinthine methodology of the Indian bureaucracy. So they hang on to benefits till they cannot go further.

These officials think they become important in the eyes of the common man, if a few black cats surround them. 'Black cats' is the name given to the high-level security staff, Special Protection Force (SPG).

Thus the list of VIPs goes on increasing with every successive government. Hence to indicate the real VIPs, the term VVIP had to be coined! It would not raise any eyebrows if you begin to hear VVVIP within a few years. India is growing!

Anand had a royal welcome on board, because the steward and air hostesses knew who he was. Other passengers did not know him, so they were surprised at the special show of respect to him. They thought this handsome young man might be a film star!

Anand eased himself into the aisle seat in business class. He preferred aisle seats. He then could get up and stroll at will without disturbing other passengers.

The plane took off in a very happy mood. The plane was almost full. But it made the staff worried, because it meant a lot of work.

Dr Tariq Azaruddin was reading the *Times of India* from the time he was seated. He was quite uneasy in his seat. He too was sitting in an aisle seat, but in the economy class. He was feeling the pinch of the revolver in his pocket.

He had very anxious moments at the security gate. But the security men had cleared him like a VVIP. He was searched, the security guard felt the gun but pretended not to have seen anything, and he was rushed through. The security guards knew that Dr Tariq was the personal physician of the king of Nepal. If money could not, connections can work wonders like this at Kathmandu, Tariq told himself. You should have connections at the right places!

His friends too were cleared at the immigration counters and security area in the same manner. All of them belonged to the Islamic Justice war group.

The plane reached the level of 30,000 feet. The seat-belt sign was switched off. Dr Tariq Azaruddin freed himself from the seat belt, stood up from his seat, and went to row

17 and murmured something in Urdu to the person in seat no. 17C. Then he proceeded to 19C and talked to that passenger for half a minute. Then he proceeded to seat no. 12C and repeated the same ritual.

Dr Tariq was an Indian physician working at the famous Kathmandu Royal Hospital. He was working in Kathmandu for the past twelve years. He had established good, friendly personal relations with the Nepalese royalty as well; his connection to the royalty was known to the airport officials as well. Today he was going home to India.

He came back to his seat, sat there for five minutes, then stood up again and proceeded to the area where the air hostesses were preparing food for the passengers, and told one of them, 'I need to talk to the pilot. Can I, please?'

He knew what she would say.

'It's not possible now. Now we have to distribute food to passengers. The pilot has to be served first. Maybe after his lunch I shall ask for his permission.'

He pressed his revolver at her side. She felt something cold rubbing harshly against her ribs. At first she did not know what that meant.

'Will you please go back to your seat, sir?' she said in a rather rough voice.

Then he pressed the gun more tightly.

'Don't make any false moves, lady. You are young. Don't you want to live longer? Just obey what I say,' he said.

She had only heard of it in the regular classes a few years back. Hijack and violence on the flying aircraft! She knew this was the rarest of things that could happen on board. She was facing it head-on now. Now she was feeling it in her body.

In a hushed but very serious voice, he said, 'Move to the pilot's cabin, open the door, and let me in. As soon as I am in, just go back to your seat, sit, and sweat. Don't do anything else,' he commanded.

She did as he said. She pulled down her seat near the food area and strapped herself with the seat belt. She was trembling from fear. Her hands were shivering. She started to perspire profusely.

As soon as he entered the cabin, he was swift in his movements. He pressed the gun on the head of the pilot and said, 'This is a hijack.' He had rehearsed it several times in his private room. 'We do not want to hurt any of you. All of your passengers will be safe, if you obey us. Our motive is just political. But don't resist us. Just obey what we say.' He had now put his revolver firmly pointed to the back of the pilot's neck. He pressed it harder so that he should feel the hardness of it; the reality should sink into his mind. Maybe the pilot thought it was some joke!

It was no joke, the pilot realized.

By the time Dr Tariq entered the pilot's cabin, the other three friends had taken position in pre-planned areas of the aircraft and flashed their guns and grenades, and told everybody to put their hands to the back of their heads, duck forward, put their faces to their laps and keep their cool.

'Nobody should move from their seats. This is a command. Our boss has taken control of the plane now. He is in the pilot's cabin. He will give you the commands now. Follow what he says.'

At the same moment, the captain's voice came through the speakers: 'Dear passengers, this is your captain speaking. This seems to be a hijack. We are asked to divert the plane to an unknown destination. We are just trying to do what the hijackers are saying. Everybody should keep their cool, and leave the matter of your safety to me. Do not move from your seats. The hijackers are armed and can harm you and the plane. Just keep calm. Pray if you wish. Everything will be OK.'

Some of the passengers made some exclamations; there was total chaos in the plane, but all of a sudden, all noises died down. There was a deadly silence all over.

One of the Chinese passengers was busy working on his laptop when the announcement came. Immediately he punched the necessary keys and got Internet connection and emailed to CNN that the Indian Airlines flight IC-345 from Nepal to New Delhi was hijacked. This happened even before the hijackers started checking the passengers. The news was a big scoop for CNN. It was immediately flashed all over the world. Indian Airlines officials and the Indian government came to know of it immediately. Unluckily, it seemed Doordarsan, the Indian government TV channel, as usual did not know about it till after many hours; it did not mention anything about it for quite some time in its news bulletins.

The entire ministry and bureaucracy were immediately alerted and were in panic. The defence minister was in Orissa on official visit. He rushed back to New Delhi in an air force plane. He knew that his son too was in the plane, but no one else knew of his travel details. The home ministry officials were busy finding out the list of passengers. Home ministry, foreign ministry, and the defence ministry were in high alert. A working group was formed with the Home Secretary, Foreign Secretary, and Defence Secretary as members. 'Let's wait and watch. We do not know where they are heading to,' said Home Minister Tilak Mardani.

Arun K. Singh was in his office. He was inspector general of police, in charge of VVIP security. He had a posh office near the South Block, in New Delhi, where the most important dignitaries live. Nothing unusual was happening on the security front. So he was in a very relaxed and happy mood. He took away his coat and put it on his chair, unbuttoned the top of his shirt, sat lazily in his chair, and dialled the number of his new girlfriend Jolly, who immediately came to the phone.

'Hi, this is Arun.'

'I know. I can quite well distinguish your voice by now,' she said.

T. K. Thakur, another IG in the Delhi police, initiated their relationship.

Jolly was tall and slim, and extremely good-looking. Her laugh was enchanting. She was efficient both in doing her job and in managing people. Thakur met her in the South Delhi TV studio, where she was an editor. He had some TV ambitions. He produced one music album, which Jolly edited. From that time, their friendship began to blossom. He used to get immense pleasure in taking her to parties and introducing her to his friends, as if she were his prized possession.

She too enjoyed his company, though she was prudent enough to avoid his undue overtures, for which he was famous. She knew about his other affairs, about his girls in Goa, Pune, and Mumbai.

Thakur was immensely rich too. He had his own police methods to amass money. If there was a very serious case, he would be there to help the victim. He would interfere in the case proceedings and let the FIRs (first information reports) of the police leave enough loopholes so that the victim could escape the worst consequences at a later point of the proceedings. In return, he would ask for and get cash and landed property. Thus he had millions of rupees in the bank accounts, but the accounts of course were in the names of his wife and children, and of his brothers and trusted cousins. He had landed property in most of the major cities of India. Besides, he owned several thriving mini industrial concerns in Delhi—of course in the names of his son and wife.

Arun Kumar Singh was thick with Thakur, and Jolly used to frequent their parties. Partying was her weakness. At the parties, she enjoyed every second and consumed whatever was served—if it was liquor, she would consume it without adding soda or water as many weak men do; she preferred pure whisky or brandy. In matters of food, her special liking went to tandoori chicken.

'What have you planned for the evening?' asked Arun.

'Actually nothing special,' she said very diplomatically. She was sitting in the South Delhi TV studio in the Noida industrial area.

'But I have some friends here, who want to get something edited quickly for Aaj Thak channel. The programme has to come on Aaj Thak day after tomorrow, so it has to reach their office at the latest by tomorrow noon. I am busy with that.'

'Is it that urgent? You are very fast at editing. You can finish it quickly, I know. So can we go out for dinner tonight?' Arun did not say what he had planned for, after the dinner.

She could read his mind, and was even more evasive. 'I may be able to finish it by midnight. Besides I do not want to disappoint the two guys who are here, who wouldn't let me go without finishing this work. What if we meet on Monday for lunch? Is that OK with you?'

'Even if it is going to be late night, I can wait. We shall meet at the Midland Elite Hotel at Connaught Place, and can have dinner there.'

She knew what he was aiming at. She did not want to give in so easily. She said, 'Arun, it's better if we met tomorrow for lunch.'

'Lunch is a difficult matter. During the day, I will be in my uniform, Jolly. I can't change into civil dress without attracting the attention of my staff, who are always with me. You know, officially I have a driver, who is always a problem. I have to convince him also. See the sad plight of an IG of police. Have mercy on him!' he begged.

'I too am in a similar dilemma. If I go away now without finishing the work, these fellows will think of all possible things, and you know film people, they are good at gossiping. So let us stick to tomorrow.'

At that moment, the red phone rang.

Arun had a battery of phones on his table. The red one was the hotline to the home ministry, the green one to the CBI (Central Bureau of Investigation), and the blue one for his DIG, and all the others were the usual off-white ones.

One of the white phones was marked for his personal communications. It was the phone he liked. Whenever he wanted to call his personal friends, he used it.

But if any of those coloured phones rang, he couldn't disregard them. The red one meant red alert.

'What a nuisance!' he cursed. 'Jols, it seems there is some emergency. I shall call you later.'

He put the white phone down, and took the red phone and attended to the call from the home ministry.

'There has been a hijacking of an Indian Airlines plane. Check the list of passengers and find out if any VIPs are on that flight.'

'To my knowledge, Anand, the son of the defence minister, is on that flight from Kathmandu.' Arun tried to show off his knowledge of affairs.

'Are you sure?'

'Of course.'

'How did you know?'

'Anand always tells me when he goes out of the country,' said Arun.

'Quickly come over to the ministry office and join the special task force for emergency operations.'

He called immediately the wife of the defence minister and told her of the matter, which she knew by now. Arun then informed the private secretary of the defence minister too about it. It was his duty to do so.

When the news of Anand's presence on the plane was known, there was much more commotion and confusion among all those concerned. The home ministry was concerned about how the hijackers knew about the movements of Anand.

Arun left the office in haste and rushed to the home ministry building. He was absolutely not in the mood. The hijack drama was only a drama, he thought. But he was disappointed that the incident forced him to break off the sweet chat he had with his sweetheart, Jols.

———◆———

When Pakistan refused permission, Dr Tariq talked to his boss, who had good connections in Tehran; he talked to the government of Iran and asked for help. The Indian government in its turn contacted the Tehran government. That paved the way for letting the hijacked plane land at Tehran International Airport. The spokesperson of Iranian foreign affairs came on line and talked to Dr Tariq in Arabic. As soon as the terms were clarified, the plane was cleared to land at Tehran airport.

The only demand India made to Iran was that the passengers should be safe, and as soon as the hijack drama was over, the hijackers too should be extradited to India.

'Follow the directions of the traffic control tower,' the spokesman of the Iran foreign ministry told Dr Tariq. The Iran foreign office gave appropriate orders to the traffic control about what to do with regard to this flight.

The plane landed safely at the Tehran airstrip and was asked to stay clear of the main runway.

The demands, negotiations, arguments, counterarguments began. The negotiators were trying their best to prolong the negotiations to gain time to make up their minds. The main demand was the release of the dreaded terrorist Mazood Nazar, who was in a high-security jail at Tihar, and five others kept in different jails of India on charges of murder, sabotage, espionage, and terrorist activities, especially the bomb blasts of the Bombay Stock Exchange.

A hotline to New Delhi was established from Tehran airport. The foreign secretary, S. B. Singh, was asked to fly to Tehran to guide the negotiations. It was his duty to keep in touch with the task force in New Delhi.

The foreign secretary S. B. Singh was always fond of flying out of India, for any flimsy reason. If possible he would like to be in the planes 24 hours a day and 365 days a year. He liked to fly out as often as possible, and enjoyed chatting with the beautiful air hostesses. He envied their husbands.

His wife, Aruna, very often complained about the frequency of his foreign travels. She complained to her father that he was rarely seen at home. Her father would console her, saying that it was part of his job. Every time the son-in-law went on a foreign trip, the father-in-law felt proud of him, and would insist that he bring him a bottle of whisky, preferably Royal Salute of Chivas Regal; the specially shaped bottle in the blue velvet cover was a beauty to look at. It had become his weakness. If his son-in-law brought a new brand of a mobile phone, perfumes, or some designer shirts, he was happy, but his Royal Salute should never be forgotten!

The proud father-in-law would exhibit the presents to his neighbours and relatives and boast that his son-in-law went every now and then to a foreign country. They enjoyed his hospitality, and prayed to all the gods that the nice son-in-law be given further opportunity to go abroad.

S. B. Singh was fond of good food. And he was lucky that his wife Aruna was a good cook. He enjoyed the food she cooked, but there ended his need of her. He didn't expect anything else from her. He could not, because she was illiterate; she had never visited a school. Though she managed the household chores expertly, the most worrying part was that she was not at all good-looking. For that reason, he never took her to parties. He abhorred looking at her.

'She is a simple village woman, very publicity shy,' he would declare to his friends.

She was the daughter of B. K. Sharma, the richest man of the Faridpur village near Rai Bareilly in Uttar Pradesh.

If you have a son, you must get a handsome dowry. That was the attitude of Bhupinder Singh, the father of S. B. Singh. Bhupinder Singh was a very ordinary farmer. He lived in the traditional house, which was constructed by his grandfather some forty-five years ago; he lived without pomp and decors. But he was lavish with his sons when it came to the matter of education. He wanted his sons to have good education, because only then could he demand thick dowries! On matters of dowry, he had an uncompromising stand.

'Jalaja, when do you think our son will finish his studies?' Bhupinder Singh used to ask his wife.

'Last time when he came for Diwali, he said he would finish before the next Diwali.'

'So we should think of arranging his marriage after next Diwali. We have to find a very suitable girl for him.' The father had laid down his plan regarding the future of his son S. B. Singh.

'My brother's daughter, Sheila, may be suitable for him,' suggested Jalaja, Bhupinder's wife.

'What dowry can her father give us?' Singh did not hide his prime consideration.

After all, marriage is the only time a father can get back at least part of the money he spent on his son's education and upbringing! Once married, the son is lost to the father; a woman, a stranger, is going to be his confidante and everything. He will forget his mother and, above all, his father in the process, so let me have at least some money back which I have spent on him.

So went on the arguments in the mind of Bhupinder Singh. He was thinking like every father in the Indian subcontinent. A son means dowry, wealth, prosperity! But a daughter means loss of wealth; the parents are always anxious about saving enough money to pay the dowry. That is why some concerned mothers cry when a daughter is born! That is why some husbands persecute the wife, if she gives birth to a daughter!

'He will give a decent dowry. I am sure of that. But I can't say how much,' shot back the cautious wife Jalaja. She wanted the son to remain in *her* family.

'After spending this much money on his education, I cannot agree to any proposal that brings less than five million rupees in dowry,' he boasted. 'With that money I will build him a new house, buy a new car, and the balance will remain with me in my bank account to care for my old age. When we become old, Jalaja, how will we live, if there is no money in the bank?' argued Bhupinder Singh.

B. K. Sharma, the father of Aruna, had specialized in marrying away his daughters to IAS or IFS or IPS officers. He was crazy about these titles.

IAS means Indian Administrative Service. Those who get trained as IAS officers take up executive positions in the government machinery. They become district collectors (who often behave like kings of the district concerned and handle a lot of government money). They become, later on, secretaries in government departments. They can go up to the level of chief secretary. Throughout their career ladder, they have a lot of means to take good bribes and amass money.

IFS means Indian Foreign Service. Persons with IFS training are posted in the foreign ministry. They may be posted in the various embassies of the country, and can become ambassadors later on in life. The IFS officers, if they are clever, can stash away big amounts from government money that goes into the embassies and consulates. They will be involved in making business deals with foreign governments, and can cleverly manage a good chunk of commissions! Of course, you should have brains!

IPS means Indian Police Service. Persons trained for IPS hold key posts in the police department. They start as assistant superintendent of police (ASP) in a district, and climb up the ladder to become superintendent of police (SP) or deputy inspector general (DIG) or inspector general (IG) or director general of police (DGP). The hierarchy of the police starts with constable, then head constable, SI (or sub-inspector), CI (circle inspector), and DySP (deputy superintendent of police); these are lower grades and meant for those who do not hold an IPS.

Because of the excessive number of IPS holders in the department and because of the automatic promotion arrangements, there are a number of SP title-holders without adequate assignments. You have even several DGPs in one state. Since the police department itself cannot use many of them, they are posted as managing directors of various public sector undertakings (PSU) of the government. Without any stake in a company, you become its managing director and handle all the assets of the company; this leads naturally to widespread corruption and malpractice. If the managing director has no stake in the company, he is not worried about the profit or loss of the company. That is why many of the PSUs run into heavy loss and bankruptcy. Most of the PSUs are sort of white elephants, kept alive just to give top jobs to IAS or IPS officers or to political leaders.

Amita, the eldest daughter of Sharma, was married to Jayakar Malhotra, an IAS officer; he was Secretary of Culture in the Central Ministry. He had built a palatial home in the outskirts of Delhi and really enjoyed life. His two sons were finishing their post-graduation from Jawaharlal Nehru University, and may follow the footsteps of their father and opt for IAS careers.

The next daughter, Anuradha, was married to Anand Sharma, another IAS officer, who held the portfolio of educational secretary in the Uttar Pradesh government. He had purchased a property of 10 acres just on the city periphery of Lucknow and was in the process of constructing a posh farmhouse with over 12,000 sq. ft. of built-up area. All the verandas and rooms had beautiful black granite on the floor. The garden in front of the house was the envy of his colleagues. Whenever the father-in-law Sharma went to Lucknow, he liked to spend at least one week with his daughter and enjoy the stylish life and uninterrupted festival mood in the house. Every day there were visitors from every walk of life. Some went there to get some favours from him, and others were there to offer him his dues!

Persons having the tag of IAS, IFS, IRS (Indian Revenue Service), or IPS really rule the country. They are the cream of the bureaucracy. Their influence and means to raise immense wealth were well known to B. K. Sharma. His offer for his third daughter, Aruna, was ten million rupees. He was just on the lookout for the best available boy in the marriage market.

Bhupinder Singh could not resist it; the amount was beyond his wildest expectations. He literally commanded his son to marry the girl he (the father) had chosen for him. S. B. Singh was fresh from the Indian Administrative College at Mussoorie and was just starting his career. His first posting was in the foreign ministry as an undersecretary at New Delhi. That was a probationary post. It was a small beginning. He, as a probationary, would get a net monthly salary of 32788 rupees after all tax deductions. With that, he could just live in New Delhi; no luxury could be entertained with that amount of money. For a bachelor, that was enough.

S. B. Singh was not in a hurry to marry, and was not enthusiastic about this proposal.

He said, 'Dadaji, I haven't even seen her!'

Bhupinder Singh shot back, 'I, your dear mother, and your dearest uncle saw her. She is good-looking. From our conversation with her, we concluded that she has a good character and is extremely intelligent. If *we* are satisfied with her, you can conclude that she is good for you too. Think of it, her sisters are all married to high-ranking IAS officials!"

S. B. Singh told his father that once he got a good posting, he might get better proposals and bigger dowry.

(He too was eyeing for money!) But the calculating father did not budge. Finally, S. B. Singh had to succumb to the command of his father, the subtle persuasions of his mother, and the lure of money.

The marriage was conducted with pomp at the behest of his father-in-law, who willingly met all the expenses of the marriage and the festive dinner for over 2,000 people from both sides. A big temporary tent was set up and was lavishly decorated. With illumination and decorations, it looked like the palace of the former king of Lucknow. The marriage party was the talk of the town for weeks.

But the married life was a catastrophe. Uneasiness started on the very first day of the marriage. When the make-up and ornaments were removed, Aruna looked horrible. The very look of Aruna without make-up annoyed him. Besides, she could not utter a single word of English. Even the Hindi she spoke was a dialect known only to some rural people; he could not understand a word she spoke. He knew he had to live with it; he had no other choice, and he decided to live with it in spite of everything. Since he felt boredom and nausea, he went to the side room and slept on the sofa.

Being an intelligent man, Singh meticulously planned out a way of life for him. First of all, he decided not to take her to any parties. Whenever invitations came for weddings, or similar functions, he went alone. He would say his wife was busy at home and looked after the children. Nobody knew that they had no issue. If there was any function in her family, she went alone. He was ashamed to accompany her! And he would say he had official duty.

So every occasion to avoid home and Aruna was heaven for S. B. Singh. At the slightest suggestion of a foreign trip,

S. B. Singh was ready. He always kept one bag ready for foreign trips. 'You do not know when the government would ask me to go abroad!' was his justification to his dear wife!

Hijack of an Indian Airlines plane created a crisis situation, a national crisis, but for S. B. Singh, it was a God-given occasion for celebration. His main consideration was that he could be away from home for a few days, a few days of peace and freedom from the thorny marriage he was in. Hotels were for him really homes away from home, even if it was in the dull wilderness of Iran.

On the way back he thought of making a stopover at Dubai. Oh, Dubai and its duty-free shops! His heart was jumping. He could be generous to himself after the hijack ordeal and take rest for two or three days in Dubai, before (unwillingly) flying back to India. 'Be happy, my soul! Let there be hijacks every month!' he told his heart.

The travel department in his ministry had made all the arrangements. His staff had already loaded his bags into the official limousine. He boarded the vehicle, and off it went to the Indira Gandhi International Airport.

———◆———

4

Om Prasad, the Minister of State in the Central Government, was a close friend of Defence Minister Charles Almeida. Almeida and Prasad had studied law together at the Bangalore Law College. Since then, Almeida was thick with his friend Prasad. They remained so, although they joined different political parties.

Both of them helped each other in every situation. If Charles Almeida needed any help, Om Prasad was there to help him, and vice versa.

By sheer coincidence, both of them became ministers in the present government of India. Almeida was defence minister, but Prasad was a junior minister in the Ministry of Finance. Almeida was a cabinet minister, whereas Prasad was MOS, in the lower echelon of power. (Cabinet ministers are senior ministers and have independent charge of major departments. They wield immense authority and power in the government. MOS are Ministers of State, junior ministers without independent charge of a department.)

Despite the difference in their grade, they kept their friendship intact; they used to meet every now and then for family celebrations like marriages, birthdays, etc. Now that Om Prasad was a junior minister, he needed the help of Almeida much more than before, and Charles Almeida would readily comply with Prasad's requests. Everybody around them knew of their close relationship.

Prasad was a Minister of State. Such ministers are known in Delhi as MOS. He was an MP (Member of Parliament) in the Lok Sabha and belonged to the BPP (Bharat People's Party).

The real Parliament or Lok Sabha is elected directly by the people. The elected representatives are called Members of Parliament or MPs. There are 550 MPs in the Lok Sabha.

Rajya Sabha is supposed to be the Parliament of the States. It is a place where the interests of each state government has to be discussed. But in India it is just a duplication of the Lok Sabha or Lower House. Party representation is strong, and state representation abysmally weak.

There had been discussion to follow the example of Germany, where the Parliament of the States—Bundesrat—is really the representation of each state of the federation; the current ministry of each state is represented there and the Chief Ministers present the case of their state in its sessions.

In India, the Rajya Sabha is the easy means for parties to get their party stalwarts elected to the Parliament without having to face the electorate. And any member of the Rajya Sabha too can become a minister. This is then an easy means to become a minister through the back door. It is a common complaint that most Rajya Sabha members do not have popular support.

Although Om Prasad was supposed to be a minister at New Delhi, he was on permanent deputation to watch the developments in Kerala State, because he belongs to that state.

At the present moment, the BPP had very little political roots in Kerala State, and they had only a few MLAs in the State Legislature and only two MPs in the central parliament from this state. Its dream was to enlarge its representation in the State Legislature and in the Parliament.

The unwritten mandate to Om Prasad was to drive a wedge between the partners of the left-wing ruling coalition of the state. The leading partner in the coalition is the Indian People's Party (IPP). There was some sort of difference of opinion between the IPP and its trade union wing. Hence, BPP and other major parties in the state were doing everything in their power to widen the rift between the IPP and their trade union wing. If a wedge could be driven between them, the supremacy of the ruling coalition could be cracked. The annual meet of the trade union was an excellent occasion to materialize the dream of BPP.

The annual meet of the trade union wing of IPP was taking place at Kottayam. The president of the trade union in Kerala was Mr C. Kannoth, and the general secretary was Mr Raman Nair. These leaders were very critical of the political leadership of the party. Their view was that the party leadership was undermining the importance of the trade union wing. The representation of the TU leaders in the affairs of the government was minimal. Further, the political leaders were unwilling to seek the opinion of TU leaders on important matters.

The TU activists considered themselves as the future of the party and considered themselves authorized to have independent opinion and working freedom, and not subservient to the whims of the aging party leadership.

The national president of the TU, Mr Sanjay Parthan, was of the same opinion, which he stated openly in his speeches. There was then jubilation among the TU delegates. But through clever manipulations in the district levels, many young people loyal to the party leadership were elected to the annual meet. There was going to be an election of the State Presidium of the TU and everybody expected a showdown on the final election day. Would the TU loyalists retain their supremacy? Would there be a split in that party?

Mr Om Prasad wished there would be some clear split. He was keenly watching every development at the TU convention of IPP. He sought the help of intelligence bureau operatives for the purpose. He arranged for the presence of plainclothes policemen at the venue to make the split evident and painful. BPP had made elaborate plans to celebrate the split in the rival party.

In every alternate year, there are elections to the presidium of the trade union, and fierce competition. The reason for the animosity is plain. The TU is rich, very rich. The TU machinery is very clever in eliciting donations from the general public and regular contributions from its members. Then they knew a lot of tactics to amass money. They had no scruples about it. The end justifies the means, so had the revolutionary Karl Marx said. So they made money at the employers' or employees' risk, by hook or by crook. They had thus a lot of immovable properties in every city and village of the state and enormous reserve funds, which could be and were conveniently manipulated by the TU leadership. Actually all the TU leaders lived from the enormous reserve funds of the TU and could afford to lead a life of plenty and luxury. Sometimes the political leaders were envious of the money power of the TU wing.

The TU leaders make a killing by organizing strikes and demonstrations. To declare a strike or demonstration, normally the members are not consulted, not even political leaders. Through such random strikes and demonstrations, the industry would lose a lot of money. In order to avoid such strikes or to minimize the damage, the proprietors or company executives tried to keep good relations with the leaders of the TU units. In the process, hundreds of thousands of rupees change hands. Through such machinations, the TU leaders had become filthy rich.

Money was behind all the political animosities. The political party leadership did not want to give up the control over the TU and over the enormous funds at its disposal. So the party leadership had acted very vigorously and behind the scenes to avoid a showdown by the TU loyalists. Even on the previous day, there was gloom among the party leadership. But Karunakara Vaidyanathan (he was endearingly called Vaidyan), the secretary general of the party, knew what to do.

The night before the election, Mr Vaidyan invited Mr Parthan for a working dinner. After the sumptuous dinner, Vaidyan accompanied Mr Parthan to his room in the five-star hotel the Kerala Regency.

'May I come in for a minute?' asked Vaidyan.

'Of course.' Mr Parthan held the door open for Vaidyan.

They eased themselves into the cosy chairs and Vaidyan opened the discussion with the words 'The party leadership is keen that there should not be a showdown between the two factions.'

'But that is unavoidable,' retorted Mr Parthan. 'The party leadership made unilateral decisions about the formation of the central committee of the TU and also about who should become the president and the secretary of the state TU. This is not a healthy trend. It is highly resented by the Young Turks. They say the election would then look like a farce.' Parthan defended the general trend of the TU loyalists.

'You see, Mr Parthan, the State Assembly elections are due in six months. The party should have the support of all the feeder organizations. There should not be a difference of opinion among the party organizations. This is our prime consideration. Do you want the party to lose the elections?'

'This is like Stalinism of Russia, pure and simple. Though we have accepted much of the Marxist ideology, we should not commit the mistakes the Russian communists committed. Stalin was ruthless in purging his party every now and then. All those who did not think the way he did were eliminated forthwith from the party, and eventually from the face of the earth. Can this be allowed in a democratic country like ours? We are not at all Russian communists.' Parthan was a staunch democrat.

'The end justifies the means, friend.' Vaidyan was pragmatic in his approach to things.

'You, Mr Vaidyan, should remember that you came into the party through the trade union. You were a toddy tapper, and you should not forget your roots. You should be loyal to the TU.'

Vaidyan was equally strong in his words: 'The end is to win the next Assembly elections. Each party member and the leaders of the feeder organizations must make sacrifices for that purpose. This time both Mr C. Kannoth and Mr Raman Nair should go, if the TU members are to fall in line with the party line. That is the general feeling of the party leadership.'

'That is not possible. Removing both of them at one stroke would be suicidal, and may create a big protest from TU members,' quipped Parthan.

'So for the time being,' Vaidyan came one step down and said, 'let us remove Kannoth from presidentship and retain Mr Raman Nair as president, and appoint Mr P. Ganeshan Nair as the general secretary.' Ganeshan Nair was a 100 per cent party loyalist. The general secretary was the most powerful person in the TU. 'The removal of Raman Nair from his position can be done after the Assembly elections. This is all that I have to say, and I need your wholehearted support.' Vaidyan explained the full strategy.

After giving his final opinion in the matter, and to show that this opinion was final, Vaidyan rose from his seat, took his briefcase, and pretended to go. He went up to the door, but then turned back, looked at Parthan one more time and placed the briefcase on the teapoy, saying, 'I almost forgot it. This is meant for you. You will find it useful. You must help us. You must do whatever you can. We depend on you.'

Vaidyan shook hands with him and held his grip firm for a few seconds longer, released his hands and abruptly left the room, and Parthan was left with the briefcase. He did not know what to say or what to do with the briefcase.

Two loyalists of Vaidyan were posted near the door of Mr Parthan to make sure Parthan did not leave his room and, if he left, to find out where he went. They waited and waited. Parthan did not come out.

Why should the party secretary give me presents like this? Maybe it contains some special traditional Kerala clothes for me and my wife.

Parthan was simply curious, he opened the briefcase. Mahatma Gandhi was smiling at him from all the bundles of currency notes inside the briefcase!

His hard feelings for Mr Vaidyan melted away in a flash under the gaze of Gandhi. *After all, we have to help each other*, he murmured to himself. *Service to the party is the service to the nation. We should not work against the party, to which we have basic allegiance!*

He closed the briefcase. He went to the door, carefully bolted it safe. Then he opened his suitcase and took out his shabby clothes and carefully unloaded the contents of Vaidyan's briefcase into his suitcase, then put his clothes over it. He thought his suitcase would burst. With the blessings of the party, it did not!

Then he went to bed. He could not sleep. *What can I do with five million rupees?* He started planning his investment possibilities: *Maybe I can renovate my house, buy a new car, and pay the fees of my daughters. Maybe . . .*

Sleep was eluding him. He took out the detective novel *The Ultimate Strategy* by Henry Stanford and started reading it. He could not concentrate. He went into the bathroom, took a shower, and eased himself into the cosy bed again. The transition to sleep was smooth. He dreamt about the Republic Day parade at New Delhi. He was flying in the air-force helicopter; the view below was splendid.

Mr Vaidyan went straight to room 304, which was occupied by Mr Aravindan Nair, the national secretary general of TU. Vaidyan made the same request to him, and left a similar briefcase in his room.

At the same time, his trusted lieutenant, Vinod Sharma, met three of the staunch supporters of Mr C. Kannoth and offered them smaller briefcases with smaller pictures of Gandhi, and asked them to do a favour for the party.

When Vaidyan reached his room it was thirty minutes after three in the morning.

The next day, the meeting started. Mr Parthan was requested to deliver the inaugural address. He gave an unusually fiery speech; he did not forget to denounce the attempt of the party leadership to destroy democratic rule within the trade union. Then he quietly took his seat.

There was jubilation among the TU loyalists. Kannoth was beaming with joy. His supporters were thrilled.

The next item on the agenda was election. Kannoth was sure that he was going to be the all-powerful president again. It would be very smooth sailing. As soon as proposals were called for, Mr Vaidyan stood up as the first and proposed the name of Raman Nair for the post of president. Kannoth was burning with anger at the temerity of the party president. The loyalists of Kannoth were outraged; there were angry outbursts and submerged heated discussions all over the place.

Kannoth too was uneasy in his seat. He knew Parthan would make his move and propose him as the president, as agreed yesterday. *Why is Parthan not making the move? Is he expecting someone else to propose his name?*

In the meantime, Mrs Sushama Ravindran stood up as instructed by Vaidyan the previous day, and seconded Raman Nair's nomination. Parthan looked uneasy in his seat, but did not make any move. He tried several times to stand up and propose the name of Kannoth, but every time he made the attempt, something was holding him back. *Gandhi's pictures in his briefcase!* He could not even utter a word. If he spoke against the wishes of Vaidyan, he knew the loyalists of Vaidyan would raid his room and bring out the currency stacked in his suitcase, and it would be flashed as the big headline in all the newspapers the next day. He himself would have to resign. So he clung to his seat.

Kannoth looked at him with a prayer and hope in his eyes. But Parthan just looked away. Aravindan Nair too looked away as if nothing of importance was happening. Kannoth sat rooted in his chair. He could not understand what really was happening. *Has Parthan forgotten his promise? Judas is his name. How sweetly he had spoken last evening. He had shaken my hands firmly for a few minutes and promised me, 'Our hour of glory is tomorrow. Don't worry, Kannoth. Everything will be OK.' Has he forgotten all that so soon?*

And had Aravindan Nair too forsaken him? *You too, Brutus?* How in the world could everything change overnight?

'What has happened to Parthan?' asked some TU loyalists. At last T. K. Ramunny proposed the name of Mr Kannoth too for the presidentship, and was readily supported by Mr D. P. Chandran from Kannur. Now that there were two candidates, equally strong, the delegates were confused. They badly looked to Mr Parthan for the final say. The decisive move had to come from Mr Parthan.

Every eye was now turned to Mr Parthan. Seconds seemed longer than usual. There was absolute silence. Which faction was going to win? Mr Parthan was the key figure who could decide the fate of either group.

At that moment, Mr Parthan rose from his seat, and Kannoth thought his moment of glory was coming at last. Kannoth watched him moving to the microphone.

Mr Parthan adjusted the mic to his level, cleared his throat one more time, and started to speak. *He will definitely support me*, thought Kannoth.

Parthan declared slowly and solemnly, 'We do not want to create a bad impression on the public. We are one party. Let us support Mr Raman Nair and be united with the political wing.' He was saying it as if he had memorised it.

TU loyalists were stunned. There were also expressions of sheer anger and frustration. Protest sounds were heard from different quarters. They were angry at the audacity of Mr Parthan to jump to the other side. The Kannoth loyalists sat rooted in their seats. 'Unbelievable,' they murmured.

But now that Mr Parthan had spoken, most of the undecided delegates had no other way than to support the proposal of Mr Vaidyan. Mr Raman Nair was elected president of the TU. Kannoth was out. The strategy of Vaidyan succeeded with the help of Gandhi's smile!

Om Prasad was anxiously walking along the corridors of the Government Guest House. He was visibly nervous. He was continuously calling every one of his trusted lieutenants for information. When some of them said that results are not encouraging, he called others for verification.

'There was no flare-up at the trade union conference?' he asked his aides.

'No,' they said unanimously.

He could not believe it. All of them confirmed what had happened. Om Prasad was simply disappointed. Despite all the efforts he had put into it, the strategy did not work out.

Something must have gone wrong somewhere, he thought.

As he was discussing the situation with his aides, his mobile phone rang. It was an emergency call from his New Delhi office.

'One Indian Airlines plane has been hijacked. The son of the defence minister is on it.'

'Oh my God!' he said aloud.

'Is the defence minister at New Delhi?' he inquired. 'Ask my private secretary to hurry to the defence minister's house; he should be there till the crisis is over. I'm coming to Delhi on the next available flight.' After giving this instruction, he asked his aide to make arrangements for the earliest flight to New Delhi.

For now, the immediate problem for Om Prasad was the hijack crisis. In a hurry, he concluded his meeting with the aides and left for the Cochin International Airport at Nedumbassery, and took the next available flight to Bombay, and from there, he would get the connecting flight to New Delhi.

Om Prasad was very perturbed. At this hour of sorrow and tension, he should be near his friend Almeida, to give him courage to face the situation and to console him.

5

Hasina was in Dubai performing at the Dubai International Convention Centre. When she came backstage in the green room, her secretary told her of the hijack drama. Fear gripped her. But she did not show any sign of it. She knew that Anand was in that fateful flight. Mishma had phoned her during the day, from Kathmandu, telling her of Anand's visit there and of his plan to fly back to India.

She changed clothes, got into her car, and asked the chauffeur to drive her to Dubai International Airport. She took the next available flight to Tehran.

Throughout her flight to Tehran, she was in a pensive mood and was planning what to do. Though she knew Anand only on a few occasions, she admired his talents and his gentlemanly behaviour. He was handsome too.

She checked into Hilton International Hotel at Tehran. As soon as she was in her room, she started to make a few phone calls. She was trying all her contacts to find out the number of Abu Salim, the trusted lieutenant of Hashim Tarif Ahmed. Finally she got the number from a friend in Pakistan, and she punched his number on her mobile phone. After several rings, he came directly on the line. He knew the number of Hasina. When it flashed on his mobile phone, he was excited. They were friends for a long time, from the time they were students at the Islamic College of International Relations at Lahore. Even after he joined the band of Hashim Tarif Ahmed, he kept his contact with her intact. It had its own advantages.

'Abu, this is Hasina,' she said.

'I know your number, dear. What is the matter? Actually I'm now in the middle of a very serious problem. Where are you calling from?'

'I'm calling from Tehran. I had a programme today at Dubai, and I'm on my way back to Islamabad. But I'm quite upset about the hijacking of the Indian Airlines plane.'

'Why? We had to do it. We have to get some of our people out from the Indian jails.'

'How is the situation, Abu? How are the passengers treated?' asked Hasina.

'What is the matter, Hasina? How do you come into the picture?'

'It's a long story, Abu. To cut it short, one Anand is on the plane. We are not really friends. We met each other a few weeks back during a function at the residence of the Nepalese Prime Minister Rana at Kathmandu. His daughter, Mishma Rana, invited me for that function. And this Anand was one of the invitees. So we met. The three of us had long discussions about fashion and music. Though I know him only casually, still at this juncture I thought I should do something to help him out. Can you help me?'

'It doesn't look good, Hasina,' Abu said. 'They are tough guys. They are not playing games. They are playing with their life. They know the rules of the game. They will be very tough. I do not know whether I should interfere at this stage.'

'Abu, you can't say that to me. You have to help me somehow. I leave it to you to devise a plan to help. But remember, I should not come into the picture. You know how embarrassing it would be for my father, if he comes to know that I interfere in such political matters. Nor should you come into the picture. Do it discreetly, tactfully. Strike the right chord. Pull the right strings. Get him out of the plane without delay and harm. And I will always remember the favour you are doing for me.'

'Hasina, I will try. I do not promise anything. No, I cannot promise. But I will just give it a try. I can give you my word that I will try.'

Abu Salim was a tough guy too. He was shaken by the emotional request of Hasina. She was not only his friend, she was not just a pop star; she was the daughter of Abdul Lateef, the president of Pakistan. *I can freely engage in such dangerous activities only because of the tacit support of Abdul Lateef and his ISI agents. Her request should be given the importance it deserves.* After all, Tarif Ahmed and he had received a lot of hospitality from Abdul Lateef and Pakistan. *She has personally given a lot of time for us. I should do it for her,* he told himself.

Immediately, Abu went to work. He called a few numbers and got the contact number of Dr Tariq and dialled him.

'Dr Tariq, this is Abu Salim. *Salaam alaikum.*'

'*Asalamu alaikum.* You know what we are into. Now we are in your territory, in Tehran. We have hijacked a plane of the Indian pigs. We need your help to get our demands accepted.'

'I shall try my best,' said Abu. 'But before that I need your help.'

'My help? What help?'

'There is one passenger by the name Anand. You have to release him somehow, immediately.'

'Why? Who is he?'

'I can explain that to you when the whole drama is over.'

'Let me see. But I need your assistance to end this drama, in a manner favourable to us and you,' said Dr Tariq.

'I will do what I can, if you do what you can. The person who made the request to me is so dear to me. So do it somehow. Everything will be OK. *Inshallah!*'

'*Inshallah!*'

Both of them clicked their phones off.

Dr Tariq carefully opened the door of the pilot's cabin and called to himself one of his assistants, Ali Abdul Sattar. 'There is one Anand among the passengers; he is dear to one of our leaders. Get him out of the plane. He should not be harmed. Deal decently with him. And hand him over safely to the Red Cross.'

Then he closed the door of the cabin and went into negotiation with people in the control tower, where Mr S. B. Singh from India and his associates were sitting.

Ali Abdul Sattar asked the air hostess to locate one Mr Anand.

'But make no commotion,' he warned her.

She knew where he was. As Anand entered the plane, the chief steward had told her who Anand was and asked her to give special attention to him.

Anand was sitting in the executive class, seat no. 4b. It was quite easy to locate him.

Sattar came up to Anand and told him, 'Put both of your hands behind your neck.'

What is he going to do? Has he found out who I am?

'Sir, I shall . . .' (He wanted to say he would use his influence in Delhi to meet all their demands, even if it seemed difficult. But words would not go out of his mouth.)

Sattar forbade him from speaking. 'Don't talk. Just do what I say.'

Anand felt the touch of death. The shadow of death was over him. He did not know what to do. Anxiety and extreme fear gripped his soul. Beads of perspiration appeared on his forehead. His hands were trembling. His mouth went dry. He had difficulty moving his tongue. His legs were going numb, he thought.

Is he going to put me as a special hostage because I'm the son of the defence minister of India? Or is he going to keep me and release all the others? The son of the defence minister of India is the best catch of the day! Or is he going to shoot me as the first victim, to press for their demands?

Fear gripped him. He was in total agony. He tried his best to keep cool. He had learned it during his MBA course. He had heard lectures on crisis management. But in such a real-life situation, theoretical things did not help. He started to perspire even more, despite the strong air conditioning in the plane.

Are all my dreams going to be shattered? My God! He prayed. After so many weeks, he said a prayer in his heart. *My God, are you there?*

Sattar bent down to Anand and spoke into his ears: 'When I am gone, pretend terrible chest pain, and call out to the air hostess for help. It must look totally real. I will come back to you in two seconds.'

Quickly, Sattar moved down three more rows and talked to his friend Abdul Kahder.

Anand did as he was told to do. He cried out in anguish.

'Shut up, you damn devil.' roared Sattar. He came running. 'No one should move. If anyone moves, I will have to shoot him,' he shouted. Then he called the air hostesses for help. Ali kept vigil over the scene.

'Don't you see he is sick?' he shouted to the air hostesses. 'We do not want anybody to die inside the plane. Take him out,' he shouted.

His friend, Muhammed Hashim, too rushed to the spot. With the help of the air hostess, they carried Anand to the door. Hashim opened the door, and Sattar managed to lower Anand carefully to the ground. The door was immediately slammed shut.

As the hijackers dropped somebody at the door of the plane, an ambulance and a military vehicle rushed to the door.

All the negotiators thought the first casualty had happened. The ambulance came prepared to give emergency service to the wounded or dead; they were ready to meet any eventuality.

The ambulance took Anand, laid him carefully on the gurney, and sped away. The personnel inside were stupefied when they saw no bloodstain on the body. They did not know what was happening.

The ambulance stopped at the first aid station, and handed over Anand to the medical team. They checked him, took his ECG, and found him healthy. Maybe he had some chest congestion due to the enormous emotional pressure. So he could be handed over to the Indian delegation.

Anand was immediately handed over to the Indian delegation. Throughout the drama, he pretended to be sick.

Anand was surprised. He was saved miraculously. He could not understand the mystery of it. *Did Dad pull some strings? Dad knows that I am on the plane, though he should be in Orissa now. If it is not him, who could that saviour be?*

Who else knew his identity? He could not find an answer.

Anand insisted that he should remain in Tehran till the end of the crisis, but the negotiators thought that it would be wise for him to leave Tehran incognito, before the news got to the world. And if it came out in the press, it would create a difficult situation for all concerned.

After he was given the necessary first aid, he was taken to the Indian Embassy building, and from there, he was flown to Dubai with a new diplomatic passport under the name Abdul Hameed, and from there, he was flown to New Delhi. One of the RAW men, Mr P. Parthasarathy, accompanied him.

Throughout the journey back home, Anand was trying to understand the mystery of his miraculous escape. 'I do not know how this could happen, so perfectly and well beyond imagination. There should be somebody who knew me and loved me behind the scenes,' Anand mused. 'Who is that? There are a lot of people who love and adore my father. He is such a just and lovable person, so it is no wonder people closely follow not only him, but also his son. Many of his admirers are anonymous. There are wealthy and highly influential people among them. It must be one such admirer of my father who had struck the right chord . . . Thank you, Dad, for being what you are!'

Charles Almeida was strolling in the garden as the car with Anand arrived. Charles Almeida came running and hugged him tight, and led him inside.

His mother came running from the kitchen and hugged and kissed him, and led him to his room. 'It's a miracle, nothing short of it. God heard my prayers and saw my tears,' said his mother. 'Now take rest. We shall talk later.'

Anand was quite restless. After lying in bed for a few minutes, he stood up, went to his table, and switched on the laptop. He wanted to share his experience with Hasina. He quickly drafted an email:

Dear Hasina,

I had a very terrible experience two days back. I was in deep trouble. The plane in which I was travelling from Kathmandu was hijacked by some terrorists. One Dr Tariq was the ringleader of the hijackers. But a real miracle happened. Somebody who knows me and loves me intervened to help me. When one of the terrorists told me to put my hands behind my head, fear gripped me. I thought he was going to execute me. Cold-blooded, without a trace of mercy, his face revealed no soft emotions. I started perspiring. I said my last prayer. By his next visit, everything was different. He appeared to be kind and considerate. He asked me to pretend that I was sick. But that was only a trick to get me out of the plane. So I was miraculously released from the hijacked plane. I'm sure somebody was working behind the scenes for me. Somebody who loved me. Since my name was not released to the press, nobody knows to this date that I was on that fateful flight. I am happy that I am alive and can write to you these lines.

Longing to see you, sometime soon,
Anand

Hasina did not receive the email. The security was tightened around Hasina. The communication lines were under surveillance. The ISI was shadowing her for quite some time. Abdul Lateef was informed of it, and he did not want to have any scandals. The email was erased before she could access it.

Abu Salim had a good relationship with the foreign minister of Iran, Mr Mohammed Hasheemi. He called up Hasheemi and negotiated an amicable settlement of the hijack drama. The five men of the Justice War group, who were in the Tihar jail in New Delhi, would be handed over to Iran and kept in custody; once Abu Salim certified that these five men were in Iranian custody, the hijackers should come out of plane, and the plane could leave.

The proposal was put to Mr S. B. Singh, who approved it. Within six hours, a special plane carrying the five prisoners with an escort of twelve security forces arrived in Tehran. The prisoners were taken into custody by Iran; Abu Salim talked to them, and they talked to Dr Tariq. After this, the hijackers got out of the plane.

The Indian Airlines plane went for refuelling and, within a few minutes, left Tehran airport.

According to international regulations, the hijackers were also taken into the custody of Iran and were kept in police custody, for further negotiations and settlements. The hijackers thought they would be freed. But they had to remain in jail, and could in all probability be extradited to India or Nepal. The Nepalese government was adamant that Dr Tariq be extradited to them, because his behaviour was seen as equivalent to high treason.

6

Pakistan Air Chief Marshal Iqbal Ali Mir was on a visit to China. The tour was planned long ago. He had an extensive talk with Mr Cheng Huan Ping, the military attaché of the Chinese Embassy at Islamabad. The voluminous literature on Chinese military hardware lay spread out on his table; he need only choose what suited Pakistan. He was convinced that the Chinese products could meet every military need of Pakistan.

For any military operation, the role of warplanes is crucial—to avoid human casualties, to avoid the difficulty in traversing ground terrain, and to have striking superiority over a larger area. Only with air superiority can you win the game. This was well known to the Pakistani military establishment. And the Pakistani air force has always measured their war-readiness by comparing their air superiority to that of India!

It is common knowledge that the Indian military gets more money than it can spend. In the name of 'national security', more money flows into the coffers of the defence department than to projects for poverty alleviation. The country has to be superior to the firepower of Pakistan; that has been the norm always. If Pakistan buys F-16s, India has to buy double the number of MIG-29s or Mirage 2000s. If Pakistan acquires a submarine, India has to get two.

Formerly, that is, till 1971, keeping watch over the borders was really difficult for India. Till that time, there was East Pakistan on the eastern front (what is now known as Bangladesh) and West Pakistan on the western sector. So India had a real hard time watching over the enemy fronts in the east and the west. By the war of 1971, India conquered the Pakistani army on the eastern front and gave independence to East Pakistan, giving it the name of Bangladesh. Bangladesh is not at all a threat to the security of India. Things took shape there to the total satisfaction of the military establishment of India. Now India needs to take care of only the western sector.

China is a traditional arms supplier to Pakistan. Though the Chinese are eager to exploit the much bigger Indian military market, there is substantive doubt in the mind of the Indian military establishment about the trustworthiness of the Chinese products and the intentions of Chinese politicians.

The Americans have cut down the military and financial assistance to Pakistan following allegations that Pakistan had clandestinely manufactured nuclear bombs and had acquired the prohibited missile technology from China and North Korea. Since then, military product development in Pakistan was in the doldrums. The only choice was to have some sort of tie-up with the Chinese. The Chinese were a willing partner. They were ready to go to any extent in providing military assistance, provided they got cash for the goods.

Pakistan Air Chief Marshal Iqbal Ali Mir was convinced of carrying on the continuous upgrading and modernisation of the Pak air force. The Indians were manufacturing and modernising the MIG-21s and MIG-27s at their own factory at Bangalore with the collaboration of the Russians. *Why not we?* Hence the Pak air force started the project of the lightweight F-7 warplanes. Its development was not progressing as expected though.

Ali Mir was especially attracted to the new version of Chendu F-7 warplanes. They were cheaper and lighter than US F-16s. F-7 is performance-wise not superior to F-16, but it has enough features, which are quite enough to counter the air superiority of the Indians. It can be a good answer to the Russian MIG-27 or MIG-29 or even to the French Mirage-2000, which were being used by the Indian air force.

The Chinese were not averse to giving some credit facility. After extensive talks, the Pak air force decided to purchase thirty Chendu F-7s from China. There was also talk of manufacturing some spare parts in Pakistan. The deal had the blessing of Abdul Lateef. Iqbal Ali Mir was now in Beijing to finalise the deal.

Finalising military purchases is the sole prerogative of the air chief marshal. He does it personally. He would have talks with the Chinese counterpart tête-à-tête; only four eyes and four ears would see and hear what was said and done there.

The sub-deals were more important. In the price of the commodity, provision for the obligatory commissions had to be included.

'The net price of the Chendu F-7 could be raised by 7 per cent,' Iqbal Ali Mir told his counterpart, 'on two conditions: (1) we should get a credit of 75 per cent which will be paid over fifteen years, and (2) our usual commission should be raised to 7 per cent; the amount so raised has to be transferred to my account in the Swiss bank, Credit Suisse Nationale, at Geneva.'

From whatever was transferred to his accounts, 2 per cent went to the account of the president, 2 per cent would go to his senior staff in the air force, 2 per cent to the numerous defence department officials; what was then left for him was just a paltry 1 per cent. But he was satisfied with that. All the percentages had to go into separate Swiss bank accounts, which was a secret that he alone knew.

'If the second condition has to be done, the credit portion has to be limited to 60 per cent only, with an interest component of LIBOR plus 1 per cent. We have no objection to giving a provision of 7 per cent for the deal and will be transferred to your account as usual. Is that agreeable?'

'Let me get the concurrence of the president. I will let you know within a few minutes.'

Actually General Ali Mir expected to have only 50 per cent credit and 5 per cent commission. But the Chinese were generous. And how could he give up such a generous offer?

Ali Mir went into his private room and talked to the president over his secure line and got his confirmation.

He came back and said, 'Agreed. We shall sign the deal during the visit of our president to your country.'

They shook hands in total agreement.

When his counterpart had gone, Mir Ali went to his private bar and poured half a glass of bourbon whisky and started sipping it. His eyes were glowing with pleasure and satisfaction. He told himself, *Now you can retire without any worry about the future.*

7

Hasina was again having a programme at Dubai. From her iPhone, she sent email to anandc@gmail.com. The text read:

My programme here was superb. The audience was marvellous. I'm proceeding to Nepal. I might be there for three days with my father; he will be there on state visit. We will go back to Islamabad on Sunday.

Hasina

She deleted it as soon as it was sent.

Abdul Lateef was on state visit to Nepal. Nepal was serving as a buffer zone between India and China. China wanted the Nepal government to be a bit soft on them so that they could use the territory for espionage and movement of arms to guerilla groups. Abdul Lateef's visit was at the request of the Nepalese prime minister. On the occasion, the cultural ministry was organizing a programme for the state guests.

The news of Hasina's visit to Nepal electrified Anand. He wanted to meet her at any cost. He wanted to tell her everything that happened on the plane and after. There is no better place for this than Nepal. He had no time to waste. He asked his agent to arrange his flight. The answer came quickly; he could not fly to Nepal, because the Indian Airlines flights were cancelled till further notice, presumably because of the state visit of Pakistan's president. So he booked a flight to Lucknow, and from there he took an air-taxi of the UP government to Gorakhpur and from there he went by road to Kathmandu. He reached Kathmandu by 3.00 p.m. and checked into the deluxe executive suite of his own resort.

Hasina was in the Kathmandu Royal Retreat with her father and entourage. He dialled the reception, but could not go further. There was tight security check on all calls. His call was not cleared. The name Anand was not familiar to them. It was the name of an Indian. So there was reason for them to block him access.

He was bitter and angry. He then rang up Mishma Rana, the daughter of the Nepalese prime minister. Even she was not available. She had gone out with state guests. She would be back in an hour, and she would reciprocate the call.

Anand waited for the call. He was growing impatient. He did not dare to go out of the room. He did not want to miss the call. She was the only person who could put him through to Hasina.

At 4.45 p.m., the phone rang. It was Charles Almeida from New Delhi. 'What are you doing there in Kathmandu? Abdul Lateef is having a state visit there. It would be difficult time for Indians to move about in Kathmandu. So be vigilant and don't get into any trouble.'

'Of course, Dad. I shall be most careful. Thank you for the advice,' said Anand.

He wanted to advise his Dad: 'Dear Dad, give up all the drama of enmity between India and Pakistan. Try to see the light. We the youngsters of both the countries wish to talk to each other, and to deal with each other. Anwar is the Pakistan high commissioner's son, but he has no problem talking to me. We are close friends, we go for a movie together, we watch cricket together . . . We the youth of both countries wish to make a change. We want to bury most of what happened once upon a time, and to look forward to the future of immense possibilities and opportunities. If we the youth could forget the borders and move freely between our two countries, why can't you elders ratify it? Please, Dad, you are the one person who can talk sense to the grey heads in your government. Please create opportunities for us youth of both countries to meet each other.'

As soon as he set the receiver down, it rang again. He jumped to take the phone. The shrill voice on the other side said, 'Hi, Anand. This is Mishma. What a pleasant surprise! How come you are here in Kathmandu?'

'Yes. Well, it was not planned. Everything happened all of a sudden. So I could not inform you in advance. Sorry.'

'Why? I am most happy that you are here. The state visit of Pakistan President is going on here. Tonight there is a cultural programme at the National Hall. Can you come? I shall reserve a seat for you. Thereafter there will be dinner for a closed circle at my father's residence. You must come for both.'

'Me? Won't it create some protocol problems for you?' Anand said.

'For me? No problem. You must come for both the functions. I'm inviting you. You just come. Don't think of official things.'

'Sure. I'll come'. He was thrilled. He thought his chest would burst for joy. He could not control his excitement. He wanted to shout for joy. Though he wanted to ask about Hasina, he could not. Before he could say anything, she said, 'Anand, we will meet this evening. Till then, bye,' and put the phone down.

'Naturally she must be busy with the guests. Well, I shall meet her and Hasina at the National Hall, and at the dinner party,' Anand consoled himself.

Anand went to the bathroom and took a shower. He put on the best clothes; Anand Jon shirts were his favourite. He combed his hair, applied his favourite perfume, Polo Ralph Lauren Blue; one more last look in the mirror, he was ready. He was proud of himself. He looked like a serious businessman.

The Mercedes-Benz of Anand came to a halt at the parking lot in the residence of Prime Minister Manickchand Rana. He was quickly escorted in. Mishma saw him from far away and ran to him, shook hands with him, and led him by the hand to the reception area. She was the real master of ceremonies.

'It's nice to see you, Anand. It is quite a surprise. The moment chosen is really good,' she said in a breath.

She led him to the prime minister, Manickchand Rana, who was happy to see him: 'Hi, Anand, how is your resort doing in our Himalayan heights?' Anand was well known in the Himalayan kingdom, especially after he started the resort in Kathmandu.

'It's doing well, thanks to your patronage.'

'Anand, I wish to introduce you to your big neighbour,' said Mishma, and took him to Mr Abdul Lateef, the president of Pakistan.

'Mr President, this is Anand, my friend from India.'

'How do you do, Mr Anand?'

'Thank you, Mr President.'

'Anand has a hill resort here just outside Kathmandu,' Mishma said. 'It is a favourite spot for us. It is a beautiful place. You should visit it, if you get time to.'

'Let me see,' said Abdul Lateef.

Anand chimed in. 'Sir, I would be immensely thankful if you can squeeze in that programme into your hectic schedule. It will be an honour and privilege for us to receive you there,' Anand pleaded.

'I'll try my best and let you know,' said Abdul Lateef.

Abdul Lateef knew that he was the one who was saved surprisingly from the hijacked Indian Airlines plane, and that he was the son of Indian Defence Minister Charles Almeida Fernandez. But he could not find out how he was released. Had the mujahideen some connections in Delhi? Maybe the mujahideen got some extra money for his release? It remained a mystery for him, and he had asked ISI to investigate, but nothing came out of it.

'You had a narrow escape, no, Anand?'

'I didn't get you.'

'I mean, at Tehran!'

How could he know that I was the one who was saved from the hijacked plane at Tehran? Since he knows it, the mystery is somehow solved!

'Sure. It was quite a miracle. I am grateful to God for it. This is my second life.'

'You are lucky.'

'Really lucky, uncle.'

He called me uncle. Abdul Lateef was pleased. He liked the young man. *Why should our two countries live as enemies, when there are likable people on both sides?* Abdul Lateef mused in his mind.

Abdul Lateef, like Charles Almeida Fernandez in India, knew it was futile to go on fighting. It would only help the arms lobby. All the wars would be fought at the expense of the poor of both the countries.

But was there a way to stop it?

Hasina saw Anand from the other corner of the ballroom; she hastily came to them, politely stood a few feet away, and waited for the signal from her father to come near them. As soon as he gave his nod, she came up to them.

'Meet Mr Anand from India,' Lateef said.

'I know, Dad.'

She shook hands with him. 'Hi, Anand, how are you?'

'Fine, fine.' Then Anand went a bit closer to her ears and murmured, 'By the way, thanks a lot.'

She was shaken by the words. Was Anand hinting at the hijack drama and his dramatic escape? Would he ask questions about how it happened? Would the cat be out of the bag? She wanted to change the subject and the venue.

'Dad, can you excuse us youngsters to chat for a few minutes?' she asked her father, Abdul Lateef.

'Of course. No problem. We elders do not wish to usurp your kingdom.' Even before Abdul Lateef finished his sentence, she moved away with Anand to where Mishma was standing.

Anand, Hasina, and Mishma moved to a corner.

Abdul Lateef looked on as they moved away from him. He liked Anand, love at first sight! Well, he was good-looking, smart, businesslike, and humble. *Nice boy*, he told himself.

The youngsters discussed films, songs, resorts, travels. About weather, about the beauty of Nepal and its mountains. All of them were itching to talk about something personal but did not know how to start and where to start, and didn't know how the others would take it.

As if to rescue them at that precise moment came Vijay Singh, the new heart-throb of the Indian teenagers; he moved close to Mishma with a beaming smile and almost dragged her from the trio talk. 'Mishma, I want you to be in my next film, *Dekho Dekho* . . . It is being directed by Anand Chopra.'

'Definitely, Vijay. Whose story is it? Whose script is it? And music by?' she asked innocently in quick succession. But she added, 'I don't care for all that. If you ask me to be in it, I will come.' She was a bit aloof to him after Vijay Singh was recently doing films with Sushmita Sen, Priya Datta, and Aishwarya Bachchan Rai.

'Everything is written and scripted with you and me in mind. We will turn out to be a good pair in this film,' shot back Vijay.

'Sure, it's my pleasure to be acting with the best ever Indian actor.' She did not spare words while praising him. Vijay enjoyed every bit of it.

As Mishma and Vijay Singh moved away, Anand and Hasina got a few moments for themselves. 'Hasina, thank you for your efforts!'

'What are you talking about?' She pretended ignorance.

'Hasina dear, you are the only one who could have pulled the strings in that situation. I got confirmation about it today!'

She did not dare to ask how. She knew he knew.

'How did you know that? Anand, please keep it a big secret. My father does not know of it until now. Nobody in the establishment in Pakistan knows of it. The ISI is in the dark. They will come to know of it only when you spill the beans. So keep it to yourself.'

'OK. But thanks.' For Anand, finally the riddle was over. *So it is Hasina! Dear Hasina, I stand here because of you. I love you!* He continued, 'You are marvellous, Hasina. I appreciate your fast and decisive move as soon as you came to know of the crisis. How did you know that I was on that plane?'

'Well, the day before, I had a talk with Mishma, and she told me you would be there in Nepal. She told me about your travel plans. And I guessed you would be on the fateful plane. I called her and confirmed that you were on that flight. Further, I got some information from your own country. I knew no one else could or would do anything at that moment. And I'm proud I could do something for you.'

'Hasina, your heart is pure love. Otherwise why should you bother about me? Now tell me, when and where are we meeting next? This time it is too official. We can't go away without being noticed. Oh, Hasina, how much I want to hold you in my hands and—'

In mid-sentence came the announcement from Mishma: 'Time for dinner!'

Anand was placed near Mishma. On the opposite side were Hasina and her cousin Mohammed Aslam. The foursome quickly imbibed the spirit of friendship and began chatting about fashion and music, films, cricket, and resorts. Anand personally was gratified that he got ample time to wonder at the beauty before him. He did not waste any moment of it. Staring into her blue eyes, he could see a new world of happiness and dreamt of a life together for eternity.

After the dinner, Anand said farewell to Abdul Lateef. 'Uncle, will we meet again? Will you visit my resort?'

'Let me see.'

'I think we should be able to meet oftener.'

'For that, the relations between our two countries have to improve, my dear son.'

The words were unintended. The moment they escaped his lips, he repented about it. He should not have talked like this. How could he call an Indian boy 'son'? He knew that emotion had overtaken his intellect. The mind has reasons that reason won't understand!

'Why don't we do something in that direction?'

Abdul Lateef was prompt in his reply: 'Why not, we but need to sit across the table and negotiate without preconditions.'

'Oh, big politics. I'm not anybody to talk about that. I'm just a humble businessman, who doesn't know much of politics,' said Anand, showing unsurpassed humility. 'I personally have nothing against anybody in Pakistan. I like the way you look at things, the way you talk to me, and above all, the way you like to call me!'

It was a good compliment. Abdul Lateef enjoyed it fully.

'Business of politics is what we do. Of course, you business people can contribute a lot to make politics businesslike,' concluded Abdul Lateef.

Anand decided to work on the project of reconciliation. It had now become very personal for him. Hasina was his love, and Abdul Lateef addressed him already as 'son'! What more motivation did he require?

8

As Anand came into the house, Almeida asked him, 'How was the trip?'

'Better than anticipated,' came the reply.

'Did you get an occasion to meet with Abdul Lateef's daughter?' There was naughtiness in his question.

'Sure, of course I did. I met her father too.'

'You met Abdul Lateef?'

'Yes. I did. He is a very nice person, very polite and decent. Well-dressed, unlike many of our political buffoons, he was in an immaculate three-piece suit. He has a good grasp of the political realities. His language is immaculate. I have a great feeling that he really wants to better the relations between India and Pakistan.'

'It is just the surface. Deep down, these Pakistani politicians are incapable of coming out of the hole they have dug for themselves. They cannot survive without anti-India slogans.'

'Why don't we try something to change that? Why can't we take the first step in the right direction?'

'We did. Our former prime minister went to Pakistan on the inaugural day of the Lahore bus service. And they did not reciprocate. No, they responded badly and started to be inimical all along the border.'

'The president of those days was a timid fellow. Abdul Lateef is different. He will do what he says.' Anand was confident.

'Well, it is a matter for Jasjit Singh Ahluwalia; he is the foreign minister. My role is to fight them, and to rebuff them if they dare to fight.'

'Throw away, Dad, this friend-enemy dichotomy in international relations,' said Anand. 'There should be an attitude of give and take. If arch-enemies France and Germany can become friends and be the cornerstone of the great European Union, why can't Pakistan and India set another example of reconciliation and regional peace?'

'This is not Europe. This is Asia. Here it can't work, Anand. Our Pakistan policy was framed after years of bitter experience. The several wars between us have taught us some bitter lessons in international politics.'

Anand shot back, 'Are you afraid you will become jobless if the two countries become friends? Or that your ministry will become redundant, or at least smaller?'

Charles Almeida said, 'I don't care.'

'If no defence is required, there would be no need for a defence minister!'

'Anand, you do not know the international ramifications of the Indo-Pak relations. If India and Pakistan become friends, India will have to confront more enemies, more formidable enemies, elsewhere.'

'I don't understand that, Dad.'

'We, India and Pakistan, are pawns in the hands of bigger powers. Even if we wanted peace, it would be difficult to achieve that. There are powers in the world who want us to remain as we are—enemies. It is just good for them!'

'So why don't both nations understand this and try to act on their own, come what may? We are neighbours and peace between us is going to be more beneficial to both the countries than to any other in the world.'

'I think I should recommend you to Jasjit Ahluwalia. Well, I shall tell him what you said. He might appoint you as his junior advisor in Indo-Pak relations! Reconciliation is better than war, I know. But it is a bookish wisdom, my son.'

Innerly, Charles Almeida was moved by the conviction of his son. And he admired his wisdom. *What he said is not wrong, after all.*

But as defence minister, he had to play the role he was supposed to play.

As his car moved along the Janpath, and to the prime minister's office, Charles Almeida was pensive. He was thinking of what he should tell the PM about the visit of Anand to Nepal.

<hr />

The day began for Captain Manish Kumar with a good omen. He knew the day would be good. There was no urgent request for flying out for any border sortie. Everything was calm and quiet along the border. He enjoyed his morning coffee. After the usual bodybuilding exercises at the gym and breakfast, he went straight to his office work.

After carefully studying all the papers and signing whatever he had to, he went home for lunch. Soundarya, his beautiful wife, had prepared a very delicious lunch for him. During their ten-year married life, he never had an occasion to complain about her food. She was very careful about his food; she knew what he liked and what he didn't. She always wanted her husband to feel good after the lunch.

Punctually at 1.15 p.m., the driver came with his jeep. Manish Kumar reached the office before time, at 1.27 p.m. He went into the inspection tower and sat with the air force traffic controllers who were watching the skies and the ground ceaselessly day and night. As soon as Koteshwar creek area came into view, they could detect some movement along the shallow waters. Immediately the order came from the command control room to start off a chopper for inspection. Manish Kumar was the immediate choice.

Yadav and three other men accompanied him for the sortie. These air force men were ready for any assault, either for defence or offence.

At the canal area, DIG Yadav asked Manish Kumar to fly a little lower. The chopper dipped its nose a bit and went in a downward direction. As they passed some two kilometres, something struck the chopper and it lost balance and went down, crashing in the field below. All the four men were wounded, but the copter pilot Manish Kumar pressed the ejection button and miraculously escaped with minor injuries. The military circles believed that Pakistani gunboats secretly roaming about in the creek must have shot down the helicopter.

An assault from the Pakistani gunboat could not be ruled out. But Air Chief Marshall A. Y. T. Tipnis refused to say categorically that the Pak boats did this. The accident happened some ten kilometres inside Indian territory. It was definitely not a missile attack from the other side.

There were a lot of radar installations along the border. The Pakistani boats might have come on a reconnaissance

9

Anand decided to meet his father's great friend Om Prasad in South India and discuss with him the issue of Indo-Pakistan relationship. His father and Om Prasad were good friends. Om Prasad could be a great influence on his father.

The phone rang and the attendant took the phone and handed it over to the minister. In his usual friendly way, he said, 'Hallooo.'

'It's me. Anand. I have a project at Cochin,' said Anand.

'How are yooou, Anannnd? How niiice to hear from yooou.' The minister tried to be extremely polite and friendly to the son of the powerful defence minister.

'It's a resort project.'

'Very gooood.'

'Well, I will ask my local manager to visit you and apprise you of the developments.'

Om Prasad was a junior minister, a Minister of State (MOS, for short, as they say); Charles Almeida was a cabinet minister and no. 2 in the cabinet. Though before the public, the Ministers of State put on a brave front and an air of importance, back in Delhi and in the ministry itself, they were just junior ministers and were ready to please their seniors in whatever way possible.

A call from Anand was equivalent to a call from Mr Charles Almeida. He had to do whatever he wanted him to.

'Tomorrow I will be at Cochin. I will be staying at the Government Guest House. In the morning hours, I am there. I will go out only in the afternoon.'

When the sun is blazing, how can a minister go out? 'Tell your manager to contact me around 11 a.m. And I shall do whatever is needed. Okaay?'

'Thank you so much, uncle.'

Yes. Om Prasad was ever ready to help Almeida and his son. Without connections, nothing would work in this part of the world. Anand wanted Om Prasad to instruct the government officials in the Cochin area to support his project in whatever way possible; they would do it, even out of the way, he knew it, if Om Prasad told them.

Anand wanted always to have some tourist project in Kerala State. Incidentally his mother, Rekha, came from Kerala. She belonged to a Brahmin family of Palakkad. Her father was in Delhi, and she had her studies there. She was a bank employee when she met the handsome Charles Almeida. Later on, she became a branch manager of the bank, when their marriage took place. Her income was the only means to keep the family from starvation. Charles Almeida was a chronic political activist and a staunch socialist. He never earned anything. He found it difficult even to have one square meal a day. But after his marriage, he could never complain. In memory of his mother, Anand always wanted to do something in Kerala. So a hotel project in Kerala was always dear to his heart.

Anand met Om Prasad at the Government Guest House and talked to him about his ideas regarding Indo-Pak relationship. Om Prasad saw the reasons and said he would talk to Charles Almeida about this when he came to Delhi.

Bu he added, 'I do not know how far the idea of reconciliation will be welcomed by other members of the Cabinet.'

Then the phone rang.

'Excuse me, uncle, it is K. C. Eapen Panicker, my project manager here; may I talk to him?'

Then he spoke into the phone 'Yes, Eapen?'

'Anand, the hotel project at Cochin is being delayed.'

'Why?'

'Simple reasons! Lame excuses. The transfer of the property into our possession is being delayed due to a bureaucratic wrangle.'

'Like?' Anand could not understand.

'The owner of the property, Mr Thomas Mathew, is in Dubai; he came down to settle the matter. He approached the village officer for possession certificate.'

'And?'

'He is not getting it for one flimsy reason or the other. That is it.'

The first day, Thomas Mathew approached the village officer, who asked him to produce the original sale document of the property. The next day when he brought it, the village officer asked him to bring the non-encumbrance certificate. Thomas Mathew said to him, 'You could have told me yesterday. I would have applied for it yesterday itself, and I would have got it by today. Now I can't apply; it is already too late. And tomorrow is a second Saturday,' (an obligatory holiday in Kerala State) 'and then Sunday. The earliest day I can apply is next Monday, and I may get it on Tuesday, if I am lucky. And I can present it to you on Wednesday. I have to leave for Dubai on a Thursday early-morning flight.'

'That is no problem. Bring all the documents on Wednesday.'

On Wednesday, Thomas Mathew brought all the original documents and non-encumbrance certificate to the village office, just to find that the village officer was on leave for two days. He would be back only on Friday.

On Friday, they had a strike. No buses were plying. And this was an excuse for the village officer to absent himself from office. He did not come on Saturday either.

'Anand, today is Monday. Thomas Mathew must have gone to the village officer today; he just wastes his time in Kerala just for this.'

'Go to the village office and call me from there. I shall talk to the officer myself', Anand was furious.

Accordingly K.C. Eapen went to the village office and called Anand from there.

'Yes, Eapen' said Anand. 'Hand over the phone to the village officer.'

Eapen told the village officer that Anand, the son of the Defense Minister, was on line.

'Sir, this is Anand. It's regarding the property of Mr. Thomas Mathew.'

Yes, sir. We shall expedite it, sir. We did not know that you are involved in it, sir.' The slave in the village officer came to light.

'Issue him the necessary documents quickly.'

'Yes, sir.'

The next day, Thomas Mathew came to the office of the village officer. The latter was in no better mood.

'To issue the possession certificate, we need the original sale document of the property and its encumbrance certificates.'

'Here they are.' Thomas gave them to the officer.

The officer sent a conspiratorial look to his colleague at the next table. 'We need to inspect your property. We have no vehicle here. So you should come with a vehicle tomorrow, so that we can come to your property. But remember to drop us back too.'

'I have come with my vehicle. Can we do it today itself?'

'No. Today we have other appointments. We will do it by tomorrow 11 a.m.'

'OK.'

The next day, Thomas Mathew came in his Mitsubishi Lancer car and took the village officer and two of his assistants to his property. They just walked a few feet along the compound wall, looked on the other side of the property, and came back and waited at the door of Thomas Mathew's house.

'Come in, sirs.'

They went in. Thomas Mathew had prepared coffee and snacks for them. But they expected a sumptuous lunch. One of the officers (he apparently was the last grade officer in the group) called Thomas Mathew to the side, and told him, 'Sir, this is lunchtime, and the officer did not have lunch, he wanted to do a favour by coming at this hour of the day for the inspection.'

'I know that,' said Thomas Mathew. He knew where he was leading to.

'So we need to take lunch.' The petty official was blunt. 'Please give them two thousand rupees; with that we will have lunch at the nearby hotel and will go on our own back to office!'

'Two thousand rupees for three lunches? That is unheard of,' said Thomas Mathew.

'You see, sir, they have come all the way from the office to conduct the inspection, just to oblige you, so you should properly reciprocate!'

'You mean, I have to grease your palms for the smooth execution of your job?'

'I did not mean that. We do you a favour and you do us a favour. That is it. It is like business. Besides, you have to show some respect to the officers.' replied the clerk.

'No, I am not prepared to pay any bribe for doing your job. I'm sorry.' Thomas Mathew was a straightforward man, honest, correct. First of all he saw that these fellows were not making any inspection; they did not even go along the compound wall, look for the boundary stones, etc. They just wanted to skip a few hours of their job at the office. And now they asked money for this trip!

'Then we are leaving. Come tomorrow morning to the office,' said the clerk curtly.

Thomas Mathew came to the office the next day.

'We do not see the receipts of your tax payments. On the contrary we see that one Mr O. V. Sunil has paid the tax of your property.'

'How could any X or Y pay my tax? If somebody paid the tax on my behalf, I thank him for his magnanimity. So what?'

'If someone paid tax for the property, he will stake a claim on the property,' said the village officer.

'How could you receive the tax from a person who is not the owner?' Thomas Mathew shot back.

'We do not keep the photos of the owners. He produced the copy of your documents and paid the tax. We received the tax. It is money. We can't deny that. On the receipt, we can put only the name of the person paying the tax.'

'How can you do that?'

'Don't get excited, Mr Thomas Mathew. That is how things are here?'

'This is lawlessness—anarchy.' Thomas Mathew was furious.

'Cool down. Don't be furious,' said the village officer. 'This is a simple matter. You can easily challenge it in the court and get a favourable verdict,' he added without remorse and shame.

Thomas Mathew inspected the tax register and found that the tax was paid only yesterday. He asked them, 'While I was here, how dare you receive the tax from another person?' Blood was welling up on his face. If he had a pistol, he would have shot both the officers point-blank.

'Anyway, the tax is paid by him. We cannot do anything. You can contest it in the court and come back with a court order showing that it was an error and that the property belongs to you.'

'It'll take years for such civil matters.' Thomas Mathew felt helpless. This was outrageous.

'We know. But we are helpless, too.'

Thomas Mathew left the office, full of rage, anger, and desperation. This country could not be saved! These petty officials were exploiting everyone. People come to them for their service, but they punished them and made things difficult for them; they were slowing down everything purposely, maliciously, for money. The pain of others did not bother them at all. These petty fellows were the ones that hampered the development of this country.

The village officer and his clerks started to laugh and shouted, 'Did that fool think that he could intimidate us by asking the office of the defence minister to call us? Then, let the defence minister come and disentangle the knot we tied!' They laughed again louder. It was like devil's laughter, thought Thomas Mathew. It was full of hate, spite, and malice.

The purchase of the plot did not come through as planned. It was getting delayed. Anand asked the private secretary of his father to call the state president of his party in Kerala to straighten out the matter. The state president of the Social Party was a man well aware of the shady tricks of such petty officials. He sent his assistant with a bunch of goondas the next day. They manhandled and damaged the village office. They practically took charge of the office; the goondas kicked the village officer and his assistants with their boots and slapped them right across their faces. Blood began oozing from their dirty noses. 'Destroy the fake tax receipt,' shouted the leader. 'We want to see that happening before our eyes. Otherwise you will not go home alive, you bastard!'

The officer obediently tore into pieces the fake tax receipt they had fabricated the other day and filled out the possession certificate with all the necessary details and handed it over to the leader of the goondas.

He then called out, 'Thomas Mathew, please come in, sir.'

As Thomas Mathew came in, the officer and his cohorts stood up in reverence. 'Sorry, sir,' they said in unison.

'If you did like this on the very first day, I could have saved a lot of time and energy. Do you know how much time I have lost, how much money I have lost? I could not fly back to Dubai and join my duty in time. I lost thousands of rupees because of you. I could have gone back and earned at least two hundred thousand rupees by this time. You are petty officials. But you are the ones who exploit the common man and slow down the progress of our country. Be ashamed of yourselves. Don't repeat this to others, especially to the poor.'

Thomas Mathew dashed out of the office in haste with the certificate. 'We need a dozen Robin Hoods in this country,' he told the party officials. The goondas too left the corrupt, malicious, haughty, officers to lick their wounds.

The sale deed of the property was signed within the next two days. The construction of the International Backwater Resort at Cochin would start one month later. Anand hoped to open its doors for tourists within twelve months.

Early morning, Anand and Minister Om Prasad got into the Mercedes-Benz car provided by the tourism department and started off to Bekal. Anand was enthralled by the scenic beauty of the places along the road to Bekal Fort.

Minister Om Prasad was a very hilarious person; at his Delhi residence, he used to host dinners for the celebrities and socialites of the city. The speciality of his parties was the Kerala delicacies, like appam, karimeen (cat fish), and tiger prawns. Almost all the MPs had been his guests at one time or another. Charles Almeida too was once his guest. At that time, Charles Almeida was the MP from Lucknow. Anand still had the sweet memories of the tasty food of those dinner parties. Anand was specially attracted by the variety of flavours and spices used in the Kerala food. He liked their smell. He liked their look. He liked their taste. The sambar (vegetables cooked with saucy yellow gram), the rasam (light tomato sauce with special spices), the aviyal (vegetables cooked without saucy ingredients), the roasted blackfish, and finally the roasted prawns (especially the tiger prawns from Kerala)—all these had been a festival for his taste buds. Since those days he always wanted to go to Kerala.

As soon as he was in his constituency, Minister Om Prasad had to hold some serious talks with one of his close party associates, Ramakrishna Warrier. So they made a stopover at the Government Guest House there.

Anand went to his room to take rest. He was very tired after the long journey. He was not used to the heat and humidity of the area.

Warrier was formerly a local heavyweight of the Indian People's Party (IPP). Through the influence of Minister Prasad, he switched over to the BPP party.

Northern part of the State is notorious for its brutal attitude towards political opponents. Formerly the fight was between the Social Secular Party (SSP) and the IPP; during the last five or six years the political rivalry is between the Bharat People's Party (BPP) and IPP. Since the ascendency of BPP to power at the Centre, the BPP had begun to flex its muscles in every part of the country where they have some sort of presence.

Many young men in the northern region shifted loyalty from IPP to BPP. This had outraged the IPP heavyweights. They carried on a vendetta against those who leave the party. Political murders had become very common. The murderers took refuge in the so-called party villages, where nobody belonging to a different party could enter or live. Nobody could go into those villages without the permission of the local leaders.

Thus there came into existence BPP villages and IPP villages; the leadership of both the parties gave their blessings lavishly to these villages. These villages had become also the haven of criminals. These villages had become states within a state. Those who live in them are safe from the opposing parties and even from the police.

Ramakrishna Warrier was formerly a staunch supporter of IPP. After a series of detailed secret talks with Minister Om Prasad, he switched his loyalty to BPP. This had antagonised the IPP leadership and local workers. They were clamouring for his blood—literally; nothing short of that would satisfy the cadres. Opponents have to be annihilated; that was the prevalent political motto in the northern region of Kerala State, the most literate state of India.

Warrier visited Minister Om Prasad to give vent to his feelings of insecurity, the real threat to his life, and to the lives of his wife, his two sons, and two daughters. The children were all grown-ups, were married, but political vendetta is merciless; it does not even exempt the children of the enemy from its wrath. Children should die with the parents or for the parents!

The minister fondly asked him, 'What can I do for you, Warrier chetta?' (*Chetta* is an endearment meaning 'elder brother'.) He was aware that Warrier was going to be a scapegoat, nay, martyr, for the party; only with the blood of martyrs can any party thrive in the northern region!

'I'm afraid for my life.' Warrier had never wept in his life. For the first time he was crying, tears flowing down his cheeks. He had been to prison during the independence agitation, and thereafter during the political activism as an IPP sympathizer. He was valiant and had always kept his composure. But now, he was not alone. He had a wife, and four dear children. There was real threat to his life, to those of his wife and children.

'And I'm scared. My life is under threat. My wife is in danger. So are all my children. The IPP people are a too dangerous tribe. I know them from close quarters,' said Warrier.

'Don't worry, Mr Warrier, we will take care of you. The party will see to it that nothing happens to you and to your dear family,' the minister chose the right words to comfort Mr Warrier and to instil in him absolute faith in the party. 'Our people will not allow anything untoward to happen. They are determined to protect every one of our members; they will pay their lives for that.'

'But the other side is watching every move of mine,' continued Warrier. 'They have their spies to find out where I go and whom I visit. For example, they know exactly that I am with you now. Is there any escape for me? I never thought I would have to pay these heavy fees for changing my political belief.' Warrier's words were full of real desperation.

Warrier was a staunch worker of IPP and so he knows well how the IPP party functions. He was one among the few who decided every move of the party in the troubled northern region. He knew how the IPP party took note of even the attitudinal change of people in the villages. He was part of that machinery.

Now that he had switched over to the other side, he came to feel the pinch of it. He came to understand how inhuman he was in those days. He was hunting others in those days; now he was the hunted, and the haunted. He regretted all that he did then, but it was now too late. He was now fated to live in permanent fear and anguish.

He knew the fate of BPP youth leader Ramachandran, who was ambushed and stabbed to death on the night of 31st December while everyone was celebrating and lighting firecrackers. The next day, the first day of the year, there lay the dead and mutilated body of Ramachandran on the small mud road leading to his house; no one knew of it until next day morning. Warrier knew of Harikumar, who was attacked with swords and bamboo sticks in broad daylight in the Thalassery market. He could count the fates of dozens of BPP workers hacked to death. He was also aware that an equal number of IPP workers too died in the same fashion. And there was no respite from the series of murders.

'Mr Warrier, I shall give strict instructions to our people and to the police to take care of your safety and that of your family.' Minister Om Prasad hugged Mr Warrier to assure him of his concern for him and to dispel his anxieties, but he (the minister) knew the threat would still be there, as long as Mr Warrier was a member of the BPP party.

Once the matter of Warrier was concluded, Minister Om Prasad invited Anand for a ride through his own constituency.

'It's quite nearby, a few kilometres from here. You could visit my home, and can have a typical Malayalee lunch there, before proceeding to Mangalore, from where you can fly back to Delhi via Bombay.' Minister Om Prasad was all courtesy while treating his friend's son.

'OK, uncle. I would love to see your place,' replied Anand.

They passed through paddy fields, coconut farms, cashew plantations. All over, there was greenery aplenty and serpentine roads.

'Fantastic!' exclaimed Anand. 'Really it is God's own country. It's green like paradise.'

Being a political being, Minister Om Prasad wanted to give Anand a taste of a typical north Kerala village. He took him to the Maraveli village. This is one of the several party villages; no one shall enter such villages without the due authorisation of the IPP (Indian People's Party). Though Anand did not know anything about this, he was curious about the way many passersby on the roads looked at them. There was an air of suspicion in everyone's face. Or was it just curiosity? He never came across such suspicious, and sometimes inimical, looks of people elsewhere in India.

The onlookers were really interested to know who these strange guys were.

'Who is this chap with the minister?' Krishnan asked one of the bystanders. He did not ask anyone specifically. The question hung in the air. He just wanted to say that he did not relish anyone from outside visiting his village. It was a village dedicated to the eternal revolution of the IPP. No one outside the village should visit it without the permission of the local IPP leaders!

Arvind was coming out of the toddy shop. (Toddy is a local alcoholic drink obtained from the sap of the coconut flower bunch.)

Krishnan asked Arvind whether he knew any of these strangers.

'Let Minister Om Prasad do what he wants. But that should be in line with the guidelines of our party. He knows it.' Arvind was very practical.

The car stopped a few feet away from the toddy shop. The travellers got out of the   car just to straighten their backs. Krishnan became more curious.

He went inside the toddy shop and told his comrades about a few newcomers. They got up and looked through the grills to assess the situation.

'No, he is not known to us. He is a total stranger,' said Balu. Balu was one of the volunteers of the party, who monitored the people who entered and went out of this IPP village.

'He could be somebody from outside Kerala. What does he want here? He has no right to pry into the secrets of our village.'

'He could be from the CID (Crime Investigation Department), or somebody from the CBI?'

'I don't think so. What have they to seek here?'

'Well then, what shall we do?' asked Krishnan.

'Let's wait and see. We shall find out what their purpose is,' said Balu.

At this moment, the driver, Minister Om Prasad, and Anand boarded the car, and the car was going to enter a side road towards the interior of the village. That made things worse!

'How could they dare do that? Minister Om Prasad must know about these matters!'

Balu, Arvind, and Krishnan came out of the toddy shop through the back door and went speedily ahead so that they could block the taxi by the next turn.

Minister Om Prasad was curious that nothing untoward happened. Anand was leisurely enjoying the serene atmosphere of the village.

As the car turned the curve, the three youngsters stood in the middle of the road and blocked the further movement of the car. They whistled and a few more youngsters came to the spot from nowhere.

'Minister Om Prasad, aren't you aware that it is not allowed to go into the interior of our village? You are not a stranger to this place. You know why. We do not want our peace to be disturbed by outsiders.'

'Of course,' said Minister Om Prasad, 'but we have no intention to disturb anybody, and the least to disturb the peace of this village. We just wanted to see the place.'

'For what? Why should you see our village?'

'Just to see its scenic beauty.'

'Minister Om Prasad, you saw the flags on that electric post, no? You know what it means.'

Minister Om Prasad showed Anand the red flag hanging from the electric post at the corner and explained to Anand that it was meant to declare that this was an exclusive IPP village, and those flags were the limit of the village. You were, so to say, entering foreign (!) territory!

Outsiders were not allowed to go beyond that post. Outsiders could not live in this village; they could not marry anyone in this village without the permission of the CPP bosses.

'Oh, that is strange,' exclaimed Anand. 'Is there anything like territorial jurisdiction for a political party inside India?' Anand could not understand that.

'Yes, Anand. It is the unwritten law of this place. This happens only in Kerala and in West Bengal.'

'That sounds curious. Unheard-of elsewhere.'

The youngsters were becoming restive. They were planning the next step they had to take to evict the intruders.

'Shall I deflate the tyres of the car?' asked Balu.

'Or shall we give the driver a small dose of punishment?' asked Aravind.

'None of it. Minister Om Prasad is in the car. It will create problems if we manhandled his driver.' said Krishnan.

'Who is he? Is he God? Let us see what will happen.' Saying this, Aravind pulled the driver's door open and dragged the driver out of the car, and slapped him hard on the cheek. As the slap landed on his face, the driver fell flat to the ground.

'What the hell are you doing?' shouted Minister Om Prasad. Anand could not comprehend what was happening.

The driver scrambled to his feet and was about to question the activists. Then Aravind pushed the driver into the car, and shouted, 'Take a U-turn and leave the place immediately. Otherwise, you will have a taste of Maraveli masala.'

Minister Om Prasad heaved a sigh of relief. After all, nothing serious happened. Anand got an inkling of what was in store if one intruded into the territory of the IPP party.

'Maraveli masala! What is that?' asked Anand.

'What you saw just now is the aperitif. What would have followed is the Maraveli masala!'

Minister Om Prasad got enough matter for his next political speech. He instructed the driver to take a U-turn. They drove the car to the main road and proceeded in the direction of NH-17 (National Highway17 going to Bombay via Mangalore).

'This is a unique political phenomenon in this part of the Kerala State. I just wanted to show you what it looks like,' said Minister Om Prasad.

'It is absolutely unheard of. I have never come across such a phenomenon in other parts of our country. This is like a sovereign state within a state,' said Anand.

'Anand. There are several such villages in this area, where the IPP has total jurisdiction. These villages are used to protect their party men who had to flee from the eyes of the police. Such villages were created during the rule of the previous state government in which IPP was a major coalition partner.'

Minister Om Prasad explained to Anand that there were also BPP villages in this part of the state, where no one could enter without the permission of the local BPP leadership. No one in that village could marry anyone inimical to the BPP, nor could anyone from these villages take part in the marriage functions of IPP workers or sympathisers, because IPP was the traditional enemy of BPP.

'This is bad,' exclaimed Anand, 'extremely bad. This is bad politics. Are people here numb? Kerala is supposed to be the most literate and civilised state of our country. And this is happening here? That people and the parties tolerate this is a very sad thing. Shame!' He paused and again said, 'Shame!'

Minister Om Prasad did not describe the tragedy the wife of the erstwhile IPP leader had to suffer at the hands of IPP. Since the death of the comrade, the IPP was having a love-hate relationship with his wife. She resented their covert attempt to interfere with her life. The IPP did not like her attitude and literally they excommunicated her from the party, and no party workers were allowed to talk to her, to sympathise with her; no labourers were allowed to work for her. She had a few coconut trees; none of the workers was willing to pluck coconuts for her. Nobody was allowed to help her in any way.

Anand wondered what these people understood by democracy.

'You know what?' Om Prasad continued, 'There are a few college campuses where rival groups are not allowed to function.'

'For example?' Anand was curious.

'A government college in one of our major cities, for example. It is the domain of the revolutionary student wing, Socialist Students Federation for Peace and Equality, SSF for short. No other student organization can function inside its campus; no one can challenge the SSF candidates, and in actual fact, no one can get admission in this college without the concurrence of the SSF leadership. SSF is the student wing of the IPP. Interesting, no?'

'Quite interesting. Is it true? If it is true, it is unheard of and strange. How can this state tolerate such brazenness? Is it compatible with the democratic principles of this country?'

'The funniest thing is that the SSF has the full support of its political party. Majority of the professors and lecturers of this college are members and/or fellow travellers of that party. The SSF has special rooms to keep their weapons too. Some criminals (who naturally belong to their parent party) find refuge in the designated rooms of the college.'

'They seem to be the Indian inheritors of the Stalinist policies prevalent in the former USSR and allied countries, where there were only a single candidate, a single party, and the candidate of the party won always with 99.9 per cent votes! The fools here do not know that that is why they fell! And miserably,' mused Anand.

'To hold on to power these tactics are practiced here. No one dares to raise his voice against it. Once, one of my nephews tried to start an independent students' association in that college. The result was that he was forcibly taken into their custody, and the SSF student leaders carved on his back the letters SSF and sent him home bleeding. This is the lesson in tolerance!'

'Is this possible and permissible in a democracy?' asked Anand.

10

The two chiefs of the border security forces normally meet once a week at the Wagah check post on the border. After the usual salutations and exchange of pleasantries, it was business as usual. This time it was pleasanter than before. They agreed to avoid confrontations. The suggestion came from Pakistan's side.

'From today, we will not shell, if no provocation happens from your side, commander,' Commander Wahab said.

'We will definitely not provoke your boys. Why should we open fire when there is no provocation? You can trust me. I do what I say.' Commander Inderjit Gupta was equally in a good mood.

'Why don't we give clear instructions to all the units along the border to keep away from firing for the next seven days? Let there be calm in the Kargil, Poonch, and other sensitive areas,' suggested Cmdr Wahab.

'Agreed. No firing from our side for the next seven days.'

'Neither from our side.'

Cmdr Wahab handed over a woollen shawl to Cmdr Inderjit. 'This is from Islamabad. It will keep you warm during the coming weeks of cold.'

Inderjit had brought a box of Punjabi sweets for Cmdr Wahab.

Both the commanders were courteous all of a sudden! They did not talk politics; they just talked about their positions and postures next week. But it helped to keep the line of control out of danger, conflict, injuries, and deaths. The governments on both sides had approved this procedure, though in public they reproached each other in consideration of their own constituencies.

Ambassador Mohammed Yasin, the Pakistani ambassador to the United States, sat in his ornate office in the NW district of Washington DC. He was a distant relative of the present president of Pakistan. His predecessor, Hafiz Aboobaker, was a cousin of the deposed President Habeebulla. During the turbulent years of army takeovers, Habeebulla was deposed and Hafiz Aboobaker sought political asylum in the United States.

The change of government in Pakistan never makes change in their attitude to India. The policy towards India is marked by animosity and enmity. All their presidents hated India, not because Pakistan is Muslim-dominated country and India a Hindu dominated country, but because Pakistan, despite all its good relationships with China and the United States, could never become strategically nor politically nor economically an equal to India. By the sheer size of the country, the size of the population, and the quality of technological achievements, India was far superior to Pakistan; the size of its industrial and intellectual base is well acclaimed even by superpowers. This has been an unsettling pain for every ruler of Pakistan.

This hate became more intensive and bitter when India succeeded in separating East Pakistan from West Pakistan.

East Pakistan became Bangladesh in 1971. India's role in the independence of Bangladesh is not a secret.

For India that was a strategic victory. Formerly, India had to divide its forces between the eastern front (along East Pakistan border) and the western front (along the West Pakistan border). When Bangladesh became independent with the support of India, half the concern and burden of border security forces was taken away from the Indian armed forces. Now it needs only to look after the western border, which is relatively easy. Because of the perennial enmity, both the countries spend lavishly on defence.

Ambassador Yasin was in a pensive mood. He took the phone and dialled a number he only knew. He could not write down certain numbers in any book nor in his electronic diary. He had to store them in his memory only.

'Hello!' There came a deep guttural voice on the line.

'This is Yasin.'

'Hi. Ambassador, how do you do?'

'I'm fine, and you?'

'I'm quite fine. I'm recovering from a tedious journey in the African continent.'

'How is your country doing?'

'We can't complain.'

'We heard you have some problem along the border with India?'

'It is the usual drama. We have to use some of our old munitions. Instead of just destroying them, we send them across to India to test their effectiveness.'

'Did you get the last consignment?'

'Of course. We got it via Turkey and Saudi Arabia.'

'The stuff is excellent. At least that is what the military says. They are happy with it. They tested them during the Kargil confrontation. Our borders function also as a test range! Our freedom fighters, who regularly cross over to the Indian side, used them very successfully.'

A turbulent border is very useful for people dealing with military hardware. Marketing promotion will be done by the turbulence—at no extra cost!

'Do you need more of them?'

'Definitely.'

'How is the payment?'

'It'll be done through our contact in Saudi Arabia. KSA has sanctioned US$300 million to buy food for the Afghan refugees in Pakistan.'

'I presume the followers of any known terrorist outfit are not connected with this. Their name or connection should not come in any transactions, because currently they are in our black list. You know our account is in the Credit Suisse Nationale?'

'Of course. We can transfer half of the Saudi money to you for your shipment. Let the containers be routed through your bases in Saudi Arabia!'

'By the by, why should you buy wheat from Australia?'

'The price is competitive, that's why. Why did you ask?'

'We can deliver you wheat a bit below their rate. Say, 5 per cent below their price. It has the advantage that the whole of Saudi money can be transferred as payment for wheat. Is that OK with you?'

'It's an idea. But I have to get clearance from Islamabad. I shall get back to you this evening. You shall quote the same price as the Australians, but the difference will be paid into my personal account in the Zuricher Credit Bank; you know my account number.'

'Of course. It can be done as you said. We give you 2 per cent on the whole transaction. Is that OK with you? 0.50 per cent for you personally, and the rest for your decision-makers in Islamabad. OK?'

'That may not be the figure my bosses would like to hear. The people in Islamabad will not be happy with below 3 per cent. So you will have to add another percentage point for me.'

'For that I have to get clearance from my boss. Call me by tomorrow evening, at seven thirty sharp. Then I shall tell you the exact percentages.'

'Sure!'

He hurriedly called Islamabad on his hotline. Abdul Nasser Malkani, the private secretary to the president, was on the line. Yasin told him of the developments. Malkani asked him to bargain hard for the percentages. 'We cannot go below 3.5 per cent. Of this, 1.5 per cent has to go into the Swiss account of the president, 1.5 per cent has to be divided among the generals, and the balance (0.5 per cent) has to go into my personal account in Banque International de Luxembourg. The dividend of the generals has to be deposited in their account in the Isle of Man, UK. They have a common account there and they have a mechanism in place to divide the spoils.'

'Then what about me?' asked Yasin.

'You will get half of what I get. Is that OK?'

'OK.'

Yasin had no objection to the percentages, provided his own cut in the deal was clear.

The next day exactly at 7.30 p.m., Yasin called his man and told him the commissions and their percentages, as transpired in the talk with Malkani.

'The total commission of 4.25 per cent will be acceptable to my boss. Yasin, you would get your 0.75 per cent and for others altogether 3.5 per cent. Is that OK?'

Yasin was more than willing to agree to the deal. His 0.75 per cent had to be transferred to his account without anyone else knowing about it. He would get another 0.25 per cent from Malkani; thus he was assured of 1 per cent, which was more than enough.

The US$300 million donated by Saudi Arabia to buy food for the Afghan refugees in Pakistan was duly transferred to the account of the Colorado Farm Enterprises (CFE). The CFE in turn arranged the wheat for Pakistan, and also other things as per the direction of Pakistan's ambassador in the United States. The commissions to the various parties involved were also transferred from the company's accounts in the Bahamas to the respective accounts in Switzerland, Luxembourg, and the Isle of Man, as directed by Yasin.

Wheat worth US$300 million arrived in Pakistan via Dubai. US$100 million worth of it was sold in the black market to finance the 'freedom fighters' on the Indian side of Kashmir. The wheat consignment was distributed to them, who in turn sold it to finance their respective area of activity.

One third of the wheat was donated to the army barracks. The weapons were hidden in those containers. After the arms and ammunition were recovered, the wheat went to the army provision store to be divided among the indigent (!) military personnel.

There were currently about three million Afghan refugees in Pakistan territory. The military invasion of the USSR, then the subsequent attempt and success of the United States in ousting the Russians from there was history. The Americans were conducting a proxy war with the other superpower, the Soviet Union. The Afghan jihadists gave the Americans the necessary cover in their fight. But these operations involved steady flow of powerful weapons into the region. Americans taught the Afghans to fight for their country in the name of Allah. Jihad was supported by the steady flow of the most effective weapons the Americans could think of.

All the American help for the poor Afghans was flowing through Pakistan. In the process, Pakistani guerillas as well as fundamentalist elements amassed the arms.

Thus the whole region was flooded with weapons, Russian and American.

When Americans were flooding the region with arms, the Russians could not hold on to this alien territory for long. When they quit, the power struggle between Dostum and Taliban broke out. Both the groups had amassed enough weapons from the Russians and from the Americans. In the melee, the Taliban succeeded in controlling Afghanistan, and eventually they turned out to be enemy number one of the United States. The rest of the story is history.

The brunt of the Afghan War was suffered both by Pakistan and India—Pakistan because of the millions of Afghan refugees. Pakistan was not at all able to feed the millions of refugees and the subsequent governments in Afghanistan were not ready to take the refugees back. But

11

Abdul Lateef was a fan of German technology. He uses only equipment made by Bosch or Siemens. His car is Mercedes-Benz. His second car is a BMW.

'If you look for technical perfection, go to the Germans,' he used to say.

He never missed the great Hannover Messe (exhibition), which is one of the finest technological exhibitions of the world. This year too, Abdul Lateef was going to Germany to take part in the millennium exhibition at Hannover. Hasina accompanied him.

On hearing of Abdul Lateef's visit to Germany, Anand took a Lufthansa flight from New Delhi to Frankfurt, and from there, he took the ICE superfast train to Hannover. Within two and a half hours, he reached Hannover and checked into the Hannover Hof, the best hotel in Hannover. As soon as he was settled in his room, he called Hasina. She had become softer, friendlier, maybe because of the change in Abdul Lateef himself. Her tone revealed it.

'How are you, dear?'

'Quite well, and you?'

'Can we somehow meet?'

'It would be difficult.'

'Why?'

'These secret service people, they are all over. If I have to meet you, it has to be arranged properly. I shall give the phone to my father. He will tell you where to meet us.'

Hasina gave the phone to Abdul Lateef. They talked matter-of-factly. Abdul Lateef gave directions to Anand and asked him to come to the Hilton International on Konrad Adenauer Strasse within thirty minutes.

Anand put on a beard and an Arab robe. He arrived in twenty minutes. His BMW 309 was flying.

He approached the reception. 'Was kann ich fuer Sie tun?' asked the lady behind the reception desk.

'I'm supposed to visit Mr Abdul Lateef in his suite,' he said.

'Ein moment, bitte.' She punched a few buttons on her computer and said in her heavily accented English, 'Can you please go to room numberrr 314?'

At room no. 314, he was asked to go to room no. 515 and wait for instructions. He did as he was told.

There was a gentle knock at the door; he opened it. He could not believe his eyes. There stood the girl of his dreams, Hasina, beautiful as ever. She stretched out her right hand; Anand grasped it, shook it, and pulled her inside and hugged her tight.

'What are you doing here?' shouted Hasina.

'I'm doing what I'm doing: hugging you, darling.' Totally emotional was Anand.

'Well, I cannot approve of this for the time being. Our culture does not permit it,' shot back Hasina.

Soon he let her go; she regained her composure and asked him to follow her. She escorted him to the room of her father. He was in a good mood.

'You are following me like a hound, young man?'

'I am. I will go on doing that. I will go any length to achieve my dream,' Anand said.

'Anand, you know I like you. But this affair cannot go on because of the sour relations between the two countries.'

'I know.'

'You must stop visiting my daughter and corresponding with her.'

'That is almost impossible, uncle.'

'It cannot be allowed, I say categorically.'

'Is there no way out, uncle?'

'No, as far as I know. I can never present the matter to my family, our all-powerful clergy, our politicians, bureaucrats, military. All of them will flay me, and burn me alive, if this continues.'

Anand did not expect this twist to the events. He came full of hopes and with a sense of anticipation. He thought Abdul Lateef would be positive as far as this relationship was concerned. He did not think of the political and religious ramifications.

'There should be some way out, uncle. May I say something?'

'Yes?'

'Why don't you make an effort to meet our prime minister somehow somewhere?'

'I cannot promise anything. My predecessor Habeebulla had declared that he would visit India, and that rogue is now sitting in jail. If I make a promise, I will keep it. At present I cannot make any promise; I do not find an occasion to meet your prime minister either.'

'Why can't you take up the initiative to create an occasion?'

'It's not possible in the immediate future.'

'It is never too late. Why don't you give a hint to the foreign minister of Germany and ask him to mediate?'

'Immediately all the other NATO partners will come to know of it and nothing tangible can be achieved. Everything has to be done in absolute secrecy, absolute diplomatic secrecy. All the powers in the world are interested in our countries, not because they like us, but because they like themselves. We are a good market to dump their old and useless weaponry. There are powers that do not want us to be friends.'

Anand was spellbound before his honesty. He could feel that he was afraid also of the US, which would not be very positive in this matter. To keep India and Pakistan as enemies is the secret agenda of the military hardware lobby. It is the most powerful lobby in the US and nobody can do anything against their wish.

'Would you let me try something at New Delhi?'

'My son, I am all for a peaceful settlement. But your people think I am just like the former rulers of Pakistan. I am really sincere about it. If it happens in my lifetime, I will be the happiest man on earth. So try. I too shall do my part.'

'Thank you, uncle. This is the happiest moment of my life.'

'Why?'

'Because you called me son.'

'Did I?'

Hasina, coming out of the connecting door said, 'You did call him so.'

'Ya, yes . . . If I did, it must have been a slip of the tongue.'

'No, Dad. You never make such mistakes. Whatever you say comes direct from your heart,' insisted Hasina.

My daughter is shrewd. She knows me. I have no way out. I must just fall in line and acknowledge it.

'Yes, that is my real feeling for you, Anand. I like you. I feel you are my unborn son. Go now. Be careful when you get out of here. In fifteen minutes, I have another appointment.'

'Thank you, uncle. We shall meet soon.'

Anand went out. The RAW men of India were waiting for him at the lobby; so were the men of ISI.

Pakistan's ISI men understood that the Indian intelligence people were also after the visitor to the president, so their waiting at the hotel lobby was worthwhile; their colleagues stayed put in their respective vehicles.

The ISI men informed Abdul Lateef of their presence in the lobby. So he called his daughter to him and told her in a very low voice, 'Hasina, tell Anand not to use the elevator, but to walk down the staircase and go through the back door and leave the country as soon as possible.'

Hasina was about to rush to the room of Anand, when her mobile rang. 'It's me. I am out of the hotel.' It was Anand.

Anand had collected his small briefcase, left the room through his window, then to the fire escape. He got out of the hotel through a back door and hailed a taxi, asked the taxi driver to proceed to the airport. On the way, Anand got down at Wurzburger Strasse, hailed another taxi, and proceeded to the railway station, where he took the next available ICE train to Hamburg, and from there, he took a KLM flight to the Schiphol Airport at Amsterdam, Holland.

The secret service men knocked on his door once, then several times, but got no reply; they called for the room boy and got it opened. They went inside to find that he had already left.

Information was passed on to their men at the lobby, who inquired about the details of the guest who was at the reception a few minutes back. The name of the guest was recorded as Abdul Hameed from Qatar. Anand used a fake passport!

Neither the Indian intelligence people nor the ISI people could find out who the visitor to Abdul Lateef was. And could they dare ask Abdul Lateef?

12

The Bofors gun deal was the biggest scandal during the time of Prime Minister Rajiv Gandhi. The Indian government imported the Swedish gun manufactured by Bofors Company, in view of its range and manoeuvrability. The scandal was that some middlemen received commissions from the Bofors Company for the successful completion of the transaction.

Everyone knows that this is no big deal. Commissions are a common feature in all business transactions. And no transaction happens without middlemen.

But in the hands of the political parties, this was an excellent cause for political manoeuvres and machinations. When you are in the opposition, you look for something to sling mud at the ruling party or parties.

The Bofors issue was very handy for the politicians of opposition parties. The opposition boosted it to a mega-scandal or scam. Politicians and media took immense pleasure in magnifying scams out of proportion. Bofors became a catchword in every political speech inside and outside Parliament, just like Watergate, after Nixon.

The enquiry into this 'scandal' has not yet been concluded, even after decades. Let the enquiry continue. Commissions and tribunals are instituted not to find any solution to the problem, but to postpone the possible solutions.

S. M. Patel, the personal assistant of General S. P. Mallick, was on a tour of Sweden, Austria, and Germany, scouting for arms purchase. He went first to Sweden. At Stockholm airport, the Indian ambassador S. K. S. Nambiar received him.

Nambiar had worked out the appointments of Mr S. M. Patel, at the request of General Mallick. His first meeting was with the military attaché at the Indian Embassy, Mr Nikhil Chopra. The discussion was regarding the enquiry of the defence ministry regarding the ammunition for the Bofors guns, which had become very popular in the army after the Kargil incident; at Kargil, the Bofors guns were the kingpin of defence in the mountain ranges.

Ambassador Nambiar had deputed his trusted Lieutenant R. S. Mani to accompany Mr Patel. After his meeting at the embassy with the military attaché, Patel went straight to the Swedish ministry of defence. The discussion was regarding the range of weapon systems that India wished to import from Sweden. The list was presented to the Swedish ministry, and they would send the quotations within two weeks.

After the meeting at the defence ministry, Patel came back to his hotel. Then he thanked Mr Mani and sent him and the chauffeur back. He said he had no other plans for that day; he would call Mani the next morning.

As soon as they were gone, Patel went down to the lobby, called a taxi, and went to 26 Vriestrad. He rang the doorbell. The 65-year-old man opened the door. It was none other than Sorensen Sune, one of the accused in the Bofors case.

Patel discussed with Sune the performance of the Bofors guns.

'Despite the mud-slinging and unnecessary political farces, don't you feel that our Bofors guns are the best?' asked Sune. Bitterness was painted in every one of his words. 'These nasty Indian politicians!'

'No doubt, the Bofors guns were our best defence in the Kargil skirmish. And the politicians, you know, they need something to talk about. If it is against one of the mightiest politicians, then it is even better.'

'Are they not taking commissions, nay, bribe, on every transaction they do, in every one of their departments? Not only in defence, but in the energy sector, in the import of any and every item, in the issue of every licence and permit?' He was bitter.

'It is public knowledge. The only thing is that some of the politicians are not clever enough to do things in the most discreet manner. They jump into things without adequate safety valves; they entrust matters to immature assistants. So a few things come to light, and the media and the opposition parties are more than willing to exploit it.'

'Now, what can I do for you, Mr Patel?'

'Let enquiries go on. Such enquiry commissions are the only way to keep the retired judges employed!' said Patel. 'I am on a private mission to locate suitable armaments for us. Urgently we need the ammunitions for the Bofors guns. We need it immediately. You know exactly where we have to go for them.'

'For your immediate needs, I can arrange them from the South African subsidiary, if the price is right,' Sune said.

'Don't worry on that count. We know the market value of things. Any single-digit percentage of fluctuation won't affect us. Our DRDO is trying to develop the required ammunition for the Bofors guns; it would be ready only in three years. So to fill that gap, we need ammunition from elsewhere.'

'That can be done. Give me a few hours. I can tell you by tomorrow morning. Call me tomorrow by eight thirty,' said Sune.

He had to consult his associates in South Africa. He knew South Africa wouldn't need them in the near future. Besides, India had the best of relations with South Africa. He knew this. But he would break the news only the next day.

'And what about the payment?' Sune asked Patel.

'Indian defence has enough money. Our trade balance is very good. So money is not at all a problem, especially for the defence ministry. The thing has to be good and the price has to be correct. And you should think of us too, when you make a hefty profit!' said Patel bluntly.

'And what about me?' asked Sune.

Patel wanted to safeguard not only himself but also Sune. The name of Sune Sorensen should not figure in any of the documents, directly or indirectly.

Finally he said, 'The offer has to come from South Africa. You will have to talk to them about the modalities; you have to ask them to put a price tag of 10 per cent above market value. In case of a price negotiation, which would definitely take place, they agree to reduce 5 per cent and you will still have 5 per cent spread to take care of our requirements. Because of the urgency and because of the known fact that the ammunition is difficult to get, the 5 per cent increase in the price won't be noted by your people.'

Patel knew that there was nothing new in this; in every government transaction in his country, this was the modus operandi. Purchasing is the big business for every ministry and department and public-sector enterprises. The more you purchase, the more you earn! Purchasing from abroad has preference in all the departments of the Indian government. The price hike is not an issue at all. There should be a credit component. Then everything will be fine. Power projects, which can be implemented with Indian technology by Indian companies, will be handed over to foreign companies for double the amount; the justification is that the foreign company will arrange also finance for the project (though in real fact, Indian banks are flush with money).

'But take care, your name shall never figure in any of the documents or transactions; don't make a mistake twice.' This was a reference to the Bofors scam being investigated in India. After a pause, Patel said, 'Of the 5 per cent, you take 1.5 per cent, and the 3.5 per cent is for us.'

'For us? What does it mean?' Sune knew how it would work out, but he wanted to hear it from Patel.

'Half a per cent is for me and it has to go into my own personal numbered account with the Zuricher Credit Bank, at Zurich, Switzerland. Balance (i.e. 3 per cent) has to go into another numbered account in the Credit Suisse Nationale at Bern.'

'Of course I know how exactly the defence purchases in India work. Normally 1 per cent goes to the personal account of the defence minister, 0.5 per cent into the campaign fund of his party; 0.5 per cent goes into the campaign fund of the ruling Indian Jana Morcha party; and 1 per cent for all the generals to divide. I am not bothered about how it is going to be divided.'

'Your one-time transaction of the Bofors guns has made you an expert on the Indian purchase system!' said Patel.

'By the way, what is your salary, Mr Patel?'

'Forty-eight thousand rupees net per month, plus benefits. Gross it will be around ninety thousand rupees; annually it will be a little above one million Indian rupees, i.e. roughly twenty thousand US dollars per year. Why did you ask?'

'I was wondering what will happen to you, if you are caught in the deal.'

A lightning chill ran through his spinal cord. He knew that could happen. He could be caught one day. He knew what would happen if he was caught.

He had done this before. He was the trusted lieutenant of General Mallick, who was the chairman of the arms purchase clearing committee. No arms purchase would happen without the consent of the general—and the general would never give his nod unless and until it was cleared by Mr Patel. But it was known to both of them. Nobody in the world knew about their relationship in this matter.

Patel was quite aware of his position. He was aware of his roots. Patels are very rich, normally. But S. M. Patel came from a very poor family. His house was not worth its name, it was just a hut in the outskirts of Kirkee township near Pune, in Maharashtra State. In the 300 sq. ft. house, there was little space for everybody. His father, Niranjan Patel, was the gatekeeper of the Kirloskar factory; he had a hard time feeding his family, with a wife and six children (four boys and two girls).

Niranjan could not think of sending his children to school; most of them dropped out after the fourth or fifth standard in school. They could not continue even if they wished to. They never had good clothes, they often had nothing to eat at noon . . . But the case of Sunder Manik Patel was different. He wanted to continue in the school; to his luck, the factory manager, Alwarez Fernando, who had observed this intelligent boy, gave him a letter of recommendation, which opened to him the gates of the famous Loyola School, at Pune. The Jesuit fathers, who are famous for educational work, ran the school. They have a lot of schools and colleges all over the world, also all over India.

Patel was a very industrious student. From Loyola School in Pune, he went to St. Xavier's College, Bombay, where he did his graduation and post-graduation in economics. He always stood first in the class, and the Jesuit principal advised him to attend the IAS (Indian Administrative Service) entrance examination, which he passed with distinction.

Patel completed his studies for the IAS at the Indian Administrative College at Mussoorie in the Himalayas. Patel wanted to be at the top in every examination; he did achieve what he wanted. He passed with flying colours and won the President's Gold Medal. He was inducted into the Central Government cadre. His first posting was at Lakshadweep as a probationary collector. There he worked for three years. Then he had a stint at Andaman and Nicobar Islands. Everywhere, Patel was known for his hard work and competence. Gradually he landed in the defence ministry.

'I'm aware of that, Mr Sune Sorensen. There is a fifty-fifty chance that someday somebody will put a note against me, and an enquiry by the Vigilance Commission will follow. If there is an enquiry, I will be suspended pending decision by the Vigilance Commission; during the period of enquiry, I will not get even my pension.'

'Will it not hurt you?'

'Of course, it will hurt me badly. But I take care of that eventuality through these deals, and this is only one of the deals. To survive, especially towards the end of my career, I have to dirty my hands a lot. My annual salary, I said, is US$20,000. For the completion of the enquiry, if ever one happens to take place they might need five years. That means I lose US$100,000. But in this present deal, the transaction volume is US$300 million. Half a per cent of it would make US$1.5 million. It is enough to keep me alive and take care of the needs of the family and the education of my children for years to come.'

'You are a clever person, Mr Patel.'

'Dear Mr Sune, even if I don't do any such deal and I work dutifully, somebody will somehow make a complaint against me towards the end of my career; it is the easiest way to take revenge. It could be my seniors or it could be my equals or even juniors, or a political rival of the minister, or a colleague belonging to another caste. We have thousands of castes, which are made to be jealous about others; this is usual in India.'

Patel thought Sune was not convinced. So he continued: 'I know of a vice chancellor of an Indian university who completed his term and retired. But he did not get his pension and other retirement benefits for several years. Do you know why? The assistant librarian of the university had a grudge against him, because the vice chancellor did not favour his undue promotion. This librarian concocted a record to show that the retired vice chancellor had not returned a book which he allegedly had taken from the library. The cost of the book was less than fifty rupees. This librarian wrote a complaint to the university and to his own trade union; the trade union took up the matter. The vice chancellor never took a book from the library. But the librarian could fabricate the case and his trade union stood by him! And eventually what happened? For years on, the retired vice chancellor could not get his pension and other benefits.'

Patel was not talking for himself. He was talking for the thousands of colleagues in various ministries and departments. The jealousies, fear, anxiety, revenge—these are also some of the reasons for the rampant corruption and bribery in Indian society.

Sune interrupted and said, 'I did not tell you about a new product of Bofors, about our TCM which can be fitted to 155-mm artillery you bought from us.'

'No, you did not tell me.'

'TCM (Trajectory Correctable Munition) is a 155-mm artillery round that has the capability to guide the projectile to the target with a very high probability of the first round hitting the target. Given such accuracy, ground forces need less ammunition to defeat the enemy. The design of the projectile shell is modular and various types of warheads can be substituted. It has an on-board guidance, navigation, and control system for adjusting the projectile during flight. The TCM uses the GPS and/or projectile tracking system information throughout the flight of the projectile.'

'Our research group in the defence ministry must be knowing that. That may be a subject matter for a future deal. This is not included in my present mission. We will deal with the old system and projectile.'

'Now that you have a nuclear arsenal, I just wanted to tell you that even micro-nuclear warheads can also be delivered with these TCM.'

'I shall keep it in mind, when I meet the generals. Thank you.'

'Well, good luck, Mr Patel. Expect my confirmation regarding the price and consignment by tomorrow morning, by eight thirty.'

'I shall call you exactly at 8.30 a.m. On confirmation, I shall give you the exact details of the bank accounts.'

'Fine.'

They happily shook hands and Patel hailed a taxi to the hotel.

There was another car parked on the opposite side. As Patel came out of the hotel, the driver switched off his recorder and started the engine. He followed Patel closely.

After one kilometre, Patel got down and waited there for three minutes and hailed another taxi to the hotel.

A third car was following both of them.

It was a usual visit of the American ambassador, Mr Crowley, to Pakistan's president. The president was waiting for Mr Crowley. Crowley was duly ushered into the office of the president. As soon as Crowley entered the room, Abdul Lateef moved towards the guest with extreme politeness (and sycophancy).

'Good morning, Mr Ambassador.'

'Good morning, Mr President.'

It was music to his ears when he heard it from the American ambassador. He wanted always to be known and respected as the president, the chief executive.

The Americans have their presidents. But to become a president there is an elaborate process. First of all, declare your candidature well in advance. Then, the primaries, then the laborious election process, meetings, conferences, conventions, TV appearances . . . How many millions of dollars are spent, how much energy is wasted before you become the president?

In contrast, here he became the president just by a declaration, and by sacking the 'inefficient and corrupt' prime minister. It was just as simple as that. It was a bloodless coup. *I did it for Pakistan. I want to make this country big.*

'How is the election of your president going?'

'Well, it takes its usual course. But this time it is very tough. The candidates are running neck and neck as far as the results are concerned. Then the whole thing is going to the courts. In the end, one of them will win, and the whole drama will be forgotten.'

'How is your health, Mr Ambassador?'

'I can't complain. My wife is very careful about what I eat and drink. She fixes my time to wake up and my time to go to bed. She insists that I spend half an hour in the morning for jogging. She will not let me munch anything between meals. She is sometimes starving me to death. So I am in good shape. And how is your health, despite all the tension inside the country and along the border?'

'By Allah's grace, I'm fine.'

'Are some of your generals making friendly overtures towards India? Will the pacifist movement have a chance in

Pakistan? Will they get enough backing from the religious and political groups?' Actually the ambassador did not want to say bluntly what he heard of the pacifist attitude of the chief executive!

'No president of Pakistan can be soft towards India. It'll be suicidal. No generals can think otherwise. Kashmir is a central issue. No one can overlook it. Unless and until a satisfactory solution to that problem is achieved, there can be no peace with India.'

'We know that. We just wanted to make sure. There were some rumours that your prime minister or somebody close to him is making overtures to India.'

'No, no. There is no basis for that. Not as far as I know. Actually the prime minister is planning to strengthen our army and air force in a big way. Recently, I did sign a request to your government to deliver us a few more F-16s to cut a balance with Indian acquisitions from other sources.'

'We are willing to give. But the sanctions regarding military hardware are still there. It will not be lifted soon. I would caution you that military and strategic vigilance is required. India is becoming more powerful. I just wanted to warn you.'

'Thank you. We are ever grateful to your country for the valuable information and suggestions. We are watchful too. Your country is the backbone of our military adequacy. With the help of your country, we are ready to face any eventuality. Our troops are fit and in the best of form. We try to keep the Indians tied down to Kashmir, so that they will not get time to think of any major offensive.'

The ambassador was convinced that Abdul Lateef was saying what he (the ambassador) wanted to hear. Actually,

Abdul Lateef had to be very careful. Through none of his words or gestures should he reveal his innermost heart. He wanted to seal peace with India and thus free Pakistan from the enormous tension and financial stress it was undergoing ever since it was formed.

He wanted to give a second liberation to Pakistan. Within one to two years, he wanted to achieve that, step by step. He planned this political strategy like a military operation.

13

Charles was taking his usual morning walk as Anand arrived from the airport.

'Good morning, Dad!'

'How was the trip to Germany?'

'Extremely rewarding!'

'Did you get an occasion to meet with the daughter of Abdul Lateef?'

'In Germany?'

'Yes, I knew she and her father were there in Germany to see the Hannover Messe!'

'So you are watching like Big Brother?'

'Yes, it's part of my duty. I will be informed about everything related to Pakistan.'

'Oh, sure, you must be informed. Then you know whom all I met!'

'Answer me the question, Anand.'

'Yes, I did meet Hasina. She is absolutely beautiful. I phoned her and she handed over the phone to her father.'

'You talked to him, just like that?'

'Yes, he asked me to meet him at Hilton International Hotel, where they were staying. I went there. The reception told me to wait for instructions in room 515.'

'And?'

'Hasina came to my room to take me to her father.'

'You really did meet him? Again?'

'Yes. I am happy about that. I met him in the palatial suite of Hilton International. This time he was extra nice and kind.'

'What did he say?'

'He has a good grasp of the political realities. I have a vague feeling that he really wants to improve the relations between our two countries.'

'Many of the previous presidents of that country have declared that. But nothing came out of it.'

'But this time I am convinced that what he says is what he means.'

'Anand, you have no idea of diplomacy'

'I am not a diplomat, I am no politician. But as a human being, as an intelligent young man, I can sense certain things which the diplomats and politicians fail to notice. Why don't you, Dad, take up something to change the impasse? Why can't we take the first step?'

'We did. Our prime minister went to Pakistan on the inaugural day of the Lahore Express service. And they did not reciprocate. Worse. They unleashed the Kargil war!'

'That was his predecessor. He was a stereotype. He in his turn just followed the path drawn by his predecessors. He had no creative ideas. He was not bold. Abdul Lateef is different. He will do what he says.' Anand was confident.

'Well, it is a matter for our prime minister to take the initiative. My role is to rebuff them, to fight them, if they dare to, as I told you.'

'Throw away this friend-enemy dichotomy in international relations. There is no permanent friend nor permanent enemy; there is only permanent self-interest. As I told you last time, Dad, if arch-enemies France and

Germany can become friends and become the cornerstone of the great European Union, why can't Pakistan and India set another example of reconciliation and co-operation?'

'This doesn't look good, Anand. You cannot take the destiny of this nation into your hands. The India-Pakistan policy was framed after years of experience and as a result of the several bitter wars waged by us.'

Anand shot back, 'Times have changed. The next era is going to be that of the young people. They are not afraid to take initiatives which might look different and dangerous. Dad, let the idealist in you awake. Please think it over. You will definitely find a way to make a difference.'

'Anand, you do not know anything about the international ramifications of the Indo-Pak relations. If India and Pakistan become friends, India will have to confront more enemies, more formidable enemies, elsewhere, as I told you last time.'

He paused for a few seconds. And slowly but surely he said, 'Remember, we, India and Pakistan, are pawns in the hands of bigger powers. Even if we wanted peace, it would be difficult to have it.'

'So why don't we realize this and act for our peace and sovereignty? If peace prevails in our two countries, it would be beneficial to our countries, more than to any other in the world.'

Almeida was convinced of what his son said, and wanted to do something in that direction, but the traditional politician in him was groping in the dark. He wanted to cut short the discussion; he said, 'That is a policy matter for the foreign ministry. Let them take the initiative.'

Almeida was moved by the conviction of his son.

His car was waiting for him. He moved out of the house and boarded the car. He eased himself into the left-side seat. After sitting comfortably, he started thinking of his conversation with his son. He went over the whole thing in his mind and wanted to find an amicable formula to settle the enmity between India and Pakistan.

***

The prime minister Loknath Singh holds a weekly durbar (public audience) every Wednesday from 11.00 a.m. to 12.30 p.m. Even if it begins a bit late, the time to terminate is sacrosanct. Loknath Singh has his lunch exactly at 12.40 p.m. every day. It cannot and does not change.

The durbar is held on the lawns of his sprawling residence. In one sense it has proved healthier for Loknath Singh. It is an occasion for him to get fresh air and to see natural environment. The Indian leaders are a much more protected (pampered) lot than their counter parts in the more industrialised countries. The loyal assistants (slaves?) and citizens (subjects?) consider the leaders as the new incarnations of the old maharajas (kings), hence the show of profound respect and/or adoration to the leaders. The higher the position, the higher the respect and near-adoration.

They too tend to feel that they are kings or demigods. They should appear to the common folk only once in a while. They give an audience only in the rarest of occasions. So the leaders, especially the president, prime minister, and similar categories live in an unreal world, away from the people they are supposed to serve. They get very few occasions to see the real world and the real people. They do sometimes see people at big meetings and rallies, but then they are just an anonymous mass. On such occasions there will be shouting of slogans and hysterical reactions; since sufferings and pains are mostly individual, they will not be manifested at such big gatherings. And the leaders get the impression that in real life, these ordinary people are the happiest lot. Despite hardship and poverty, our people are the happiest in the world, they would declare.

Sharma is participating in the durbar of Loknath Singh. He came from a village in Uttar Pradesh. He is a farmer. He, his wife, two daughters, and two sons are happy with their life as farmers. The third son, the youngest, Harikrishnan, made a mistake. He went to school; he completed not only the school, but also the college. He possesses a degree in commerce from Lucknow University. It was real occasion for the family to celebrate. He is the first man in that village ever to obtain a degree from a university.

Once the celebration was over, the pangs of having an educated son began. Poor villagers thought a degree meant a sure job. They started asking him when he was going to join duty. So the search for a job began. Harikrishnan needed a job. At last he got one at the nearby village office. Getting an appointment in a government department is a big blessing. It gives security for life; you will never be terminated from the job. Even if the post is not required, there is no provision to lay you off. Isn't it a blessing! So everyone is after government jobs. But there is one catch. Getting such jobs is costly.

Formerly such appointments were done at local level, by the district collector or by the district head of the concerned department. But there was room for corruption, partiality, and hegemonizing. In order to avoid this, the government decided to make the appointments centrally. There would be a central examination, on the basis of which a list of selectable candidates would be prepared, then the actual selection is done by the Public Service Commission; the final approval comes from the minister. This gave the concerned minister a strong hold on all appointments.

This system paved way for centralisation of corruption. Take the example of the appointment of sweepers. There would be hundreds of thousands of applicants for the few posts. All these candidates should appear at a central place for examination. That it costs enormous money in transport and otherwise has not occurred to the government. There should be people to prepare the question papers; some of the mischievous from among them would leak the questions on the eve of the examination day (of course for money, good money), so there would be squads to supervise those who prepare the question papers. Then there are people on examination duty, who could also be corrupt. The examiners are checked by what they call examination squads. They come in groups and check whether the examination supervisors are doing their job.

Then the answer papers have to be evaluated. Again, jobs for thousands of persons. Then the results have to be tabulated and finalised. Again jobs. Thus the system produces job opportunities, on one side, and scope for corruption on the other.

The final results have to come before the Public Service Commission for its approval. In the Public Service Commission, there will be nominees of all the political parties; each party nominee has to look after the interests of the party and its members in awarding appointments.

So each member has a say or a share in the distribution of spoils.

Spoils? Yes, spoils. The appointment of the sweepers or clerks or other junior staff depends on the decision of the members of the PSC. So all those who have party affiliation will have already pulled the strings. But you have to pull the right strings.

Now, Harikrishnan, the son of farmer Sharma, wrote the test of the Public Service Commission (PSC) examination. He passed the examination with flying colours; he held rank number 18. There were 175 vacancies for the post of lower division clerks. And he was sure to be appointed, he thought. He waited for the appointment letter for one week, then for two, three, four weeks. But no letter came. He inquired at the PSC office. He was told, 'You fool, all the appointments are over. Where were you?'

'I was at home. But no letters came,' he innocently replied.

'The letter will not come unless you make the necessary procedure for that.'

'But no one told me about it!' was his answer.

The officer was a kindly man. He said, 'My son, you should have met one of the members of the PSC and gotten his blessings, if you were to get the appointment.'

'But no one told me about it!' he said.

'Nobody will tell you that. It is known to everybody. And it involves also a little bit of money. You have to give some gift to the PSC member.'

'How much?' he asked.

'What is your post?'

'Lower division clerk.'

'What would be your salary?'

'I heard it would be around 6,000 rupees.'

'Then you have to pay three months' salary: 18,000 rupees.'

'That is a lot of money. Even if we sell our farmland, we will not get that much money.' He told of his plight.

'Then you will not get a job.'

He and his father approached the head of the panchayat (village council). He recommended his case to Mr Raj Kumar, the local MLA (Member of Legislative Assembly or State Legislature).

The local MLA was a known leader of the area. He was a man known for his ruthlessness. If he wanted something, he would get it. For achieving his goal, he did not shy from using force either. He has a band of healthy volunteers to help him; they are also amply armed. The journalists call it a private army. It is true they carry some sort of weapons, and use them occasionally when things can't be achieved by persuasion of words. When people see the volunteers, they know they have to surrender to the wishes of the MLA.

Mr Raj Kumar called one of the members of the PSC. 'Hello! Balraj Gujral?'

'Yes, Gujral here.'

'Well, I'm sending one Harikrishnan to you. He wrote the Central Public Service Commission examination and got the eighteenth rank also. But he did not get the job. So would you please help him?'

He put the phone down and told the farmer, 'He will help you, Sharmaji.' (You add 'ji' to the names of persons you respect.)

But nothing happened. Sharmaji started wondering if there was a real Gujral.

Disappointed Harikrishnan and father Sharma went to the house of the MP (Member of Parliament). At first they were appalled by the bigness of his house, with big compound walls around. At the gate, there was a Nepali security guard with a big moustache and a dagger in his waist.

'Hm? What do you want?'

'We wish to see the MP sahib.'

'Wait here. Let me ask.'

He got clearance from inside and he took the farmers inside to the office of the MP. He was sitting in his hanging bed, and was chewing the pan masala, a mixture of betel leaf, areca nut, and lime; it has a mild intoxication effect. Some such masalas are mixed with cocaine or similar stuff.

'Sharmaji, tell me what is happening in your village.'

'Everything is fine, sir,' Sharma said with his innocent smile. 'But what great things can happen in a village, sir?'

'Village is everything, Sharmaji. I know that 70 per cent of the people in our country are living in villages. So how can we neglect villages?'

'With your blessing everything is going fine, Sarkar,' said farmer Sharma.

'Well then, what is the reason of your journey to my poor hut?' asked the MP.

'Sir, we have a special request.'

'I know. Your MLA told me about it. You see, Sharmaji, there are 540 MPs, and if each MP recommends one person there should be at least 550 vacancies, one for each of us. It doesn't look bright. I will do one thing. I shall give you a letter for the prime minister's office. They have every power in their hands. They can pull some strings and get your son the post.'

'Isn't it far off, sir? Will they let us in? We are all small people, old-fashioned villagers!'

'Don't worry. I will write a letter to the private secretary of the prime minster. We are good friends. He will definitely do what he can.'

He did write the letter and got an appointment for Mr Sharma and son. They could present their case to the prime minister in person on Wednesday during his weekly durbar.

Loknath Singh read the petition carefully, and asked his personal assistant, 'Do you think I can do anything about this?'

'Sir, they have come from a village. If you put in a word to the CPSU (Central Public Service Commission) they will do the needful.'

'OK, then. Write a letter to the concerned CPSU for these people,' he told his private secretary. And turning to the peasant, he said, 'I will do what I can. Go back to your village. Tell your people that we care for them. You will get a reply within ten days.'

The farmer and his son were happy not only because they knew that the prime minister was going to interfere for them, but also because of the sheer fact that they could meet the prime minister in person. It would be big news in his village and all around. There would be visitors to hear city news from them.

There were about 150 persons with pressing needs; all of them got a chance to present their case before the prime minister, who in his friendly manner heard them and consoled them, and offered to help them.

After the durbar, Loknath Singh went back to his residence for lunch.

As his car moved along the Janpath, and to the prime minister's office, Charles was in a pensive mood. He was thinking of what he should tell the PM about the visit of Anand to Hannover.

He reached the prime minister's house in time for the appointment. Last time when he spoke about Anand's visit to Nepal, Almeida was searching for words to express his indignation, though in real fact he had no indignation at all. This time, he was more convinced of the good intentions of Anand and did not know what to say.

'Anand has brought a present for you from Germany.'

'From Germany?'

'Yes. He had gone the other day to Hannover. He wanted to have a look at the famous Hannover Messe. He is on the lookout for some tie-ups to expand his hotel industry.'

'How did he enjoy the trip?'

Charles was choosing the correct words. 'He enjoyed the trip very much. But this time on his return, I noticed that he is a changed man. He is no more the young man I knew.'

'Why? Is it a change for good or bad? Has he met some girls?' asked Loknath Singh innocently. Loknath Singh was still young at heart. He knows what a young man of Anand's age would do or look for.

'It could be.' Charles knew of the affair between Hasina and Anand but did not want to disclose the secret now. Let it mature, and become public on its own, at the proper time.

'That is good news,' said Loknath Singh. 'How old is he now?'

'Twenty-seven.'

'It's high time he married,' said Loknath Singh. He did not forget that he himself was still a bachelor; because he did not think about it at the right time. 'Otherwise he will be a perennial bachelor like me!'

'Experientia docet?' Charles mumbled the Latin dictum from his seminary days.

'What does it mean, Charles?' Loknath Singh had never learned a word of Latin language.

'"Experience is the best teacher," so we may translate. It is a famous Latin dictum,' said Charles. He was proud of his knowledge of Latin language.

14

When Charles Almeida entered the house, Anand was watching news on PTV (Pakistan Television).

'You have now become a fan of Pakistan, and I am condemned to fight them! Isn't it ironical?'

Anand quipped, 'Then, why don't you get out of this mess?'

'What do you mean, Anand?'

'Innerly you do not believe in what you say before the TV cameras. Every one of you, I mean, all the ministers, MPs, and other bureaucrats (excepting a few hard-core haters) wish to get out of this forced enmity with Pakistan.'

'How do you know that?'

'Once out of India, Indians have no qualm in making friends with Pakistanis; in Canada, in the USA or in Europe, and in Gulf countries, Indians have good Pakistani friends.'

'They are exceptions,' quipped Charles Almeida.

'Look, I have no problem with the Pakistanis!'

'I know you like Abdul Lateef's daughter. But that is an emotional affair. It will find its natural death in a few weeks' time.'

Almeida was sending a covert indication that he did not approve of Anand's affair with Hasina.

'No, it'll never go. Besides, I like her father too. Our meeting at Hannover has sealed our relationship.'

'Oh, I don't believe it will last.'

'At Hannover, I had a long talk with him. He is not like the former rulers of Pakistan. He wants change. He wants better relations with India. If possible, he wants to get the Nobel Peace Prize too—if not this year, sometime soon! Why don't you try to share it with him?'

'This is too much, Anand. How dare you meddle with such complicated political matters?'

'What complication? Is it a bad thing to talk to your enemies? Is reconciliation a bad thing? "Blessed are the peacemakers, for they shall inherit heaven." You remember that line from your seminary days?'

'I also remember the sentence "I am sending you like sheep among wolves!" Anand, what I mean is that there are risks involved in such rendezvous. It can be dangerous even to your life. ISI is a terrible organization. You do not know them.'

'I know that. I am extra careful. They will not get me. I went to Germany as Abdul Hameed, and got out as Anand.'

'You have a different passport?'

'Yes, the one I was given by the government after being saved from the Tehran hijack.'

Just then, the phone rang. Once. Twice. And it went dead. Almeida knew it was from his personal security officer. It was a signal that someone was on the line.

Charles Almeida dialed his secretary, then he put the phone down and told Anand, 'Anyhow, keep it a top secret. Also this conversation, and your conversation with Abdul Lateef.

'Tomorrow morning, I have the weekly private session with the prime minister. We discuss everything related to defence in that meeting. I have to be there by seven thirty in the morning. So it is enough for today; let us have dinner. After dinner, I have to go through the files.'

They moved to the dining table. Rekha had prepared delicious Kerala-style vegetarian food for them, with sambar, rasam, thoran, pachadi, kitchadi, varieties of pickles, etc. At dining table, they did not discuss serious matters, and never politics. They speak only about home affairs, the taste of food, functions in the family or in the family of friends.

They enjoyed the food, cracked jokes, and felt free in the intimacy of their home. Rekha had prepared also a special desert, ada pradhaman.

15

Loknath Singh was reading the Bhagavadgita as Charles Almeida entered his room. Whenever he had to face serious problems, Loknath took to Bhagavadgita and read a few pages. It gave him peace, he claimed.

'Good morning, defence minister.' The PM greeted him with unusual joy.

'Good morning, sir,' Charles Almeida replied respectfully.

'Please be seated.'

Loknath Singh sat on his ornate seat, and Charles took the chair next to him.

Loknath Singh went straight to the problem. The Uttar Pradesh Aryan Force (a new radical outfit) had made a public statement just fifteen minutes ago that they would demolish the Taj Mahal, because it stood on the site of a temple.

This declaration at this moment of the year was unexpected. The government was nervous about how to tackle the issue. Though new, the UAF had tremendous influence among the northern Hindi belt. Without them, the BPP government could not function, and the UAF leadership seemed to take on a belligerent attitude.

'I think we should talk to Dharmendra Raj about this,' said Charles Almeida. Dharmendra Raj was a monk turned politician. He stood at the core of the hard-core Hinduists. But he had a soft corner for Loknath Singh.

Loknath Singh rang the bell at his seat and signalled for his PA (personal assistant) to come over.

'Could you please get me Dharmendra Raj on line? No, you better tell him that I invite him for dinner tonight,' Loknath Singh told his PA, who left immediately to make the call.

When Loknath had postponed the discussion on the imminent issues, Charles was ready with his ideas. 'What worries me are the borders,' said Charles Almeida. 'The situation along the Rajasthan border is becoming very tense. The other side says the intelligence (ours as well as that of the Americans) is amassing weapons and moving hardware along that vulnerable border.'

'Haven't you too moved hardware and personnel to that region?' asked Loknath Singh.

'They are in place and are on blue alert,' replied Charles Almeida, and continued, 'but this game plan is getting on my nerves.'

'What do you mean?' Loknath Singh was shaken by the words of the defence minister. Charles Almeida was supposed to be tough. Very tough.

'May I say something about our foreign policy?' asked Charles Almeida.

'Mr Almeida, what is this? Do you need to ask my permission for opening up your heart? You are the keeper of my conscience,' replied Loknath Singh.

'I think we should show much more statesmanship in our foreign policy, especially towards Pakistan. We should try to come out of the rut in which we are,' said Charles Almeida in one breath.

Loknath Singh was taken aback. He never thought that Charles Almeida would speak in such soft terms when Pakistan is in question. After all, he was the defence minister. He had to be a hawk in matters of defence.

'It is strange that a defence minister could be so soft. What do you mean?' said Loknath Singh, without revealing what he had in his mind. Singh was an intellectual, unlike the other politicians. He was open to ideas and suggestions. Charles Almeida always had plenty of them. That was why Singh kept Charles Almeida close to himself, and let him have his say in his decision-making process.

'I think, it is my very personal opinion, we should cut a new and innovative path in our relations with our immediate neighbour, Pakistan.'

'What could that be?'

'We should have a long-term policy of achieving friendship and real co-operation between Pakistan and India, something that was possible between France and Germany, the arch-enemies for several centuries. Both of them fought several wars, bloody wars, and finally the Second World War. After the Second World War, France took pains to get Germany and Berlin divided into two. You know, the Russians conquered Berlin, and France and the Allies conquered the rest of Germany. And what did France do? The French said they would give half of Germany to the Russians, if they could get half of Berlin. That was the last nail in the coffin of a German nation. This was immediately after the Second World War.

'But, though France did such a mean thing to the Germans, when the fire of enmity and war-related animosity died down, France and Germany became friends; they became the cornerstone of the new European Union. If they could do this, why can't we?' Charles Almeida finished in one breath.

Was he talking, or was his son talking through him? The one year of logic in the seminary had taught him to reason with force and convincing arguments.

'How do you think that is possible given the border situation and Kashmir problem? It is a warlike situation there. Isn't it?' asked Loknath Singh. He did not want to give in so fast, though as a real statesman, he saw the logic of Almeida's argumentation.

'In small steps. In the European nations, change happened through small steps of reconciliation, through constant contact between the peoples,' said Charles Almeida.

'How could we plan something similar here, if at all it is possible?' asked Loknath Singh feigning ignorance.

'We should at least make a beginning. First of all, you and I should make a firm personal decision that we would turn the tables and make friendship with Pakistan through a series of silent secret agenda as long as we are in the government, and work towards its fulfilment.' Charles Almeida remembered Mikhail Gorbachev, who meticulously wrote the script of the disintegration of the erstwhile Soviet Union and got it done with accurate precision. Gorbachev was giving the Russian people freedom in a well-planned scheme; he took time to achieve it, and he did achieve it through a meticulous planning.

'Once we can make such a decision, everything else is going to be easy,' continued Charles Almeida.

'But this idea can never be sold in our political marketplace, Mr Almeida.' Loknath Singh was cautious.

'Let us not declare the product with fanfare, let us just market it in small doses,' said Charles, 'in such small doses as would not be perceivable to the political pundits. Slowly but constantly, the dosage should be increased, and the net result should be a smooth transition from enmity to friendship. It should be administered like certain medicines. Slowly it will take its effect and the other side also will respond,' said Charles Almeida.

The conversation he had with his son was alive in his mind. Ever since his conversation with Anand, he wanted to talk out what was taking shape in his mind. He had spent long hours thinking out strategies. As defence minister, he was well aware of the military strategies, which are planned meticulously so that everything is in place and the total effect would be the success of the plan. This diplomatic strategy too should be meticulously planned, and carefully executed.

'In four to five years, we should achieve it,' continued Charles Almeida. 'The trend we set should be such that even the successive governments should not be able to reverse it.'

'In small steps?' asked Loknath Singh. 'I should sleep on it. Let my brain work on it for a day. Let us meet again tomorrow at this time.'

Loknath Singh could not imagine that such a soft pacifistic and diplomatic lecture would come from the lips of the defense minister Charles Almeida.

Charles Almeida came from a very poor Catholic family of Meerut. His father was landless, and poor. The only way out was to secure a government job somewhere. He got one at Lucknow as a peon in a government school. Charles was the third of the eleven children his father had brought into the world. The six girls and the five boys grew up as good and God-fearing Christians. The staunch Catholic Almeida senior and his wife Cathy taught the children just two lessons: remember God always and be a friend to every other human being; this, they said, is the gist of Christianity. His father's nearness to the school too was a boon to his children. Though his wife was illiterate, she would tell her husband that all of them should get good education so that life will be kind to them at least.

Charles Almeida did schooling in the same government school. He passed high school with flying colours. In his parish church, he was an altar boy. He was always punctual for the holy mass at six in the morning every day. He was liked both by his peers and by the parish priest, Patricio Donato, who was an Italian. As soon as he heard that Charles Almeida had passed the matriculation, Pastor Donato called for him.

'God has some good plan for you, son,' said the parish priest. Charles Almeida kept silent and stood devout before him. 'What do you think that could be?' asked the parish priest. Charles was still silent, ready to obey whatever the parish priest said.

'I told the bishop about you,' went on Father Donato. 'And he says you will make a very good priest.'

Charles did not expect this. He thought that the parish priest would arrange some scholarship for him for his higher studies in a college. He wanted really to become something else.

So he said without hesitation, 'Oh, father, I thought I should become a doctor.'

It was unexpected. Father Donato had no answer. But he asked him, 'Why do you want to become a doctor?'

'Because I can help the poor and downtrodden, treat the sick people who are poor and have no one to help them,' replied young Charles Almeida.

'Well, that is a fine intention, Charles. But you can help much more by becoming a priest,' said the parish priest.

'How is that possible? Priests can only say mass and preach.'

'No, no, priests can and should do much more. They do not treat the sick, but they can very well treat the minds and bestow peace and solace to the poor, and to the rich. Peace of mind and peace of heart is the ultimate thing which everyone craves. What is the use if you are rich and have no peace of mind? People can confide in a priest their sorrows and worries. He will be able to give them appropriate advice and consolation,' lectured the parish priest.

'That is a correct argument, father,' said Charles Almeida. 'But give me some time to think it over.'

Charles Almeida came back after a week and told the parish priest that he had decided to join the seminary. He studied for two years at the minor seminary of Lucknow, got proficiency in Latin and English. Then he joined the Papal Seminary at Pune and studied philosophy for three years. He avidly read the history of philosophy. He came across such luminaries as Socrates, Plato, Aristotle, Spinoza, Descartes, Leibniz, Emmanuel Kant, Hegel, Bertrand Russell, John

Dewey, and Jean-Paul Sartre. From Jean-Paul Sartre, he went straight to Karl Marx. And that was the turning point. He found similarity between the Marxist philosophy and Christian philosophy. He avidly read the works of Karl Marx. He finished *Das Kapital* in one week.

That year by the end of March, the annual vacation began. Like all fellow seminarians, Charles Almeida too went home. But after the vacation, he did not go back to the seminary; instead he joined the communist party, which was prohibited at that time. So he worked underground. Twice he was arrested and put in jail. The life in jail made him a real politician. He decided to be more active in politics. Socialism was in his blood, and was not alien to his Christian upbringing. He wanted to help the poor and downtrodden; he wanted to make India a country where everybody had equal opportunity.

He worked among workers and became a good organizer of factory workers. The working conditions, the salary, the facilities given were all inadequate. He staunchly supported the workers in their struggles. He slowly became a noted trade union leader.

He was not a pacifist. The urgency of the hour and heat of the situation sometimes carried him away. He had to use violence many a time to achieve the goal. The end justifies the means, he thought, like Marx.

Slowly he built up relationships, and was a prominent member in the Indian Jana Morcha Party, which came to power in the last two elections. Since then he was always a political power to reckon with. He was very active and sincere in his convictions; he was always a Member of

Parliament (MP) either in the opposition or in the ruling alliance.

Charles Almeida was always outspoken, and tough, as he was simple in his lifestyle. He used to go in his bicycle unlike many of his politician friends, who wanted to show pomp and lavishness in their dresses and appearance. Loknath Singh liked him for his high thinking and low living, and made him the defence minister.

A defence minister should think of enemies. If he doesn't have one, he should create one. That is the accepted role of a defence minister. And always, Indian defence ministers had plenty of them just across the border.

But now, Loknath Singh was wondering how this man could become soft on Pakistan all of a sudden.

Anyhow, Loknath Singh decided to think over the matter and would discuss with Charles Almeida the next day.

<hr />

Loknath Singh just finished his weekly sitting with his security advisor, Mr Ram Murthy, when Charles Almeida's car entered the gates. Murthy took away much of the problems from Loknath Singh and tried to solve them as and when they came; often he came with a report of problems solved. Murthy knew the mind of Loknath Singh and Loknath Singh trusted Murthy fully.

When Charles Almeida arrived, Mr Murthy retired to his office. Charles Almeida was ushered into the office of the prime minister.

'Good morning Mr Prime Ministerji,' said Charles Almeida with utmost respect.

'Good morning, dear defence minister,' replied Loknath Singh. Loknath Singh was in a very good mood. He cracked a few jokes, which surprised Charles Almeida. Loknath Singh did it only during his political speeches before mammoth gatherings.

This is unusual, thought Charles Almeida. *I rarely hear him cracking jokes in private.*

All of a sudden, Loknath became serious and came to the pivotal point that he wanted to discuss with Charles.

'Charles, what do you think about your proposal of yesterday?' Loknath Singh was forthright in his approach. He went straight to the subject.

'What do you think of it?' asked Charles Almeida.

'I think it is worth giving a thought. But I need your assistance. I need more details, I mean we need detailed and meticulous planning. If we initiate it, we should succeed,' said Loknath Singh.

'That is what I too thought. We should constitute a small, a very small, group and discuss the pros and cons, the details of it, and work out a meticulous plan for its execution,' said Charles Almeida.

'Where should we start first?'

'We can start with us ministers. Why doesn't one of our ministers go to Pakistan, and invite his counterpart to visit India?'

'Who will go first? In any case it should not be the prime minister; it would be big news.'

'Let us send the minister of energy, Mr Narayana Rao. He is not much known even here in India. Pakistan has never heard of him. He is innocuous as well, but has a lot of Muslim friends. Let him just visit the important tourist spots of Pakistan, hold no political talks; he may meet President Abdul Lateef, but no press conference or briefing. Let him invite his Pakistani counterpart for a return visit to India, just for a pleasure trip of two weeks or so.'

The idea is not bad, thought the Prime Minister. 'Give it a try, Charles Almeida. Let it be between us. I do not tell anyone about this. It is up to you to make Mr Rao interested in the trip. Let the aim of the journey be in our mind.'

Charles Almeida did not spare any moment. He went back to his office, and asked his PA to phone up MOS (i.e. Minister of State), Mr Narayana Rao.

The phone rang again. 'MOS is on the line, sir,' said his PA.

'Hallo! Mr Narayana Rao?'

'Yes, Narayana Rao speaking,' said he in a very inaudible soft voice. Charles Almeida would on another occasion have mistaken it for the voice of a woman.

'Mr Narayana Rao? Sir, are you busy?'

'Not at all. An MOS has nothing much to do. Just wait for his senior and execute his orders,' came back the pathetic voice. Actually, many an MOS has nothing to do but help his cabinet minister in moving the files. He is often sort of a secretary.

'Well, an MOS is still a minister, you should remember that,' quipped Charles Almeida. He did want him to feel important. The Ministry of the Central Government of India has more than seventy ministers. Most of them are appointed for political reasons. The present government is supported by a coalition of thirteen political parties. Each party has staked claims for a number of ministries. These claims too are based on the inner-party compulsions and equations. If a particular person is not given the berth of ministership, he/she would desert the party and try to form a splinter party, and can try to become important. If more than one third of the Members of Parliament of a particular party so decide, it can desert the mother party and form a (splinter) party of their own with total impunity.

There are parties which have two hundred members, and there are parties which have five members or even less. Since the majority of the government is so slender, numbers do matter; every one of the MPs counts. The prime minister depends on each and every one of the Members of Parliament for his continuance as leader of the ruling coalition. So the ministerial berths are allotted to coalition members according to the proportionate number of the MPs. Actually it is difficult to run the government with such a flood of ministers. But there is no other way. So there is a rank called cabinet ministers; only a handpicked few are cabinet ministers; the others are called Minister of State (MOS for short), with or without independent charge of their portfolio.

Narayana Rao is one of those hapless Ministers of State.

Why did Charles Almeida call me? It is quite intriguing. Actually, Charles Almeida is running the government. He is number two in the Cabinet and the chief advisor of the prime minister. Whatever Charles Almeida says is a golden rule for Loknath Singh. Now if Charles Almeida calls me, it must be regarding something very important.

'Of course, still sometimes you feel you are just a secretary of another minister. But I am satisfied with what I am. I do what I can,' said the hapless MOS.

'Can you come over for a cup of coffee?' asked Charles Almeida.

There is something important. Either I am losing my ministry or I am getting a better slot. Anyway it is important to meet Charles Almeida. Normally you do not get easy access to him. There is something good or bad waiting for me!

'I will be there by 4 p.m., sir.' He tried to be deprecative and humble before Almeida. *You have to be in his favour always; he is number two in the Cabinet!* That is a trait of the Indian public life. Everyone tries to be servile. Why court trouble! If you are not servile, you will definitely be stamped as arrogant. Being arrogant, you can't survive in the oligarchic society that India is. The superior (be it in political parties, government offices, or religious institutions) will use all the means at his disposal first to discredit and then to destroy his inferiors or his juniors, just because they are not servile. This slavery eats into every segment of the Indian society. Undeclared slavery persists in the system.

Mr Narayana Rao seldom travelled alone. He would have with him a bunch of followers. They look like (and really are) his bodyguards. But to boost his importance in the public eyes, he had asked for the service of four SPG men (black cats). Black cats are a Special Protection Group (SPG), created after the murder of Indira Gandhi. SPG is instituted to protect the endangered political personalities. SPG protection is given to the president of India, the Speaker, the Cabinet ministers, the governors, the former prime ministers, etc. Because of its show of pomp, everyone in the government tries to get SPG protection, often just to make others believe they are important! So some of the MOS (they are dubbed also as junior ministers) have chosen this path to make themselves more important than they actually are.

As soon as his car stopped at the gate of the defence minister's office, the bodyguards and the SPG men jumped out of the car, and were looking around for possible danger to the life of this junior minister; then they escorted him to the gate of the ministry. The gate was opened. The followers of the minister as well as the SPG men were told to wait outside. The minister was led to the visitors' room.

Actually, Mr Narayana Rao was in total confusion. Either he was getting a better post or he was going to lose his ministry. Anyway, he made up his mind. If he was offered a better ministry, he would accept it even if it was not to his liking. But if he was going to be thrown out of the ministry, he should threaten to form a splinter party with the support of his three friendly MPs.

His nervousness was very visible as Charles Almeida's secretary came to take him to the drawing room of Mr Charles Almeida. *This is a sign of something good.* He soothed his soul.

'Good evening, Minister Narayana Rao!' said Charles Almeida.

Narayana Rao was elated by the addressing. 'Good evening, Hon'ble Defence Minister. I am really honoured to be invited by you.' This was the first time that he was invited for private coffee with the defence minister.

'How is the ministry doing?'

'We are on target in everything.'

In India, setting targets is a big exercise. It is an accepted fact that no one is really willing to put in some effort to improve the situation of the country. An MP wants to be a minister sometime in his life. Once he is made a minister, he falls back and relaxes!

All the work of the government, of the ministries, has to be done by the IAS officers. (IAS means Indian Administrative Service.) Smart youngsters are selected yearly to undergo training in the Indian Administrative Service College. On the basis of the results in the exams, they are selected to IAS (Indian Administrative Service), IPS (Indian Police Service), IRS (Indian Revenue Service), IFS (Indian Foreign Service), IPS (Indian Postal Service), etc. and are posted in the respective branches of the government. They are senior officers in any branch of the government, and have a lifetime warranty for their job in government. They may change their portfolios, but seldom are they sent home (terminated). These officers of the government do much of the dirty work in the various departments of the government; the ministers do not study the subject of their ministry; they are there just to sign papers. Most of them do not know what they are signing. The IAS officers explain to the ministers what the papers or documents are. The former even write the speeches of the ministers. If anybody asks a minister some details about his ministry, he will be unable to answer them. He will have to have the ready-made answer written by his officers and delivered to him.

Since nobody seems to work, the government assigns targets to officers and even to ministers. For example, the ministry of telecommunication has the target that four million telephone connections are to be given this year.

Most often, the targets are achieved only on paper. The officials of the ministry concoct the targets, and declare that so many connections were given, so that it exceeds target. For example the ministry of family welfare is given the target that in one year, five million sterilizations have to be conducted in the government hospitals; each sterilization is rewarded with Rs.1,000 for the patient and Rs.200 for the doctor. The doctors collude with their junior officers and simply concoct the numbers and collect the entire money earmarked for sterilization promotion. In actual fact, not even one tenth of the target might have been achieved. All these false data add up, and the minister will declare that he has overachieved his target.

'In that case, how many solar panels have been distributed during the past three months, Mr Rao?' asked Charles Almeida.

'I do not remember the numbers, but we have achieved our targets. That is what my secretary told me the other day.'

Charles Almeida knew what that meant.

'Our power position is not good. But our neighbour Pakistan has enough energy, and is seemingly doing well on the energy front,' said Charles Almeida.

'That might be true. But who knows whether what the reports say is true?' quipped Narayana Rao. He knew how things were happening in India.

'Why don't you make a visit to Pakistan?' asked Charles Almeida casually, 'And find out for yourself how the energy sector is working there.'

'Pakistan is out of the question. Does anyone dare to go there? Especially a minister? Our relationship with Pakistan is at present very bad. The Lahore bus is plying only occasionally. Armies on both sides are on permanent alert,' said Rao.

'I think the energy sector is important. We can at least learn a few things from Pakistan. I shall make arrangements for your trip to Pakistan. I shall talk to the PM. He will let you go. What do you say about that?'

'No. I don't dare go. Maybe somebody will kidnap me, or murder me. Then that is the end of it,' said Rao. *Does he want to get rid of me? Or is Charles Almeida plotting something else?*

'I thought you would be interested,' said Charles Almeida.

'I am not at all interested.' Rao was quick.

Charles Almeida quickly changed the subject. *This fellow is no good. He can't be sent to Pakistan. He has no initiative, no imagination. If we sent him, it might even be counterproductive.*

They then discussed about the Jana Morcha Party, to which Mr Rao belonged, its internal squabbling and bickering. And it was time for Rao to take leave.

'Thank you for coming, Minister Rao. Keep in touch,' said Charles Almeida. Narayana Rao left the place with his entourage of followers and SPG.

Charles Almeida called Amar Kant, the MOS in the defence ministry, and entrusted him with the job of making meticulous plans for a rapprochement between India and Pakistan; he was answerable only to the defence minister.

16

In the meantime, the election in the United States had made things difficult. The USA was a firm ally of Pakistan. But recently after the overthrow of the previous president, the relationship had become a little cooler and the USA had begun to tilt towards India.

That the Americans were tilting towards India had been of some concern to the politicians, the military, and the economists of Pakistan. But the general public did not have any admiration for the Americans. They as a whole hate the Americans; Western civilization in general is haram (horribly objectionable) to Muslims.

Because of the frozen relationships, Pakistan was not keen as far as the results of the US election were concerned. Once the election was over and a new president was in place, Pakistanis would have to seek the blessings (though ceremonious) of the US for every foreign affairs undertaking.

Now was the right time. Now was the right time to make a deal with India. The total attention of American politics was now on the election process. *Let us make a fait accompli*, thought Abdul Lateef.

Abdul Lateef strolled in the presidential garden with Jack, his Doberman dog, at his side. He was considering the pros and cons of a new, totally new, relationship with India. Since the visit of Anand, this thought was consuming him.

Abdul Lateef was aware of the danger and the opportunity in charting a new course of relationship with India. He was convinced that the advantages were many, and disadvantages less. The major disadvantage was that friendship with India brought, as a natural corollary, hatred from United States.

What can happen if we went ahead with the normalization process? At most, the US may stop military privileges and may stop supply of military hardware and support, which might not be that critical if the arch-enemy, India, becomes a friend. The main advantage will be the considerable reduction in military spending; besides, trade and tourism will flourish.

Wheat required by Pakistan can easily, for less transport cost, be purchased from India, like many other commodities. And India might buy leather, sports goods, textile and agricultural products from Pakistan. A pipeline from Iran or any other Gulf countries to India will have to pass through Pakistan, and it will be beneficial also for Pakistan.

He dialled Dr Muhammed Aslam, his most trusted lieutenant. Abdul Lateef could talk to him freely and discuss critical matters and arrive at some solution. Aslam had always been the keeper of Abdul Lateef's secrets. He was an expert in international relations. After his graduation from the University of Karachi, he studied international relations at the London School of Economics; he did his post-graduation and doctorate there. After a stint of teaching at the London School of Economics, he came back to Pakistan and was appointed professor of international relations at Karachi University. It was Zulfikar Ali Bhutto who brought Aslam into politics. Aslam was the chief advisor of Bhutto on international relations. After the execution of Bhutto, Aslam went back to Karachi University, where he concentrated on teaching and research. Abdul Lateef was his classmate in Karachi University, and both were friends since then.

As soon as Abdul Lateef took over the reins of Pakistan, he brought Dr Muhammed Aslam back from anonymity and put him in political limelight as his principal policy advisor.

'Aslam, do you think we can disarm India in the near future?'

'It would be a difficult proposition. India is too big for us to chew. But we can keep the tiger in check—by not allowing him to concentrate on development and by making him spend profusely on military acquisitions.'

'Even the British could not keep India in check.'

'Now that it is one of the IT superpowers, we cannot disarm it as much as before.'

'Still, I think, we should devise a means to disarm India.'

'Any definite idea? You must be kidding.'

'I am not kidding. Can we disarm him by embracing him?'

'The thought is too strange. It borders on madness. It is a dreamy solution,' said Dr Aslam. 'Especially now that the Hindu chauvinists are hyperactive in that country, any rapprochement would be difficult and misinterpreted.'

'I have no definite plans. Just a stray thought. Why don't you give some thought to it? You will definitely come up with some fine ideas that would be advantages to Pakistan without in any way losing face in the process.'

'My pleasure. I had occasionally mulled over the idea. But every time it was rebuffed by events of daily occurrence. I shall think over it for a day or two, and get back to you.'

Dr Aslam said goodbye to the president, and was about to leave. Then the president asked him, 'By the way, what is the fate of our state visit to Nepal? Is the foreign ministry seriously working on it?'

'I will check it out.'

17

'Hello! Who is on the line please?' Hasina was awakened from her sleep. It was just 5.00 a.m. She had gone late to bed. Who must that be?

'This is Abdul Hameed! Do you remember me, lady?'

'Abdul Hameed?' Hasina couldn't recall the name. 'Who is that?'

'Hasina, is it you? It's me. Anand.'

'Well, I guessed. No one else would dare trouble me like this. Where are you calling from?'

'Paris.'

'Paris? You are always travelling?'

'You too are travelling all the time.'

'There is a wine festival at Monte Carlo next Monday. I have to visit it. My resorts and hotels have to keep in touch with the developments in the beverages industry everywhere in the world. On that trip if I wish to see you, is it something wrong?'

'I have a programme at London. But only next Sunday. I was planning to fly out only on Saturday night. Let me see. Call me after two hours. I shall give you exact details by then.'

'You must find a way. I must meet you. It's important, very important.'

At nine thirty, she was ready with the plan. She would fly Saturday morning to Paris. She would reach Paris in three hours, and would put in a break there. *I shall fly to London at around noon on Sunday.*

'Well then, we shall meet at Hotel Chateaubriand near Eiffel Tower,' said Anand. 'I'm in room 412. As soon as you land, give me a call on my mobile number. Where will you be staying?'

'I will be as usual at Hotel Bordeaux near Arc de Triomphe. I would rather call you after settling down in my room. That's better.'

There should not be any room for rumours and gossip.

'Tres bien. A bientot.' Anand wanted to show off his knowledge of French.

'A bientot!' replied Hasina and pressed the button to end the call.

Anand had been waiting at the entrance to the Moulin Rouge since 6.15 p.m. He was getting anxious. Anything could happen. She was the daughter of Abdul Lateef. ISI people must be all over the place.

Anand was dressed up as Abdul Hameed, in an Arab robe. She had put on her usual veil; no one could find out who she was. She had a T-shirt and jeans underneath. She did recognize him, but ignored him and went straight inside the theatre for the show. Anand could guess it was she from her body language, so he too went in but could not locate her. So he took a row in the back.

The show had already started at seven sharp. She scrambled for her seat, got settled, and watched the performances for ten minutes. The ISI people were following her. After a few minutes, they were absorbed in the typical Moulin Rouge dances and performances. They had never seen so much female flesh on the stage. They were captivated by the dress and the lack of it.

She knew they were lost in the show. Abruptly and without making any room for suspicion, she took off her veil, put it into her handbag, and went out in her jeans and T-shirt. Anand followed her. Before he could catch up with her, she took a taxi and went to Hotel Chateaubriand. She rang up Anand on his mobile phone and asked him to go immediately to his room at Hotel Chateaubriand and stay inside his room.

Looking out the window of the car, Anand marvelled at the beauty of Paris. This was perhaps the most beautiful city of the world, culturally rich, extraordinarily tasty culinary style, heavenly Bordeaux wines and champagne, and the typical streets and buildings. *If I am to settle down anywhere, Paris will be my first choice*, thought Anand. Eiffel Tower, Notre-Dame Cathedral, Sacré Coeur, Champs-Élysées, Musée du Louvre . . . unforgettable monuments!

The taxi stopped at the entrance of Chateaubriand. She paid the fare and quickly went inside. She went to the restroom for a while to kill time and came out with a hat to camouflage her appearance. She took one of the elevators and rushed to the room of Anand. She knocked on the door, and Anand opened the door and quickly pulled her inside. His taxi was flying through the streets of Paris, when he was in the dream world of Parisian beauty.

'I think the ISI may not have seen me coming out of the Moulin Rouge,' Hasina said. 'Our life is becoming dramatic. We are acting in real life. Aren't we?'

'We will have to do things like this for some more time. Soon everything will work out to our advantage, I'm sure.'

'What did your dad say about our ideas?'

'I talked to my father. He is adamant in his attitude and stuck to his usual position. He said his mission and office is to fight Pakistan.'

'Humbug. Is he such a belligerent person? Why can't he be like you?' Hasina was surprised at the strong language she used.

'How is your father, Hasina? Is he like you?' quipped Anand.

'Almost. I think we think along the same lines. We have almost the same taste in food, clothing, lifestyle, attitudes, etc.'

'Except in the matter of international relations! Let us be clear about it. Only two of us know that there is in actual fact no problem. All this enmity between India and Pakistan is the creation of politicians and of some interested foreign countries. We should work out some means to break the ice. We will succeed. Are you hopeful, Hasina?' Anand said in a breath.

Anand continued, 'My dad! He is only acting. He is convinced of my position. He will act on it, but he can't admit that he is acting on it. In the meantime, he met our prime minister, Loknath Singh, and held secret talks with him. Loknath Singh will discuss the matter with his foreign secretary, Raj Pagodia Vasvani, and his security advisor Rama Murthy. In a few days, we will know what will come out of it. My sure guess is that it will be positive.'

'My father too has become soft on India,' said Hasina.

'How to break the ice?'

'In small steps. In small gestures of friendship.'

'Maybe the strategy of Willy Brandt of Germany would be feasible.'

'That is?'

'First, establish people-to-people contact and friendship. There should be a lot of visits across the border. Then friendship on the political level would be easy. That was how the West Germans accomplished the unification of Germany. Why don't we too think of some similar steps, like some exchange programme? Say, at first on the academic level, between professors or writers,' said Anand.

'That might break the ice. You talk to your dad about it. I will do my part,' said Hasina.

'He already thinks along that line. He had confided to me that he would encourage the idea of sending an Indian writer and an Indian professor to Islamabad.'

'In that case, we will send some of our writers and/or professors to India too. I shall talk to my dad about it.'

———◆———

While addressing a meeting of his party men, belonging to Kashmir World Conference, at Arnia in the border belt of R. S. Pura after inaugurating a 160-metre bridge across the rivulet there, Ahmed Shah, the Kashmir chief minister, declared that he would go ahead with the border fencing and electronic sensing system to check infiltration and cross-border terrorism.

He asked Pakistan to appreciate the importance of the restoration of normalcy in the region and to stop cross-border terrorism. He said that while the border shelling had uprooted vast chunks of population from their habitats along the line of control at Pallanwala sector, militant activities have driven out a sizeable population of Kashmiri pandits from the valley.

The interest of the Muslim militants was just that; they wanted to drive out the Hindu pandits from the Srinagar area, and to divide Kashmir into Srinagar and Jammu—Srinagar for the Muslims and Jammu for the Hindus.

Ahmed Shah had said, 'India is growing as a superpower both militarily and economically. Some external powers cannot reconcile themselves with this development; they conspire to dismantle this great nation. Like the erstwhile USSR, they want to break India into diverse nations; they start with Kashmir, but their dreams will not be realized.'

He called upon the people to stand like a rock and not allow such sinister plans to succeed.

Ahmed Shah promised the people of the state that every one of them would get equal opportunity and justice. He promised that the power projects at Baghliar, Sewa, and Baramula would go ahead as planned; this would ease the power situation in the state.

Charles Almeida decided that it would be a great idea to send a writer or a university professor, preferably a Muslim, to Pakistan. He would visit some Pakistani writers; he could hold discussions with some universities there, which might pave the way for research collaborations. He could be asked to invite one or two Pakistani writers or professors to visit India. It would be a non-political move. When this writer or professor came to India, he should feel at home; he should be given receptions wherever he went. He should be sent also to several states to visit the writers there and the universities or places of interest so that when he went back, he should have something vivid, happy memories to share, and a few nice words to say about India.

When he met Loknath Singh the next time, he told him about this idea, which was immediately found acceptable to him as well. And things began to move, and events began to roll.

Dr Iqbal Sultan, Dean of the Faculty of Philosophy at the JNU, Delhi, was chosen to make a visit to Pakistan. He always wanted to visit Karachi, Islamabad, and Lahore. He had read a lot of Pakistan during the past few years. Despite all the wars and war preparations, he used to keep a cool mind and was positive about the improvement in the relations between India and Pakistan. He used to tell his colleagues and friends that one day India and Pakistan would become friends and collaborators.

Loknath Singh had a meeting with Akhilesh Sharma, the human resource minister, and asked him about the propriety of sending one university professor to Pakistan on a goodwill mission. Loknath suggested the name of Dr Iqbal Sultan since Dr Sultan was well known as the dean of the faculty of philosophy at JNU, and he was respected and loved by colleagues and students for his highly intelligent attitudes about life. Akhilesh Sharma had no objection to accepting the proposal and he agreed to do everything for organizing the visit of Dr Iqbal to Pakistan.

The visit of Dr Iqbal Sultan was well received by the people and media of that country. It was the front-page news of almost every newspaper in Pakistan. His visits to Lahore, Karachi, and Islamabad were reported at length every day. His photos with professors of universities of Lahore, Karachi, and Islamabad were favourite items in the newspapers for days on. His visit to the home of Jinnah was well covered by all the TV channels and was the leading news of the day. To top it all, his visit to the ministry of culture, and his encounter with the minister for human resource development, Dr Akbar Khan, were favourite news in the newspapers and TV channels.

Two weeks went flying. He wanted to stay on for a few more days. But duty called; he had a lot of work waiting at JNU department of philosophy. He came back with wonderful memories.

———✦———

Prof. Dr Abdul Rahim Wahab (of Lahore University) always wanted to visit India and visit all the places he knew from books and from TV news; it was his life's ambition. He knew, the relationship between India and Pakistan being what it was, he would never have the chance to have this pleasure. He waited and waited. Whenever he got a chance, he would tell this to his friend Dr Chandra Sekhar of ISRO.

Now everything happened in a swift move. The visit of the Indian scholar Dr Iqbal Sultan had given a big spurt to the idea of a return visit to India. The initiative came from none other than the Pakistan president himself. He asked the ministry of culture to select two eminent scholars for the return visit. When Prof. Abdul Rahim Wahab heard that he and his friend Subinullah Zacharia (of Karachi University) were selected for the visit to India, his joy was boundless. Though the two countries are not on good terms, and had even fought wars, Zacharia and Wahab were aware of the academic professionalism in India, and wanted very much to visit India and talk to some of the academic luminaries they knew from international journals.

There is no air traffic between India and Pakistan. The only means of transportation was bus through the outpost at Wagah. The two scholars left Lahore at 4.50 a.m. and by 9.40 a.m., they were at Wagah post; the formalities at the Pakistan border were simple and fast. On the Indian side, every passenger was asked to alight from the bus and had to stand in a queue to meet the immigration officials, who were always eager to find something wrong in the passports and/or visas of the visitors from Pakistan. In the case of the two scholars, they could find nothing wrong, and the scholars were readily and speedily checked and papers were returned to them to proceed to the bus. The immigration officials were gratified and felt proud that two eminent Pakistani scholars were visiting Indian universities.

When the two scholars arrived in Delhi, there was a crowd of scholars to receive them. Many professors from IIT (Indian Institute of Technology) Delhi and JNU (Jawaharlal Nehru University) Delhi were present at the bus station to offer the academicians from Pakistan a very warm welcome. Wahab and Zacharia were overwhelmed by the magnitude and the warmth of the reception. They were driven directly to the Hotel Maurya, Delhi.

Prof. Wahab and Prof. Zacharia were enjoying every bit of the landscape during their bus ride and the taxi ride to the hotel. They were happy that Delhi had changed a lot, and had become a neat and beautiful world-city. The next day, they visited the IIT, Delhi, and had a meeting with the faculty of computer science and the faculty of telecommunication engineering. They had a special meeting with the president of IIT, and with the vice chancellor of Delhi University. The student associations organized a meeting in which the two professors were felicitated; this gave the visitors a lively engagement with the student community. After the talks of the two professors, students had a chance to pose questions; mundane things, from the university canteens in Pakistan to the interest of Pakistani students with regard to social media, were discussed. Naturally politics was not an issue in any of the questions. Many students expressed their wish to visit Pakistan and to meet the students there.

Greatly elated by the reception given to them wherever they visited and greatly surprised at the maturity of Indian students, the two professors went back to Pakistan with the firm resolve to come back again—soon. But before going back, they requested Delhi University and IIT, Delhi, to take the initiative to send for one month a batch of students to Pakistan as the beginning of a student exchange programme. Back in Pakistan, the two professors, Wahab and Zacharia, took the initiative to organize a student exchange programme between India and Pakistan; through their concerted effort, they could get the approval of the ministry of culture for the student exchange programme. They sent out the invitation to Delhi University and Delhi IIT, requesting them to send the first group of Indian students to visit Pakistan. The students would be guests of the Lahore and Karachi universities; they could spend one month in Pakistan, visit places, and hold discussions with students there.

The first batch of twenty students doing post-graduation in computer science in Delhi IIT went to Pakistan; a son of the Cricket Board chairman was also among them. They spent one month in Lahore, Karachi, and Islamabad, and returned with pleasant memories, friendly relationships, and the wish to revisit Pakistan soon.

This was followed by a return visit by twenty students of Islamabad University, Pakistan.

Three months after the student visits, the Football Club of Islamabad was invited to India to play at Delhi, Bombay, Bangalore, and Cochin. The Mohan Bagan Club of Kolkata did the return visit, and played with clubs in Islamabad, Karachi, and Lahore.

Cricket games between the two nations were neglected for a long time. But it had awoken to the new situation, and test cricket games were conducted in Pakistan and India.

FICCI (Federation of Indian Chambers of Commerce and Industry) sent a delegation of thirty to Pakistan to see the business situation in Pakistan, to hold talks with the Pakistan Chamber of Commerce and Industry. Mr Mukesh Ambani of Reliance Industries, Mr Narayana Murthy of Infosys, Mr Azim Premji of Wipro, Dr Ravi Pillai, and Mr Joy Alukkas were among them.

The FICCI delegation offered to establish computer centres in Karachi and Islamabad to train the young IT professionals; it had agreed to offer annual scholarships of US$12,000 each to fifty Pakistani students to come for studies in India in computer science, MBA, medicine, and engineering. Correspondingly, the Pakistan Chamber of Commerce on their part offered fifty scholarships to Indian students to study in Pakistan universities.

The exchange programme found good response from the academic community and from students. The programme was executed on both sides, and the response and enthusiasm had surprised the political players.

The parents of the scholarship holders were also allowed to visit Pakistan. They travelled in three luxury coaches to Pakistan. They toured the entire length and breadth of Pakistan. They were received with fanfare from the different universities.

The parents of fifty Pakistani students made the counter-visit to India in five tourist buses. Guest department of Delhi IIT had planned and organized their stay and visit. The group visited Delhi, Jaipur, Agra, Udaipur, Hyderabad, Bangalore, and Mysore. They were astonished at the number of Muslim mosques in India, and on several occasions, they could take part in the Friday prayers.

An Indo-Pak society took shape in Islamabad, in which all those who visited India became members; many political and business leaders were anxious to join the club. The members of the Indo-Pak Society and thirty like-minded MPs visited India.

All these gave Abdul Lateef extraordinary satisfaction and he foresaw the beautiful Indo-Pak relations of tomorrow.

In a reciprocal gesture, while the Indo-Pak delegation was in India, the Indo-Pak Friendship Society was established in New Delhi. Abdul Habeebulla was the president, and Dr Ananthakrishna Menon the secretary.

Dolphin International (a private hotel group in Islamabad) had offered to set up an international hotel at New Delhi (in association with Anand).

Things were moving at such a speed and tempo that the political leadership also were, so to say, forced to move with it.

Pakistan President Abdul Lateef called a meeting of his confidants and explored the possibility and opportunity of meeting the prime minister of India.

The president Abdul Lateef and Indian Prime Minister Loknath Singh met at Nepal on the sidelines of the SAARC conference held at Kathmandu. They held secret parleys and asked their respective delegates to prepare the treaty of friendship and peace between the two countries; the treaty should be comprehensive and should lead to some sort of economic union between the two countries. The treaty should be formally ratified before the next Independence Day (August 15). It would be known as the Nepal Treaty.

Even before the formalization of the treaty, the two nations started to move according to the spirit of the treaty.

Pakistan had unilaterally instructed its army personnel along the LOC never to shoot to the Indian side; it had also decreased the number of military personnel along the line of control. The Indian defence minister dismissed the idea, saying that Pakistan is not serious and that India can't believe that the Pak can remove the military installations that fast.

The new Pak high commissioner in Delhi, Dr Ashraf Jehangir Qazi, said that India should follow Pakistan and accept the ceasefire offer and also set up modalities for talks on Kashmir.

Indian government too declared a ceasefire in connection with Ramzan for a month. It might be extended further, if the climate was conducive to that.

Indian government held talks with militant outfits in Kashmir. The militants welcomed the ceasefire, especially the All Kashmir Global Conference (AKGC). It is the umbrella organization of all the Muslim militant outfits in Kashmir.

Mr Amar Kant, MOS in the defence ministry, sat with the militant organizations. Through the mediation of AKGC, a line of contact was established with all militant outfits, except a few radical ones.

Discussions were fruitful and peaceful. All seemed to imbibe the spirit of union and togetherness.

'It is high time the roar of guns should be mixed with the sound of politics. To be very honest, the goal of AKGC and other militant outfits is the same. While we fight with arguments, they fight with guns.'

'We do not have to talk peace. We will have to buy it. To buy peace, we will have to pay a price. That price is the ability to forget the bitter yesterday and dream of a better bright tomorrow.'

AKGC leader Abdul Jaleel returned to India after his three-week stay in Pakistan. On his return, he spent one week in New Delhi (more to do medical check-up than to do political negotiations).

'I look forward to sharing my experience in Pakistan and particularly in Azad Kashmir. There are vested interests both in India and in Pakistan, who do not want to solve the Kashmir problem. They are the extremist organizations, intelligence agencies, and some sections of the armed forces.'

Apart from religious freedom, people in Pakistan and Azad Kashmir could not boast of any other freedom. In his interaction with Pakistani leaders in Islamabad, Rawalpindi, and Lahore, Mr Jaleel was brutally frank in telling his hosts that a country like Pakistan with no democracy could not be relied upon to help the cause of Kashmiris.

18

General Mohammed Yusuf Geelani was the one sure link between the Pakistan military establishment and the Pentagon.

The 'friendship' started when Mohammed Yusuf was selected for military training in the United States of America. At that time, he was young and just a lieutenant.

He came from the border town of Wana in South Waziristan. When Yusuf was two years old, his father had said talaq to his mother and sent her away. It was hard for his mother to take care of him and to send him to school. But she had decided to send him to school, and he was good at studies and was luckily admitted to the military school in Islamabad. During his days of training, he was a model cadet and was always ready to take up difficult tasks. He was ever ready to please his superiors, and was conscientious in accomplishing correctly the jobs entrusted to him. He passed with flying colours and was drafted as lieutenant in the army. He was then sent to the prestigious Army War Academy, where young lieutenants are given training to perform important functions of evaluation of concepts and doctrines in the fields of tactics and operational logistics. They are given the complete spectrum of tactical drills and concepts pertaining to infantry operating in varied terrain and environment. They were given training also in the sub-unit level in tactical and special mission techniques to enable them to carry out assigned operational missions.

Even before passing the Army War Academy, Lieutenant Mohammed Yusuf Geelani was selected to go to the United States for further military training.

In the United States too, he won the friendship of every one of his colleagues through his humble attitude and pleasing manners. His humble origin helped him to be thankful for even the smallest favours he received.

The CIA, which has an eye on every foreign trainee in the United States, did not miss the pleasing personality of Mohammed Yusuf Geelani. Everybody called him Yusuf. To say the complete name was difficult.

On the first of February1989 as Yusuf was sipping his coffee in the military canteen, Lt. Alfred Hopkins came to him with his cup of coffee and asked politely, 'Shall I sit with you, if you don't mind?' Yusuf nodded his consent.

'Lieutenant Mohammed Yusuf Geelani, we have met several times in our classrooms. But we never had the occasion to talk. If I may ask, which is your native place?' asked Hopkins.

'Of course, Pakistan,' replied Geelani.

'I know that. Which is your exact native city?'

'Oh, it is a very small village. It is no city. It is Wana on the western border of Pakistan, quite close to Afghanistan,' replied Yusuf.

'Myself, I come from the very small city of St. Benedict, in the state of Oregon. I had my studies in the school run by the Benedictine fathers of St. Angel Abbey. So both of us come from the western part of our countries. How do you like the United States?'

'Oh, I love it. It's like heaven. I came to know of freedom only after coming here. In Pakistan, there are only restrictions and limitations. Here there is nothing like that. If you abide by the laws, which are not difficult to follow, you have no problem here. It is the finest thing about the United States.'

Lt. Hopkins and Yusuf met oftener. Hopkins became thick with Yusuf. They exchanged information about each one's family and background, each one's tastes and future plans. But Yusuf did not know one thing: that Hopkins was deputed by Gen. Frederick Hughes to canvas at least one faithful lieutenant from among the Pakistani trainees.

Keeping tabs on whatever is happening in the Pakistani military establishment was important to the United States. Knowledge is power. In Pakistan, the military has immense power and influence. No politician can ever ignore the military establishment. Pakistan was for the most part ruled by the military.

If ever any civil government came to power, it never ignored the advice and wishes of the military. The military had complete control of the governance, even when the civilians ruled the country. So good and lasting contact with the military establishment is a must for safeguarding the larger interests of the United States in Pakistan. They had several links in Pakistani military. Yusuf was a good addition to the list.

After the celebration of independence on the 15th of August by the Pakistani trainees, Lt. Hopkins dutifully introduced Yusuf to Gen. Frederick Hughes, who was the chief guest for the celebrations.

'How do you do, Lieutenant Mohammed Yusuf Geelani?' asked Gen. Hughes.

Yusuf was surprised that the general knew his complete name. And he pronounced it properly. 'How come, how do you remember our difficult names?' asked Yusuf.

'Shall I call you Yusuf? It's easier to say.'

'Of course,' replied Yusuf. 'Lt. Hopkins and others call me by that name.'

'We are happy to have you here, lieutenant,' said Gen. Hughes. 'If you can, please meet me in my office at Washington DC NE. Lieutenant Alfred Hopkins will tell you exactly where it is.'

Yusuf was enthralled by the invitation. He was proud that he was invited by a general of the United States army to his office. It was an honour. Yusuf was completely nervous. Gen. Hughes said farewell and went along the hall, saying hello to everyone whom he knew.

Yusuf could not believe his ears. He went straight to Lt. Hopkins, who was busy with the pieces of Kentucky Fried Chicken served for the buffet.

'Lieutenant Hopkins, do you know what the general said?' asked Yusuf. 'I'm excited. He invited me to his office. I have to meet him tomorrow at his Washington DC NE office.'

'Fantastic! It's really an honour. It's rare that you are invited by a general.' Hopkins went on to explain the importance of Gen. Hughes, and the esteem he enjoyed in the military establishment of the USA. 'Do you know where his office is?' asked Hopkins.

'No. General Hughes told me that you would know the place. Would you tell me exactly how to get there? I am simply nervous. I think it would be difficult for me to sleep this night. Well, it is very nice of him that he invited me. I am at a loss to find a reason why he should invite me.'

'There need not be any reason. The general is like that. He is a very approachable person. If he likes somebody, he will heap favours on him,' said Hopkins. He was careful not to mention the fact that he too was invited by the general six weeks before. He was invited for a very special purpose. 'Get the smartest Pakistani trainee for me. Establish a strong friendship with him, and when it is time, introduce him to me. We need people in Pakistan military who will work with us,' the general had said then.

'I've done my job. Now it is for the general to do the rest,' thought Hopkins.

General Hughes did the rest. He spoke to Yusuf about the cordial relationship between the US and Pakistan since the time of Nixon: the service of Pakistan in connecting the USA to China, the assistance of Pakistan and its territory in routing the Russians from Afghanistan, and on the part of the US, the immense military support given to Pakistan.

'We wish that this cordial relationship should last,' said Hughes.

'Sure.' Yusuf did not know what else to say.

Gen. Hughes presented him with a laptop computer and a cover with US$10,000 in it. 'This is a humble gift from me. The laptop will help you in your days ahead. I am impressed by your military acumen and dedication. Keep in touch with me,' concluded Gen. Hughes. He shook hands with Yusuf and dialled the intercom. His secretary ushered Yusuf out of the general's office.

As soon as Yusuf left, the general replayed the whole scene and analysed the words and facial expression of Yusuf. 'He is our man,' declared Hughes.

Every alternate week, Gen. Hughes used to call Yusuf to his office, and each time he would give him some gift, and a cheque. Thus Yusuf got a camera, a VCR, and other valuable things a Pakistani would like. And each time, everything was videotaped.

After one year, Yusuf became thick with Gen. Hughes. Yusuf had a filial feeling towards him, love and respect bundled together.

On their tenth meeting, Gen. Hughes said casually, 'Yusuf, I hope you would love to see how our first visit went.'

'I know how it went. I remember every detail, and I thank you for your kindness,' said Yusuf in utter supplication.

'Well, look there,' Gen. Hughes pointed to the TV screen. 'You were so meek and hesitating when you came first.'

Yusuf seemed to enjoy the scenes, until they reached the part showing his receiving the laptop and the cover. The cover was very prominent in the picture. Yusuf knew he was in. He could no longer escape.

Have I a choice? Can I quit now? If I quit, I will be betrayed and possibly court-martialled. I can expect a sentence of twenty or thirty years in prison. At any rate, my military and civil career would be over if I quit. It is better to live in permanent internal conflict than perish as a traitor.

It was a moment of decision about life and death. He did not want to disappoint himself, nor his parents, and spend the rest of his youth in jails. Hopkins and Hughes were trapping him. All the niceties they said were traps. The gentlemen succeeded in achieving what they wanted.

There was nothing like sincerity, friendliness, decency. It was all business. The end justifies the means. Means can be cruel and brutal.

Not even for a moment did he think that he was being led like a lamb to the slaughterhouse by the two US army personnel.

He regained his composure. He said calmly, 'I knew what was coming.' He wanted at least to show that he was not a fool. He was an intelligent officer. He knew what this replay meant.

'Don't worry, lieutenant. You are in safe hands. Your career will only get a boost. Your association with us will be only useful to you,' Gen. Hughes said without any sign of guilt or remorse in trapping Yusuf.

Yusuf had decided to co-operate with Gen. Hughes. (In his mind, he despised him for what he did to him.)

From now own I do not own myself. My country does not own me. I am owned by the US military. I am a slave. I have been caught, bought. Slave trading is going on.

From then on, he understood his role. And from then on, the filial feeling gave way to the dispassionate feeling of dutifulness of a collaborator. From now on, it was sheer business. As a military man, he understood what it meant.

Before going home after his training, Yusuf visited Gen. Hughes, who gave Yusuf a small video camera (he had no other choice than visit him). 'Ask some of your trusted friends to make pictures of scenes which would be of interest to us. And mail the cassette to us through our embassy at Islamabad. I shall instruct the embassy to help you,' instructed the general, as if he were talking to one of his subordinates.

Yusuf dutifully continued to serve the interests of the USA in Pakistan. He regularly sent email to the general, and sent photos and videocassettes. And like a good partner, Gen. Hughes sent back covers with thousands of dollars each time. Yusuf could afford a decent life in the city of Islamabad, with his own posh house, cars, servants, and all the luxuries a middle-class businessman could think of.

During the last twenty years, a lot of things happened in Pakistan and in the United States. But nothing happened in Pakistan without the prior knowledge (if not consent) of the United States. General Hughes and his men in the Pakistani army were in close contact. He had more than two dozen Yusufs in the Pakistani army.

Gen. Hughes retired in 1998, and General Arnold Richards took his place. Gen. Hughes had given him a detailed analysis of the Indian subcontinent and its military-political situation, especially in Pakistan and India. He dutifully gave the list of the confidants in the two countries. Gen. Mohammed Yusuf Geelani was on the list.

Gen. Richards dialled the private number of Gen. Yusuf. 'Good afternoon, general. This is General Richards from Washington.'

'Good afternoon, general. Yusuf here. What a surprise. What can I do for you, general?' Yusuf was ever ready to do anything for Richards. Gen. Richards had kept up the warm relationship with Yusuf. He has become a general recently. He was one of the key players in Pakistani politics now.

'Any new developments, General Yusuf?'

'Nothing special. General Abdul Lateef is very secure in his position as the president of Pakistan and as the head of the defence forces.'

'We welcome that. He has the tacit blessing of the previous and present Presidents of the United States. He is doing his job well. How is your relationship with India? Has it become worse, or better? I know, the Indians always hated Pakistani leaders and Abdul Lateef is no exception. Especially the Indian military, hates him like anything.' said Gen. Richards in a breath.

'The Indians, especially their defence minister Charles Almeida, really hate him. He has not made any overtures to the Indians yet. He tells us that we should wait for some more time so that the heat of the war cools down.'

'We heard that General Abdul Lateef had some informal talks with some Indian emissaries, especially with the Indian Ambassador Vijay Menon.'

'Yes, he had some talks. But they are informal and unimportant,' replied Yusuf.

'Our political leadership has to encourage mutual discussion and dialogue between India and Pakistan. You know, the politicians have to take care of the public opinion. But we the strategists are aware that India will become the supreme power in the South Indian subcontinent, if left unchecked. Strategically it is not in our interest. Any lull in the border will help India to concentrate on its economy; that will be a problem for our military as well as consumer industries. I hope you understand what I mean.' Gen. Richards explained his priorities.

'Of course, Mr Richards. I am here to represent your interest in Pakistan and Indo-Pak relations. Our special group of generals will see to it that there is no peace on the long border with India.'

Actually, Gen. Yusuf and all the other generals were not aware of what Gen. Abdul Lateef was thinking. He knew that a strategy given out is no longer a strategy. The military has to surprise the enemy. In politics too, surprise has its unique importance.

'Thank you, General Yusuf, for your time. Please keep me posted. You can send me emails from your laptop. I hope even now it is a good tool' Richard concluded.

'Yes, general,' replied Yusuf like a dutiful vassal.

Gen. Richards rang up US Ambassador Aaron Kemper in Islamabad and told him about his conversation with Gen. Yusuf, and asked him to contact Gen. Abdul Azeez about his impression of Abdul Lateef's rule and Indo-Pak relationship.

The CIA was also told about the talk and he requested the CIA to post additional men at Islamabad, Karachi, and Azad Kashmir to watch the developments.

Gen. Richards phoned US Ambassador Abraham Montgomery at New Delhi and talked about the feeling that something was happening in India and Pakistan, and advised him to find out what that could be.

⚜

Vladimir Pushkin was convalescing from the severe cold he had after his return from his villa in Leningrad. The memo on his office table signalled that something was happening in South Asia. What could that be? To his knowledge, there was no big problem between the two traditional enemies, India and Pakistan, at present. Was a war going to take place between them?

Or, could it be that some external forces were trying to do some sort of a coup in India or in Pakistan? In Pakistan, it could be possible. They were used to it. But in India? If anything of the sort happened there, it could have far-reaching consequences in the whole region, nay, in the whole world. Who was behind it? Could be the USA or China. (Who else would dare such manoeuvres in other countries?)

He buzzed for his secretary. Alexandriev Petrovski came rushing in. He said, 'The head of the KGB called here twice this morning and asked me about the time of your return.'

'That is fine.' He had learned to be cool and quiet especially in times of upheaval and crisis.

'Has he left any inkling about what that could be?'

'No. Not at all. He just asked in his usual emotionless fashion. But I have the feeling that something is happening in South Asia. That's why I left the memo on your table,' said Petrovski.

19

Arthur Fitzgerald Mason had come up the ladder through years of sweat. Every step was won through sheer willpower and hard work. He had witnessed and was part of the several crises of enormous magnitude in international relations. He lived through the dismantling of the USSR, the unification of the two Germanies, the Balkan crisis, Kosovo, Serbia, Afghan War, Iraq War . . . From the beginning of the crack in the Russian iron curtain till the levelling off with the independence of the slave states like Estonia, Latvia, Czechoslovakia, Hungary, Yugoslavia, Poland, etc., he was actively involved, not only for the gathering of information, but also for speeding up the process of the collapse of the Soviet empire. Now that he was the chief of the Asia desk of the CIA, he felt that he held responsibility for the well-being of all the countries in that part of the world.

At present, India was a major concern of the CIA. Not because it was a big military power, but because it is a fast-growing economy, the most potential trade partner in the long run, a big market for consumer goods and for sophisticated costly military hardware. For the sale of military hardware, the best marketing strategy is to keep borders burning and to support the least costly cross-border terrorism.

India is very vulnerable on all the three sides of its borders. In the north, China is perceived as a threat, even if no one says it aloud. On the eastern front, terrorism and separatism are active in most of the north-eastern states; add to it the bases of terrorist outfits along the border of Bangladesh and Myanmar. In the west, Pakistan and its associate Kashmiri terrorists are a permanent headache for India. India must have the feeling that it is being contained from all the three sides. This will drive it mad to buy profusely sophisticated military hardware in order to reach the required comfort level. Formerly the Indians wanted to buy everything military from the Russians. Now that Indo-Soviet myth is gone, India is emerging as the biggest market for US and European military manufacturers. In the long run, the competition for this market may be between the US and Europe.

Any rapprochement between India and Pakistan would signal catastrophic consequences for the military hardware sales. The military lobby is the biggest one in Washington. Its interests are intertwined with that of the USA.

From reliable sources in New Delhi, Bombay, Islamabad, and Karachi, Arthur Fitzgerald Mason had come to know that the relationship between the two countries was going to be different. Smooth. Friendly.

'It is preposterous,' he told himself.

'Some secret parleys are said to be going on between Abdul Lateef and some secret service men of India,' Yusuf had informed him last week in his short phone call.

'Outwardly nothing is happening as far as the relationship between India and Pakistan is concerned.' This was what Sunil Choudhry, his informant in India, reported from New Delhi.

'These Indians cannot be trusted. They blasted the nuclear device in Pokhran without anybody in CIA knowing about it. They had even fooled our spy satellites,' cautioned Larry Dumkopf, the CIA man in charge of South Asia. 'Better have a close watch on the developments there. Even if nothing is seen on the periphery, something could be brewing up in their secret corridors.'

After a week of intense research, eavesdropping, and highly technical espionage of conversations in the north and south blocks of New Delhi, the CIA was sure that nothing was happening on the Indian front.

But all the reports from Pakistan tended to say that something was really happening. Abdul Lateef had become softer as far as India was concerned. And he was reported to have unknown visitors when he went to Nepal, Germany, etc.

Two weeks of research into the dark and labyrinthine avenues of events had revealed that really Abdul Lateef planned a sort of rapprochement. But there was no hard and fast evidence.

Mason had been wondering why the Indians had become less belligerent. During the Kargil war, they did not at all follow a military strategy. Though they defended their territory, they did not extend the attack behind the lines, to cut off the supply of men and materials to the border on Pakistan side. It was quite a non-military strategy.

All this showed that some sort of cooling off was taking place.

Better to be on the safer side!

Mason called up his South Asian team and asked them to plot strategies to thwart any possible rapprochement between the two. Rtd. General Ed Whitewash was of the opinion that nothing needed to be undertaken in the absence of hard evidence to prove the rapprochement.

But Mason trusted his intuition much more than the logic of his lieutenants. He had made up his mind. He asked the team to work out strategies. He cautioned them: 'We will put the strategy into action only when we get clear-cut evidence and clearance from the government for its execution.'

He dialled the number of his boss, Lester Hoffkins, and apprised him of what he thought about the Indo-Pak situation.

The arms dealers are better parameters to gauge the situation in a given country. They have a well-knit system of information. They have contact with the men who handle the purchase of military hardware. They give great care to keep this relationship cordial and happy. They were disturbed at the statistical data available with them.

Pakistan was buying less. Not because they have financial crunch. They do get financial support from the Arab world and even from the US. Saudi Arabia is always sympathetic to Pakistan; Iran too has a soft corner for Pakistan. These Arab nations do give adequate funds directly or indirectly to Pakistan. Still, Pakistan was now buying more industrial and consumer goods than military hardware.

These statistics correspond to the cooling off on the actual line of control (LOC). The Pakistani military establishment was not inclined to create trouble for Indians. You seldom heard the roaring guns at the borders. No shelling. Wasn't it strange!

The academic seminar on 'Global Consequences of the Star Wars (Strategic Defense Initiative)' held at Washington

University offered an apt occasion for Beneditto Passavanti to bring the South Asian situation to the notice of the defence secretary, Juliano D'Amato.

Beneditto Passavanti was the representative of the arms lobby for the past few decades. He began from the lowest level and came to the present position through hard work and luck. When it was the question of military hardware, Passavanti was the man. He was well-known to industry and politics equally. He was looking for a suitable occasion to get the private ears of the defence secretary.

Dr Conrado Kennfield from the University of Pennsylvania just finished his talk on 'Anti Ballistic Missile Treaty and Missile Defence System'. As the participants were moving to the coffee tables, Passavanti moved to the defence secretary, Mr Juliano D'Amato.

'May I have the favour of your ears for a while?' asked Passavanti. Passavanti was the main spokesman of the arms lobby. He was well-known to D'Amato. Passavanti was soft-spoken, but a hard bargainer.

'Of course, Mr Passavanti. I had already seen you in the crowd; it was good that you came,' said the defence secretary politely, though he did not like the bossy attitude of the arms dealer.

'You must be aware of the South Asian situation.' Passavanti went straight to the crux of the matter.

'Of course. Rather than South Asia, Afghanistan is the headache at the moment.' The defence secretary built up his defence; he did not want to leak any sensitive news to him. 'We have a good government in place. But the Afghans are a thankless people. They do not remember all the help we gave them to get rid of the Russian occupation, and then the oppressive regime of the Taliban, the sacrifice of man and materials by us for their cause. The present mood of the people is still a pain in the ass for the administration. In the Afghan involvement, all of you have made good money, no?' The defence minister was well aware of the preoccupations of the arms lobby, but wanted to hear it from them.

'But we the arms dealers are at present worried about the lull in the South Asian market in general,' replied Passavanti. 'The arms purchase from the Pakistan side has gone down considerably and consistently during the last six months. Isn't it surprising?' asked Passavanti. 'You know, the bloody Indians are not our regular customers.'

'Not very surprising, given the poor economic situation of Pakistan.' The defence secretary was quite careful not to give out unnecessary information; at the same time, he prodded the arms dealer to come out with more information. It could give him a clue as to what his friends in the business too think.

'It is surprising, if you analyse systematically the track record of Pakistan. Money has never been a problem for them. The Pakis find some patrons somehow or other. If not the USA, they have their oil-rich sheiks and kings,' quipped Passavanti. 'But now the trend seems to be that they do not want to purchase!'

'You find the situation alarming?' asked D'Amato quite innocently.

'Yes. Yes. We do, I mean, the whole arms lobby. We are disturbed by the trend. We follow the projects and statistics of our experts, who keep close watch on the arms deals all over the world. We give orders for production on the basis of our prognosis in sensitive markets. The development in Pakistan is serious and unexplainable.' Passavanti tried to convince the defence secretary about the gravity of the situation.

Passavanti was very active in spearheading the wishes of his lobby; he wanted to keep every member of his exclusive club happy. He wished to be re-elected next year also. What was required for this is volume, the sales volume of arms. The better the results, the better his chance for re-election.

It was his lobby which donated millions of dollars for the campaign fund of D'Amato when he ran for the governorship of Oklahoma. Now he would need their support in the next elections, when he intended to run again for the governorship when his term with the president was over.

On the whole, D'Amato was happy with the global turnover of arms deals in the first quarter of this year. Keeping hot spots alive is a need of the arms lobby. The Middle East crisis is a consistent promoter of arms movement; how can it stop all of a sudden? The Sri Lankan conflict between government and LTTE was paying good dividends; both sides bought arms in huge quantities as well as used and abused them. The Chechen conflict too brought happiness to the arms dealers. Northern Ireland was a flourishing market for small arms, so also the internal conflicts in Indonesia and Malaysia. The tribal conflicts in almost all the African countries expedited the sale of small- and middle-level arms. The hot spot China-Taiwan is a most fertile market, and the volume is big. Every conflict in any corner of the world gives sleepless nights to politicians, but the arms dealers go home with a song in their hearts. The newest avatar of violence, ISIS, is a God-given gift to the arms lobby.

The very long stretch of hot spots along the Indo-Pakistan border is not as unimportant as one might think; arms dealers are happy about the sporadic and occasional eruption of conflicts and mini-wars all along the border. When people die from grenade attacks or bomb explosions in the Kashmir valley, the arms dealers are jubilant.

Pakistan had been a traditional buyer of defence hardware from the USA. Any slowdown in the Pakistan market will disturb the production strategies of their principals. (After the collapse of the Soviet Union, the Indians had started to purchase conventional arms as well as high-tech dual technology from the USA in considerable quantities.) South Asia had become a very fertile market for the arms lobby. Now that the Indians have improved their economic situation due to the flourishing business in the information technology segment, quantities have become bigger.

Hence the present trend in Pakistan is alarming news to them. Arms lobby is not just a few individuals and corporations, but it is one of the major industries of the nation. Arms deals are in billions of dollars. Even the so-called poor countries of the world are good buyers. The government cannot forget the fact that a lot of employees depend on this branch of industry.

Hence the arms lobby always gets the support of the government machinery. Arms trade is one of the major components of foreign trade and foreign policy as well.

'Well, I shall look into the matter. I shall also have a word with the Secretary of State, Dr Conrad Paulovski.'

Back in his office after the seminar, the defence secretary phoned the Secretary of State and inquired about possible strategic changes in South Asia.

'There is a lull in the arms purchase deals from Pakistan's side. But that is not alarming. Anyway, I shall look into the matter and get back to you the same time tomorrow,' concluded the Secretary of State.

The Secretary of State asked his officials to get in touch with Pakistan's ambassador and to ask him to find out whether anything (untoward!) was happening.

———◆———

Hectic discussions were taking place both at Islamabad and at New Delhi. The final draft of the agreement was approved by the foreign ministers of both countries. The prime minister of India and the president of Pakistan had to give their final approval to the text. At a convenient date, they would hold a videoconference to discuss and agree on the final draft.

The main objective of the agreement was to have lasting peace in the subcontinent. In a dramatic and historical move, India and Pakistan will become an economic union—Indo-Pak Union (IPU); it is in many ways similar to the formation of Benelux in Europe. (In Benelux, the three small countries Belgium, Netherlands, and Luxembourg were members, and it was actually the beginning of the present European Union.) Just as it happened in the case of Benelux, the border between Pakistan and India would be practically fully open. The requirement for visa would be done away with. Visas issued by the Indo-Pak Union would be valid for both the countries. The movement of people and goods would increase. There would be peace between the nations and free movement for their people. There would still be terrorist activities. But without official support, they will die a natural death in the course of a few years.

Pakistan agreed not to send militants to Indian side, nor to help them in any way. Regular bus service to Lahore, Karachi, and Islamabad would be introduced. The train link between the two countries would be restored. Flights between New Delhi/Bombay and Islamabad/Karachi/Lahore had to become regular.

There would be mutual exchange of politicians, academicians, students, etc.

India and Pakistan agreed to honour the LOC. If people from both the parts can travel and trade with each other without any hindrance, what is the relevance of having to fight for a few square metres of land along the borders?

As a result of these measures, trade was to pick up. Pak buys Indian wheat, instead of from New Zealand and Australia. India buys Pak sports goods, leather goods, onions, etc.

India and Pakistan should co-operate in building an oil pipeline from Iran to India.

Both the countries should take initiative to declare the countries of SAARC as a common economic zone and pave the way for a union of South Asia.

This in nutshell was the agreement. The text of the agreement was kept as a top secret.

It was tentatively decided to sign the agreement at Jaipur on the morning of the 14th of August. But the date and place of signing was kept as a great secret by both the countries. It was known only to the Indian prime minister, Pakistani president, the foreign ministers, and their immediate entourage.

Though the treaty was supposed to be a great secret, the USA knew of it within three hours. Within a day, China and Russia too came to know of it. Among the European nations, it was France which knew of it within forty-eight hours. The French are known to be for co-operation and peaceful coexistence between India and Pakistan.

Despite the moves towards peace, terrorist activities by various militant groups were somehow gathering momentum. It made the leaderships of both the countries a bit nervous.

The ceasefire and movement towards peace was being thwarted by some radical separatist organizations. They carried out a rocket attack on an army installation, whereby three Special Police officers were killed. The attack damaged a house; a woman and her daughter were injured.

In another incident, five BSF Jawans were wounded when their jeep was blown up at Matka Chowk, Parimpora downtown in the afternoon.

SPO Abdul Qadoos Khan was killed and his wife and daughter injured when the militants fired a rocket at his house in Lalpora, Kupwara. One of the rockets landed in Khan's bedroom and exploded.

At Kakarhamam, Baramula district, counter-insurgent Parvaiz Ahmad was killed by militants. Formerly, Ahmad was a militant and had retired from terrorist activities.

At Dhandak, Poonch district, Jammu, Mohammad Sadiq, SPO, was gunned down by militants. At Danadi Dhara, Poonch, a civilian died from the bullets of a militant.

20

The trend of normalization in South Asia had unnerved many officials in the CIA. The CIA in the US Embassy at New Delhi had become more active. The bigwigs in the CIA think that friendly relationship between India and Pakistan is not in their interest. The arms lobby would suffer; there would be less military hardware purchase by Pakistan; there will be less dual-technology purchase by India. On the agricultural front, the grain lobby of the USA will suffer, because Pakistan can import wheat and rice from India at cheaper rates, now that India has a buffer of millions of tons of grain more than it can store. There is tremendous advantage also on the transport cost. Further, Pakistan need not stockpile wheat; it can buy as and when it requires wheat from just over the border. Pakistan would feel more independent, as India already is, despite the recent tilt towards the USA.

A very confusing situation was emerging. That the economic interests of the USA would suffer if both the countries buried their hatchets was giving a headache to the officials in the CIA establishment. Now that India was becoming more powerful technologically, the coexistence between the two countries with the possible blessing of China would make them forget the importance of the USA. Russia is by all means a friend of India and would put in their weight and make some sort of alliance with the

Indo-Pak union. The global power balance too might shift in favour of an Asian axis. The thought of it became heady day by day.

———◆———

The US ambassador in Islamabad has the highest priority access to the president of Pakistan, especially ever since the Afghan War. The right-wing fundamentalists are a headache to every ruler in Pakistan; they oppose tooth and nail any collusion with the Americans. The US assured Abdul Lateef all support, and asked him to consolidate his position in the politics. As per the advice of US 'consultants', first he started with the extension of his presidency for five years. Then he repeated the feat again. This was his third term. He had practically become the sheik of Pakistan, who cannot be removed. If almost all the Arab countries are ruled by kings, why not a semi-king in Pakistan?

And the Americans are happy that they have in Pakistan a ruler who will bend to any extent. He is a big help for them in any strategic move in the Gulf area. In the Iraq War too, Pakistan was a reliable ally. The next target is Iran; Pakistan is highly strategic for that operation.

When the US ambassador called, he was prompt in giving him the required appointment as per his wish: 9 a.m.

On that sunny Monday, the ambassador arrived punctually in his official car and entered the office of the president. Receiving the US ambassador is almost like receiving a head of state. Everywhere there is reverence and respect, sometimes to the extent of slavishness.

'Good morning, Mr President,' said the ambassador. His tone spoke volumes about his assertiveness.

'Very good morning, Your Excellency,' replied the president. His tone and gestures were exuberant expression of his thankfulness to the US government throughout his career as the (immovable) president of Pakistan.

'By the way, the Secretary of State phoned me yesterday night, and asked me to meet you as soon as possible,' said the ambassador.

The president was a bit uneasy when he heard of the phone call from the Secretary of State.

Is there any covert plan for his ouster? Is there any coup brewing up among our military establishment? If anything untoward were happening there, General Abdul Sattar would have told me. Then what could be the urgency of a phone call from the Secretary of State?

'He wanted me to convey his best wishes for the holy month of Ramzan, which begins tomorrow,' said the ambassador, without trying to open up the real issue.

'Thank you, thank you. It is the month that I long for all the year. I am a strict observer of the Ramzan like any other genuine Muslim. During this month, I never make any state visit outside Pakistan. I spend most of the time in Islamabad itself. And I pray a lot,' the President explained. He was also relieved.

'*Who wants to hear about Ramzan and his holy fasting and prayers!*' said the ambassador in his mind. '*There are more pressing issues than fasting.*'

'How is the border situation? Are the bloody Indians still showing their muscle? We have some intelligence report about some arms movement, some serious hardware movement, along the Rajasthan border.'

'Of course, I know that.'

'Then what I heard is right too. Our defence department has reliable information regarding this. And our satellites are doing their job properly,' said the ambassador.

'But there is nothing to worry about. Our people are well aware of the quantities of the hardware and the number of personnel moving along the border area. The Indian side informed us about it. We cross-checked it. There is nothing to worry about,' explained the president.

So it is known to him! There is no concern in his voice! It's strange. The suspicion of the Secretary of State might be true.

'You can never trust them. Years back before, the Indians exploded their atomic device at Pokhran, who thought they were moving a nuclear device, though we and you noticed some vehicle movement?' said the ambassador casually. *Maybe the name of Pokhran would send shock waves in the president,* he thought. He continued, 'Now they are trying to be friendly with us. But we know where to put them. We have some marketing strategies. Once that is achieved, they will belong to where they belong: in the dustbin of history.' The ambassador laughed with a conspiratorial look.

'Of course, we know from history the machinations of the fanatic Hindus. We are always meticulously careful about our relation to them,' said the president. *This infidel need not know about our economic and strategic compulsions. We shall keep it a secret in our hearts. Friendship with India is not one of sincerity, but one of expediency.*

'*Isn't he hiding something?*' thought the ambassador. '*If he is, we will have to change our attitude to this bastard.*'

'Well, I thought I would just convey the good wishes of our Secretary of State for the holy month of Ramzan,' concluded the ambassador.

'Thank you. Convey my personal gratitude to him. Tell him also that there is nothing to worry about the borders with Indians. It is as strong as before. We know well how to thwart any foolish move of the Indians,' responded the president.

Already the ambassador was on his feet. The door to the presidential offices opened. They shook hands and the ambassador exited in unusual haste.

The Chinese ambassador Ho Dung Fung, in Islamabad, was nervous that the American CIA presence in Pakistan had increased substantially in the recent weeks. He contacted his counterpart in New Delhi; he too confirmed that there was unusual CIA activity all over India. Was it a signal of something ominous? Did it mean that something serious was going to happen in South Asia? Were they planning a toppling game in China or in Pakistan? Were they going to change the Pakistani president? Or did they plan some dirty politics in India? These days, the Americans could do what they wished. They are now the policemen of the world. The UN had become a useless institution; it did not raise a finger against whatever the USA wished or did. Nay, it was there just to support the machinations of the United States and its allies. The Chinese ambassador reported his nervousness about the situation to Beijing.

Upon the instructions from Beijing, the Chinese ambassador fixed up an appointment with Foreign Minister Abdul Sattar of Pakistan. 'I must find out what is going on,' he told himself.

———◆———

Wherever there is some conflict or a move towards one, the Israeli secret service Mossad will be there. They are interested in everything that happens in the world, and they are very good at gathering information, and are a good informant for other secret services. If Israeli secret service gets some inkling of what is going on, it gives partial information first thing to the CIA.

Moshe Dayan (not the former famous one-eyed Israeli defence minister) was walking along the streets of Old Delhi. He was following a thread of information he got from his informant. He went to the fruit stall and pretended to buy a fruit juice. Orange from Himachal had just arrived.

From the corner of his eye, he could see the strange movement of two figures on the other side of the road. There was something unusual about the way they were walking. They were carrying something unwieldy. It would appear they were protecting themselves from the extreme cold of Delhi in the month of January. But the protruding rifle did not escape his attention.

Dayan continued drinking his juice and continued watching the two figures. Dayan sat down on the floor as some villagers do and watched carefully what was going on. He finished his juice and wanted to stand up to give back the glass, when a Maruti van with darkened glass screeched to a halt and, in the next second, sped away. The two strange figures too disappeared. They must have entered the van, or may have been pulled into it.

Suddenly, Dayan pressed his camera button and recorded what was left of the event, and he just got the back of the van with the number plate. But he was sure it must be a false number. At least the colour of the vehicle would help. He switched on his mobile phone and dialled.

'Yes, Dayan,' said the other side.

'A blue van has just rushed in the direction of Connaught Place. It has at least two persons in it with automatic rifles or rocket launchers. There may be more people in the van and more weapons,' said Dayan in one breath.

'Thank you, Dayan,' said the other end. "I am passing on the information to the nearest possible man, who will be able to spot the vehicle in question and maybe also follow it. In the meantime, you quickly go over to New Delhi railway station and wait in the waiting hall. Our man will meet you there.'

Dayan was relieved. His facial expression betrayed his satisfaction that he had at last done something worthwhile during that day. He always feared that he would be retrenched if he were not sharp enough, if he were not fast enough, if he were not seeing enough, if he were not communicating enough.

Immediately he boarded an autorickshaw that came that way and sped to New Delhi railway station.

Dayan had served in Delhi from 1996 to 2001. He had a thrilling assignment also during the Kargil war between India and Pakistan. He knew Hindi and Urdu perfectly well. It helped him to mingle easily with the common people of India. With some handiwork on his hair, he could very well pass for a Punjabi.

The duo in the Maruti van proceeded to Race Course Road, where the prime minister's office and residence were situated. Mr Ariel Perez was clutching his mobile phone and was standing idly at the junction. As soon as he spotted the Maruti van, he pressed one button on his mobile and the signal had already gone to the concerned attaché in the Israeli embassy. He knew what Ariel wanted to say. Ariel had an array of symbolic signals when he was on external duty. Signals are coded information.

Ariel expected that something would happen there. He quickly took out his mobile phone and pressed the camera button. But to his disappointment, the Maruti van proceeded beyond Race Course Road; it took a right turn into Asoka Road, and again a right to enter the Janpath. He was puzzled. What were they going to do?

But suddenly it had slowed down; the occupants were, perhaps, enjoying the scenery around. Maybe, Ariel thought, they too had the type of camera he held in his hand. Then the next moment, they sped away in haste. Now Ariel Perez was at a loss to figure out where they were heading to or what they were planning. He again called his officer and told him what he saw and what he thought. The officer too was without any clues, but asked Ariel to keep track of the van. Ariel kick-started his bike and followed the van up to the airport road, until the van vanished from his sight.

21

'Good morning, Mr Almeida. How are you?' He did not think that he would get Charles Almeida that easily over the phone.

'I'm fine, thank you. And how are you?'

'How is your family? Your son?'

'All are doing well. Thank you for your presidential concern.' Almeida did not want to disclose that he had given his consent to Anand.

'When children decide, we parents turn out to be just onlookers. No?'

'Sometimes it is true, Mr President.'

None of them was willing to give out what he had in his mind.

'How is Anand, Mr Almeida?' asked Abdul Lateef.

'Thank you, Mr President. He is doing fine. His hotel business is thriving. He is at present at Kathmandu to review the working of his resort there. It was during the inauguration of that resort that you met him for the first time.'

'Well, things have developed fast and I think we should give our blessings to our children,' said Lateef in one breath.

'Mr President, is it easy to have such political marriages?' asked Almeida, feigning ignorance of what was going on between Anand and Hasina and trying to hide the fact that he had given his consent to Anand.

Abdul Lateef was shocked to hear what Mr Almeida said. *Doesn't he know of their relationship? Is he against it? Is he scheming to avert it somehow?*

'Anyway, thanks for the time you spent on the phone, Mr Almeida. Let things develop to a level when our intervention may be needed,' Abdul Lateef concluded.

Anand was returning from Manali. As soon as his Mercedes-Benz screeched to a halt at his residence, he ran to his father, and said, 'Dad, why do you continue with your pretence? You politicians cannot look straight at truth and call a spade a spade? But there is a limit to this hypocrisy.' He was exasperated that when Abdul Lateef called his father, he (his father) was playing hide and seek. He hadn't let him (President Lateef) know that he had given his consent for his son.

Hasina was with him when Abdul Lateef called Charles Almeida. As soon as Abdul Lateef put down the phone, she called up Anand to say what she overheard. She was wondering whether their marriage would ever take place, if this was the attitude of his father.

'Don't worry, darling,' Anand told her. His father was a politician. Politicians have to act; they are real dramatists. They think they should act also in real life. They are reluctant to face realities, and accept them as they are.

'I shall talk to him as soon as I am home,' Anand assured her.

'I am not worried. But I have to call him Dad in the near future. So I should know what goes on in his mind and what type of person he is. That is all.'

'Actually, Hasina dear, my dad is a very simple person, very nice and friendly. You will like him the day you meet him. Despite the pretences and the urge to act, he is in the core of his heart a very likable person. I am sure once you come to know him, you will adore him, the way I do.'

'I have no doubt about that. Let us hope for the best. By the way, how was your trip to Manali? How is the hotel doing there?'

'Everything goes as per script. Fantastic results. Everything functions perfectly. The team is excellent. I can fully trust them.'

He wanted to meet his father without further delay. He came out of the airport terminal and boarded his Mercedes-Benz. Unlike previously, Anand was preoccupied and silent throughout the half-hour journey to his residence.

'Well, my son, when President Abdul Lateef called and spoke about your marriage, I was totally surprised. So I had to give myself some more time to choose the correct words and to decide the correct course of action.'

'But you could at least tell him that you would talk to me and then get back to him. Instead, you asked him whether it was easy to have such political marriages, as if it won't work out.'

'I did not mean that. You know that I approve of your relationship with Hasina and that I like her. Because of that, I begin also to like Abdul Lateef. But think of my political persona. I was his enemy number one till now. So it is not easy to do away with that mask so easily and so quickly. But don't worry, I will call him right away.'

Charles Almeida dialled up Abdul Lateef and informed him of the arrival of Anand from Kathmandu and announced to him formally his intention to let the children get married. Both of them talked for over half an hour about each one's family and also about politics. It was also decided that the marriage of Anand and Hasina could take place at Agra on the evening of the 14th of August after the signing of the treaty at Jaipur. The exact time and location of this historical event was to be a secret between the foursome (Abdul Lateef, Charles Almeida, Hasina, and Anand.). No one else knew of it. It should be, they thought, a very private event. No politicians would be invited; only their closest relations would be invited. Otherwise this historical event would not take place, they thought.

'He, this Abdul Lateef, is really a nice man!' he mused as he put down the phone.

Anand could not control himself. He ran to his dad, hugged him tight, and said, 'I love you, Dad.' He held on to him for a few seconds. *How lucky I am to have such a nice dad!*

The United States is as friendly to Pakistan as to India; at least things have to appear so. It cannot alienate either of them. The Pentagon almost tightly controls the Pakistan military establishment. Almost all the officers in the top echelons of military power in Pakistan have had special military training in the USA during their initial years in the army. Besides, they are recipients of monthly emoluments and occasional largesse of the CIA through the innumerable channels it has. Now that the US foreign policy has become more aggressive after the incidents in the year 2001, the CIA has enough funds and means to manipulate world events to the advantage of the USA.

For the CIA, the prime concern is the USA, its supremacy in the world, its defence productions, and their markets in the whole world. On this depend thousands of US citizens and scientists for their livelihood. The provisions of this giant establishment for largesse towards politicians and political machineries in other countries are incomparable. They give help even to unsuspecting political parties like communist parties; this will help them acquire some sensitive information.

It may be of great interest for the macropolitics of the USA that India and Pakistan are becoming friends. This is what the US administration always says in public and in private. But the reason why the CIA has to be active in the world is for the benefit of US citizens and its nation. Lester Hoffkins, the chief of the Asia and Pacific Desk of the CIA, has massive powers to make decisions and initiate actions. He is responsible only to the president, and sometimes even the president is briefed only post factum. Then the president is left with no other option than to give to the course of action *sanatio a radice*.

'What do you say?' Hoffkins asked his lieutenant, Abrahams Rocco. Rocco could be trusted like a rock. 'As you wish. It is the nation that comes first. Defence is our bread and butter.'

'OK then, here it goes. Tell Mr Francis Sweetwater to contact me this afternoon and book for him a ticket to Baghdad on the night flight under the name Cater Karaberis. He should come here at 6.45 p.m. sharp and shall go straight to the airport. You shall be with him till he takes off. Make sure he goes. Put also Henry Salvatori (under the name Heinrich Pitzen) in the same plane to see what this fucking informer is going to do.

'After boarding the plane, Salvatori should check whether Sweetwater is making phone calls from the plane; if yes, he should immediately call you, and you shall verify where the call of Sweetwater went. Have an eye on the plane till it lands at Baghdad.

'At the same time, Rocco, you should call the retired general Henry Rogers, who enjoys his retired life in his villa (a former palace of Saddam Hussein) at Baghdad. He should send somebody to the Baghdad international airport to keep a watch on Sweetwater.'

Rocco did as Hoffkins said. At 7.25 p.m. sharp, the plane took off, and both the men boarded the plane; none of them made a phone call before landing.

Sweetwater landed safely and Abdulla Ahmasa received him. He told him he was instructed to take him to the house of Asmi Yara, reporter of the *Baghdad Times*.

Sweetwater knocked on the door twice. No response. And then a third time. Then a shrill female voice came from inside. 'I'm coming! Who's that?'

An extremely beautiful figure opened the door. She was presumably taking a shower when he rang the bell. She had the towel around her and had pulled her overalls over it. Sweetwater was at a loss for words. The beauty before him stunned him. He did not know whether to admire her beauty first or to do his mission first.

'I hope you are Asmi Yara?'

'Yes, I am.'

'I still remember your photo in the newspapers when the US army invaded Baghdad in 2003. You were then magnificent. You pointed your finger straight at the US soldier and asked him to quit. Had you no fear then?'

'Well, it is long time back. I did what I should do then. I was young and impetuous. Who could look on such events without saying a word of protest? Well, what can I do for you now?'

'Oh, I forgot my mission actually. I have just to hand over this cover to you.'

'Who gave it to you?'

'Oh, that is unimportant. You could open it and know the secret, if any. It may be a piece of hot news.'

'Well, thank you. You did not say your name.'

'Oh, sorry. I am Cater Karaberis. I'm an American. I will be here in Baghdad for a few weeks.'

'Well, who sends me this cover, if I may ask?'

'Oh, I do not know the fellow. He knocked at my door just like I did here, and handed over this cover to me. He told me to give it to you. He might be somebody big. Before I could ask his name, he was gone.'

'I hope there is no bomb inside!'

'Definitely not.'

'Thank you, Mr Karaberis.'

Without saying another word, he turned back and walked away briskly. He was really sad that he could not spend more time with that beauty.

As soon as Karaberis went, she closed the door, locked it, and went to her table to open the letter. Her heart was pounding. She was very curious. Maybe she was also afraid.

A letter coming from somebody important! Or another attempt on her life? The content should be important.

There was just one A4-size white paper and a cheque for US$5,000. On it was printed in bold: 'Contact immediately Abdul Hameed Malik, and give him the information written in the next paragraph.' It was not the first time that she received such information from secret service people.

She dressed up quickly, put on her parda and went into her car. She briskly drove through the maze of streets and lanes and stopped her car in front of a dilapidated house, and slid the letter under the door, into the courtyard. She was not supposed to knock at the door nor try to meet Abdul Hameed Malik. If needed, he would call her or meet her. That was the agreed arrangement between the two.

The next paragraph in that letter said, 'Inform the Kashmir Revolutionary Party, Kashmir Liberation Union, and United Kashmir Party that Pakistan is preparing to give up its claim on the Kashmir occupied by Indians. The actual line of control is going to become the international border. For more information, contact me through the agreed route as soon as possible.'

The signature was in Arabic. After the signature, there was a code number.

Abdul Hameed Malik knew the signature. The secret code after the signature told him who exactly was sending him this message.

Officially, Abdul Hameed Malik was the chief negotiator of many terrorist outfits around the world. It was his duty to get the required military hardware for these groups from anywhere in the world. His main personal interest in this war of attrition was his arms deals with the Yugoslav republics. In actual fact, he was known as the chief of the United Kashmir Party, and was loved by all terrorist outfits because of his financial clout and his ability to procure arms for the groups. His connections to important people were known. He was one of the richest Kashmiris in the world. Think of the money he accumulated through arms deal. He was disturbed that his interests would be in jeopardy if Pakistan was going to be soft on India. The CIA kept track of his moves through a number of special intelligence networks.

Formerly he could rely on the Taliban. They were ruthless and would give any help needed for the Muslim cause, but now they seemed to be shattered. Iraq was another source, and it fell too. Pakistan could be the only country that could give some cover and some secret assistance. If Pakistan was soft, then the whole military strategy of the freedom struggle and the personal interests of Malik would fall flat; this was the line of argumentation of Malik.

This piece of information would create hectic consultation among the Kashmiri militant groups. They might agree to make a concerted effort, despite all the difference of opinion and methodology, to thwart any move to placate India. They had a good network of agents and militants, who were ready to sacrifice anything for their leadership. Malik took his satellite phone and dialled a number in Lahore. He told his man at Lahore about this piece of information and asked him to make a very extensive search to verify the information.

Malik was desperate. He made a call to the Serbian arms dealer Yuran Milosevic.

'Milosevic, it is very urgent. We need some hardware for our operations. We need the usual things. Money, you know, is not a problem. Tell me, how and when can you deliver them to us?'

'You did not specify your needs. If you can send your boy here, I can show him some of the beautiful pieces that we have inherited from the erstwhile Soviet Union. It is in the possession of our army, but it can be purchased if adequate money is there.'

'I know. I am sending Mohammed Danladi, the Nigerian lawyer, to you. He will tell you what we want. He is my man. He will give you a number; if it tallies with the number I give you now, you can trust him.'

'But if he gives me a wrong number, what should I do? You remember the case of the Afghan Ahmed Abdulla Bin Farhani, who approached me in your name last December?'

'You remember what we did to him?' asked Malik.

'Of course.'

'So in this case too, follow the same routine. Eliminate him the way you did Farhani, then and there. He knows more than he should. If he shifts stand now, it will be suicidal for you and for me.'

'If Mohammed Danladi is not trustworthy, you should call Abdulla Qussai in Amman and tell him what happened. He will contact me and I shall tell you what to do next.'

'At any rate, within the next fifteen days we need some nice pieces of hardware for our operations on the eastern front. It is most urgent. This is a life-and-death operation. We have to win, inshallah.'

22

Hasina was used to the Western style of life and table manners.

'Butler, please bring me another fork.' She did not like the one set on the table.

The butler dressed in English style, today in an immaculately pressed white shirt, white pants, and white coat, walked in style to the kitchen, took another fork, placed it on his small tray, and brought it to her left-hand side. Politely he bowed 15 degrees and reverently said, 'Madam, the fork.' Gracefully she took the fork, and he bowed again and went back to the kitchen door and dutifully waited for further orders.

She gracefully took the fork and started working on her breakfast. She took one slice of bread, placed it on her plate. Butter was ready in its tray, soft at room temperature; the butler had taken it out from the fridge one hour before breakfast time and placed it on its appropriate place on the table. She took the knife, took some butter, and smeared it lightly on the slice of bread. Then she placed two thin slices of ham on the bread, then placed another slice of bread and cut the sandwich from corner to corner, took one piece of it, and started eating it.

Then she poured coffee into her cup, put two cubes of sugar into it and a little milk, stirred it, and took a sip of coffee. Then she worked on her sandwich.

This morning, her dad was not there; he had to meet the foreign minister of Saudi Arabia. He left home at 7 a.m., would have breakfast with the foreign minister.

Most of the days were like this. Since her mother's death a few years back, she had always had breakfast alone. She would sit in the dining room, facing the window open to the sprawling green garden, with innumerable sorts of exotic trees, plants, and flowers. The gentle breeze of the morning gave her refreshing positive energy.

She finished her breakfast, placed the fork and knife and teaspoon properly on the plate, pushed the plate three inches forward, and stood up. A stack of newspapers and magazines was laid out on the table in the spacious beautifully decorated sit out. Along the walls hang large oil paintings of world-famous artists, including one by M. F. Husain.

She was dressed in the white-and-violet gown which dragged on the floor, giving exceptional beauty and elegance to her moves. She sat at the table to read the newspapers laid out systematically in alphabetical order. Setting aside every one, she went down to T and took the *Times of India*. Since last night, she was thinking of Anand and his project.

Last night she couldn't sleep. His image, his stature, his beautiful, attractive eyes were beckoning her. His soft voice, mature words, occasional looks sideways, his elegant dress . . . everything about him came vividly into her mind, flooding it with memories, unforgettable memories, and sensuous feelings. She turned to the window side, closed her eyes, and tried to ease into sleep. From nowhere, his figure stood there behind the window curtain. ... What was he doing here? He slowly moved the curtain to the side, and called out 'Hasinaaa!' The melodious voice released a spring of emotions in her and she quickly stood up, just to realize that she was alone in her room.

Disappointed at her folly, she went back to the side table, took the mobile phone, and called Anand. 'Hey, Hasina, why, you are still awake?'

'Ya, still awake. Just memories about you. So I thought I should call you.'

'That's nice of you.'

'Where are you?'

'Home. During the day, I had a fight with my dad.'

'Why do you fight with him always?'

'It was about you?'

'He is still apprehensive of the consequences?'

'Yes, something like that. But I prevailed over him. He had no real arguments.'

'And finally, what did he say?'

'To forget you, like a foolish unrealizable dream,' he said.

'Dreams do come true, Dad.' I concluded the sitting.

'That may be true. But you have work for it.' So said he in conclusion, and he stood up, gave me a tight hug (which he never does normally) with a smile of inner approval. I did not leave the hold for a moment longer, to let my happiness sink in.'

'Oh!'

'What, oh. It means that he says it without saying it. It is the language of politics and diplomacy.'

'Ya, that's nice to hear. Your dad is really a great lovable person.'

'So is your dad too. Great and lovable. You remember, unknowingly he called me "my son". Do you still remember that?'

'Yes, he was saying it without saying—language of politics.' Both of them burst out laughing in the middle of the night.

As she laughed aloud, the *Times of India* slipped out of her hands; she tried to catch it, and woke up to the fact that she was about to read the newspapers after breakfast!

She moved the chair a bit from the table and lowered herself into it, and spread the newspaper to read. On the front page in six-column bold letters was the news '6 terrorists shot down'. She knew it, and it was about a border clash along Kashmir. And on the right-hand corner stood the quarter-page advertisement for Manali International Hotel of Anand. She was wondering why he didn't mention it yesterday. She thought of calling and chiding him for not telling her about the new advertisement. Not now. He told her yesterday that he would be going to Mumbai in the morning; he must be on the plane now. She went ahead scanning through the papers and magazines.

Malik took his satellite phone and called Ahmed bin Abdulla bin Habeebi, the key figure in all subversive activities in the mid-Asian region.

Abdulla was perturbed by the unexpected call. He called his close associate Omar bin Habeebullah Mohammed and asked him to come straightaway to his house for an urgent meeting. Both of them discussed the matter, weighed all the pros and cons, and decided to go to Jalalabad near Khyber

Pass, in order to inform the jihad groups there about the development and to decide on the course of action.

Instruction went out to all jihad groups that activities had to be increased, that operations directed at Kashmir should be tightened, and that a new front had to be opened on the western front of India with the help of friends. Clearer instructions would be given within a few days, as to the exact course of action to be followed.

Information for increased activity was sent also to other operatives in the other parts of India and around India. A big concerted offensive was required. The offensive should shatter all hopes of a reconciliation and normalization between India and Pakistan.

In the multi-pronged action targets should be the big Hindu temples at Varanasi, Madhura, Kolkata, Ahmedabad, Mumbai, Varanasi, Nagpur, Lucknow, Patna, Surat, Coimbatore, Chennai, Old Delhi, Hyderabad, Bangalore, and Trivandrum. For the first step, the operatives were instructed to select the targets now, and directives would be given as to how and when the operation would have to be done. The result of the strikes was clear. Communal fights should erupt in those cities and should slowly spread to other parts of the country, and should grow into a big conflagration.

The Indian government and its agencies, especially the IB, were appalled at the sudden spurt of terrorist activities. Many of the intercepted telephone calls were foreboding catastrophe. Prime Minister Loknath Singh asked the home minister to alert central intelligence agencies and their state counterparts to watch out. States came up with suggestions, and the central forces were deployed in all possible trouble spots at the request of state governments. The Rapid Action Force was fully deployed in sensitive areas.

The investigative teams came upon a first decisive clue when a terrorist, Chinthamani Bhrammasivan, was nabbed at Coimbatore. Continuous interrogation revealed his strong links to the erstwhile LTTE and its underground operatives. A number of his associates were nabbed from different parts of the country. Further questioning by the investigative agencies was carried out. Even high-handed methods were employed. The result was amazing.

The series of blasts on the first day and the series of blasts on the second day were to be organized. and carried out by a breakaway group of the former LTTE group and its associates. The key organizer Aruvi Ponnusamy was nabbed from his hideout in the suburb of Rameswaram.

Police raided his hideout, and two of his associates committed suicide, consuming cyanide when they were caught. A large quantity of raw materials for the manufacture of country bombs was recovered from his residence, and other locations occupied by him. Sophisticated communication instruments were also recovered. His mobile phones revealed the numbers of many of the culprits in other parts of the country. A few phone calls were made to Jaffna. The numbers in Jaffna are being investigated. At least fourteen calls were made to the Santhi Path area of New Delhi. The numbers in Delhi are kept as a closely guarded secret.

There was a big news splash in all the newspapers, on the front page with eight-column headlines about the proposed terrorist activities throughout India. TV channels were continuously keeping the tempo through revelations and conjectures and 'learned' opinion of 'knowledgeable' experts.

There was a big uproar in the Parliament and in the state assemblies across the country over the leaked reports of probable terrorist strikes in many parts of the country. The central government made a statement in the Lok Sabha and Rajya Sabha, detailing the result of investigations so far. The statement made clear that certain details couldn't be divulged because it would jeopardize the ongoing investigation and other sensitive national interests. Loknath Singh, Charles Almeida, and the opposition leader, as well as the top officials of RAW, CBI, and IB knew about these details. Clear instructions were given by Loknath Singh to these people that this secret information should in no circumstance go beyond this limited circle.

23

Abdul Lateef called a meeting of the religious leaders of the country and had a heart-to-heart talk. The religious leaders saw the wisdom of having peace in the region; they saw the immense possibility to collaborate with their brethren in India, who were more than 140 million in number. A consensus was arrived at that terrorist and violent movements would not be encouraged. After the meeting, Lateef rebuked the religious fundamentalists who were calling for jihad against India. The terrorists' groups that were disobeying had been brought under strict military control.

Given the peace-loving situation in Pakistan, the terrorist activities moved their base to the Afghan territory. Ahmed bin Abdulla bin Habeebi understood that Abdul Lateef was going ahead with the peace proposal between India and Pakistan. The best occasion to eliminate him was his trip to Agra for the marriage of his daughter Hasina to Anand.

He organized four separate suicide squads for the Agra operation. He mused, 'At one stroke, all the important leaders of both the countries will be finished. Loknath Singh, Charles Almeida, opposition leader, leaders of main political parties, and the top brass of the military establishments, Abdul Lateef and his generals as well as governors.' He was exuberant of the ghastly outcome of the operation.

245

The marriage should not take place. The signing of the treaty should not take place. If it happened, it would be the biggest tragedy of the century for his group and for himself! The haughtiness of Abdul Lateef in prohibiting the activities of Afghan mercenaries inside Pakistan was simply not acceptable!

Ahmed bin Abdulla bin Habeebi contacted Aruvi Ponnusamy for assistance. Ponnusamy had become cautious after years of fighting and hiding. The fact that he was not more than forty years old had begun to say volumes about his reaction to events in world politics. He did not think that this would be a trap into which his lifelong plan would fall.

'Well, we are willing to co-operate in anything to make India look small. They sent military against us under the sweet name Peace Force. They thought that they could establish peace in Sri Lanka by eliminating the Tamils. They were wrong. We are looking for every occasion to humiliate India,' said Ponnusamy.

'I shall send my envoy to Jaffna. The time and place will be communicated to you within the next ten days,' said Ahmed bin Abdulla bin Habeebi.

'But I have my own conditions. They have to be safeguarded,' quipped Ponnusamy.

'Definitely,' said Habeebi.

Ahmed bin Abdulla bin Habeebi started planning. He sent his trusted lieutenant Abu Sadique Anwar to Tajikistan, and Abu Sayyed Geelani to Uzbekistan. What he needed were the handheld multiple rocket launchers. He needed 200 of them. Perhaps they could deliver two rockets at a time. Money was not a problem. His numbered account in the Swiss banks was doing its job as per his instructions.

General Ubaid of Tajikistan was hard-pressed for money. His military was in bad shape. He could not afford to pay the salary in time. The government had given him blanket permission to sell military hardware or know-how for hard currency payments. 'Sell them in the open market or in the black one; hard currency is what we need.'

He had also a secret weapon: a crude version of a cruise missile, developed from the blueprint he had hidden away during the upheaval and collapse of the Soviet Union.

Ahmed bin Abdulla bin Habeebi advised his associates to use any amount of dummy plans to divert attention from the main plan. For this, they were advised to bomb and/or to organize small attacks on military installations in Srinagar, Anandnag, Baramula, etc. in the Kashmir region. This should be done two days before the Independence Day bash of August 15. After the bomb attacks, the concerned persons should give phone messages to important newspapers that the presidential palace would be the next target, and that the Independence Day parade would be disrupted.

He advised another team to target some locations in New Delhi, Gurgaon, etc.

The Al-Samoud 2 missiles reached the Afghanistan border a few months back. It was a handiwork of perfection. They had seen similar missiles in Afghanistan before the US attack in Afghanistan.

Now these missiles were added to the arsenal through the friends of Abdul Malik in the former Yugoslavia. Now the task was to bring these to the destination for the operation on 14th August. Habeebi had a plan for this difficult task.

First they dismantled the four missiles completely, marked every part carefully, packed everything perfectly, and sent them through the thousands of 'refugees' who were fleeing from Afghanistan into Pakistan. Each one carried just one or two pieces at a time. The deluge of 'refugees' transported all the stuff in a matter of days.

When all the pieces arrived at the collection point, they were checked and rechecked to make sure that all the parts are there. Then started the second leg of the transportation, over ponies and lorries filled with hay.

At Mmahwa, the lorry turned to the right in the direction of the village of Hindaun. At Hindaun, the small hillock was ideal for their hideout. Everybody in the camps was anxiously waiting for the signals from the commander Habeebi.

The way to its destination was arduous and dangerous. From Kandahar, the trail went to Spin Boldak. From there, they did not take the obvious and better route to Quetta. Instead they went south to Magzai Bedawan, and went along the Pishin Lora River, crossed over to Burj, and from there, they came to the destined camp in Quetta. This was the second checking point. Each component had to pass through the security check at this secret camp just outside Quetta. Abdulla had put his security agents at all vital places. Once each component arrived, its number was noted, and the 'refugee' was asked to go further.

From Quetta, the transport vehicles (lorries) proceeded to the Bolan Pass, and from there to Sibi and Jacobabad. The journey in this area was easier, because it was all plain land. From Jacobabad, they crossed to Shikarpur and from there to the security checkpoint at Sukkur. Just outside the city, the security agent was waiting for each of the carrier 'refugees'. At Sukkur, only these security agents knew where the 'refugees' exactly had to go.

From Sukkur, they had to travel north to Rahmiyar Khan, from there to Khairpur. From Khairpur, they travelled south along the plain to Khairgarh. The open wheat fields were a blessing for them. They could tread along the rough roads the farmers had built for agriculture. And the farmers were kind towards the unlucky 'refugees' fleeing from Afghanistan. Food and shelter was no problem. The hospitality of that region was a boon to the 'refugees'.

From Khairgarh, they went east to the destinations. One group, as per the strict direction of the commanders, went to Nawaskot and the other group went to Bukanpur. The Nawaskot group had with them the parts of Al-Samoud and Taepodong missiles, and the Bukanpur group had the parts of the Igor-II version of the SA-20 Russian missiles.

By the grace of Allah, all the parts of the missiles reached the two destinations intact, though the trek took them almost four months. The day the last pieces arrived, Abdul Hameed Malik imposed on himself a day of prayer and fasting in thanksgiving to Allah. It was not an easy job to transport such delicate parts of a missile, and without losing any piece on the way. It was almost a wonder, which only Allah can accomplish.

Now that all the parts had arrived, engineer Habeebullah Muthuvakkil and his three assistants who arrived at the scene as 'refugees' in rags started working day and night to assemble the missiles. It took them twenty-six days to complete the assembly of the four missiles.

The base for the rocket launch was ready. And people required for the operation were in place. Malik had real reason to be happy and to celebrate.

But he was not a type who is interested in celebrating. He wanted only to do the job, the job of Allah, which means annihilation of all the infidels from the face of this earth.

Both Nawaskot and Bukanpur were strategically important. A few trees that stood here and there in the expansive wheat fields gave the refugees enough camouflage, and also solitude.

Both the places were some fifty kilometres away from the Indian border along Rajasthan. Both the places were within the 500-km distance to Delhi and Agra. This was the strategic location for any serious missile operation against the targets of Delhi and Agra.

Underneath it was all activity. The missiles have a range of 500 km. Delhi and Agra came within the clear range of these missiles. And these would hit the targets with utmost precision. This is at least what the Yugoslav dealer had promised them.

The trench was perfect. The underground silo could not be seen from any vantage point. On the outside, it looked like a small hut. People came and went out of it in rags and looked like poor peasants or unlucky refugees.

The scattered hillocks in the region were an ideal place for Abdul Malik. He liked the place on his first visit itself some six months back. He posted his trusted lieutenant Ahmed Badun to look after the affairs there. Ahmed Badun looked like a real Pathan worker with bony figure and large build-up. He would never say he was tired. He worked like a machine. He had kept continuous contact with Malik with the help of his satellite phone. Without this equipment, he could not have kept close contact with his men along the pony route.

In five months, his workers created a perfect missile silo there, and a tunnel to the site of the Taepodong missiles one kilometre away.

The Taepodong missiles were imported from North Korea with the help of Abdul Malik's friends. The dreaded Taepodong missile has a range of 900 km. From this border silo, many important places in India, like Delhi, Agra, Jaipur, Bhopal, Baroda, Chandigarh, and Shimla come within the range of this missile. Not even the Pakistan military had this missile. The Pakistan government is bound by certain agreements with India and the international community. But the terrorist outfits are not bound by any of them. So they have a free hand and the arms dealers are happy about the situation.

The launch pad of Taepodong missiles too was ready.

Since the beginning of this year, the Indian satellite Insat-2G, which was sent into orbit just last year, had noticed small but regular traffic along the Bahawalpur plateau. The images were handed over to the RAW. The strategic analysts of the RAW did not find anything harmful or dangerous in the pictures. Mostly ponies and trucks were going this route, often with hay and firewood, and hence were not given the attention they deserved.

Now that the important function was going to be held at Agra, there were more serious reconnaissance operations and within the entire 1,000-km range.

Ahmed bin Abdulla bin Habeebi contacted Ahmed Afzal Noorudeen in Rassal Khaima and asked him to fly down to Bangalore to co-ordinate the southern states. Noorudeen hailed from Karnataka and was the key figure in terrorist operations in the southern region of India.

Noorudeen was based in Oman. He had business concerns there. He was dealing in the import and export of fresh vegetables and other food products. From Kerala, he imported rice and fresh vegetables, and exported consumer electronic goods. Together with the exports, he had cleverly managed to smuggle into Kerala vital chemicals and electronic gadgets required for building miniature bombs.

Baiju Kottar was his right-hand man. He was a timid fellow. But he would do anything for money, and Noorudeen had plenty of it. Noorudeen was always a good friend; he had even arranged a trip for Baiju and family to Oman. The trip cemented their friendship still further. Baiju had never seen such abundance of consumer goods in his life. He enjoyed the two weeks of hospitality and in return he pledged to help Noorudeen in his business. Slowly he was introduced into the shady deals and treacherous designs of Noorudeen. By that time, Baiju had no other way than to co-operate with Noorudeen.

Noorudeen had amassed enough materials to fabricate five powerful bombs, which could blow up massive buildings. The targets were none other than the Sree Padmanabha

Swami temple at Trivandrum, Sri Krishna Temple at Guruvayoor, the Holy of Holies at Sabarimala, Vaikom Subramania Temple, and the Ettumanoor Shiva Kshetram.

The bombs were in place by the end of July. They were stored in the rented building at Vattiyurkavu. Baiju Kottar, with his operatives, was waiting for orders from Noorudeen.

The frequent visits of Noorudeen to Kerala through the Chennai and Nedumbassery airports had alerted the Kerala police about his movements. Mr Asokan Nair, a sub-inspector in the CID branch of police, had been closely following his movements within the state; his stay at Mughal Park Hotel, his meetings with local businessmen, the vehicles he used were closely watched. This time, Asokan put up a 24-hour watch on Noorudeen. His regular meetings with Baiju Kottar and his trips with Noorudeen in his Mahindra XUV raised curiosity in Sub-inspector Asokan. They were seen several times going around Cochin City. All these details were reported to SP Sukumaran, who was heading the antiterrorist operations in the state.

Sukumaran told Asokan to inform him immediately of any suspicious moves by the duo.

Nadeem Baig made a phone call to Musalampetti Senthil Paramasivan, the breakaway Sri Lankan terrorist contact in Chennai, and fixed up an appointment with him for next Friday. The discussion was fruitful. Full co-operation from his cadres in the southern state of Tamil Nadu was assured.

The 'fishing boats' from Jafna arrived in time with the materials. They stayed in the sea till 2 a.m., and when they received the signals from the beach, they started moving onto the beach. Thirty youngsters were waiting for them ashore. These boys had extensive training in handling explosives and complicated AK-47s.

The cargo was released and was immediately taken in lorries and trucks to an unknown destination. There were 150 AK-47s with enough munitions, and an unspecified number of hand grenades and 20 handheld rocket launchers with enough munitions to blow off any important building within seconds.

The goods were transported to a packing hall at Vadapalani where a rented container was waiting. The whole lot was loaded onto the container. The boys were blindfolded and taken to a flat nearby, where Sundaranar gave them detailed instructions about how to behave during the next four weeks. In the thick of the night, they were taken into a waiting bus. They did not know where they were going. The bus finally reached Madurai.

All of them were offloaded into the three flats rented in the fifteen-storeyed Meenakshi Towers near the Madurai Meenakshi Temple. The windows were all darkened with black films. They would be served food at appropriate hours, and they were psychologically prepared to go into action in a very vital strategic operation. The boys were only thrilled to do something 'worthwhile'. They were paid Rupees 5,000 each before they were recruited. Their parents were immensely thankful to Senthil Paramasivan's man that he gave such a huge amount for a work of one month.

All the weapons were transported to their flats and were kept ready.

Senthil Paramasivan received the call from Nadeem Baig that evening. He was told that his operation had to take place on the 12th August at 8 a.m. That was exactly forty-eight hours before the historic treaty was going to be signed between India and Pakistan at Jaipur, and thereafter the wedding of the century was going to take place at Agra. Sundaranar was not aware of the connection with this event. He was just told to give a helping hand to do one operation, namely to destroy with one mighty strike the Meenakshi Temple. The rockets and bombs in their possession were enough for that.

If he did this work, there was a promise from Malik that his people would get cash or arms and ammunition worth US$5 million, five days after the terrorist strikes. It would be delivered at Jaffna, or off the Rameshwaram coast. Sundaranar got the firm assurance for this, which he communicated to Paramasivan's assistant Anandan.

Paramasivan was but quite unaware that the sleuths of DGP Wellington Devar were following him. His clever anti-insurgent unit got the entire message Sundaranar got. They knew the consequence of the action that was going to be undertaken by the gang. Wellington had enough information to set in motion his loyal antiterrorist task force, which helped him gun down the notorious forest pirate Veerapandi.

The task force under the leadership of Muthukrishnan was ready near the Meenakshi Towers, to foil the attempts of the gang. At the instruction of Devar, Operation Island would take place as they had meticulously planned.

Mohammood Jalani was entrusted with the work on the north-eastern area of India. Jalani phoned the key leader of the Myanmar insurgents along the north-eastern borders to India and asked for help. The Anawrahthy activists would be the ideal players. They would receive adequate munitions within the next few days, and have to wait along the border areas of Myanmar. Despite the combing operations of the Myanmar army recently, enough Anawrahthy activists had taken refuge in the deep jungles and co-operated with the jihadist operatives and Jalani. At the order of Mr Jalani, they would cross over to India in the second week of August. Two groups were ready—one would blow up the Kali Temple at Kolkata and the other group would concentrate on Mother Teresa Street and create enough of a bomb scare on the crowded street.

24

IB gets news of increased terrorist movements throughout India. Enough information was coming in to say that something massive was going to happen within the next few days or weeks. The RAW and IB had informed all the states about the importance of this year's independence celebration and about some important function which would be held at Agra on the previous day.

Each state was asked to double the number of plain-clothes policemen. They were sent out into the field to get information about any and every suspicious operation. All the information was to be sent to RAW New Delhi immediately through fax or secret email routes.

There were plans meant for political parties to make demonstrations against the USA and Israel embassies. The Coca-Cola factory distribution vans should be destroyed. Pepsi Company should be assaulted. A large demonstration before the American Embassy also was on the list.

When the terrorists are caught, the picture becomes different. It was Ahmed bin Abdulla bin Habeebi who was doing all these activities with the help of willing Indians, in which Hindus and Muslims were equally involved.

Two suicide squads skipped the attention of the CIDs. They planned a rocket launch on the Taj Mahal, President's Palace, the Parliament building, and Jaipur Hawa Mahal.

The timely intervention of the RAW sleuths got hold of the terrorists at the last moment as they were readying their rockets to target the Taj Mahal, the President's Palace, the Parliament building, and the Supreme Court buildings. The rockets and bombs were recovered and neutralized.

Simultaneously jihadists were aiming for the life of Gen. Abdul Lateef, which was unearthed by the CIA sleuths.

The real big bang came from Trivandrum. The task force of the superintendent of police, Mr Sukumaran, had on August 10 captured the vehicle of Mr Baiju Kottar, while he was going along the NH 47. The Highway Patrol unit noticed the excessive speed of the vehicle and suspicious moves of the passengers; it relayed information to the police stations at Kayamkulam and Chavara. The police of Kayamkulam were waiting just before Al-Ammen College to get hold of the vehicle of Mr Kottar. As soon as the vehicle entered their territory, the police followed the Mahindra XUV vehicle. Just before the police station, Sub-inspector Rajan Pillai radioed to his colleagues in the other waiting jeep to block the vehicle. The waiting policemen signalled to the Mahindra XUV to stop. Mr Kottar was driving. When he saw the signal, he was perturbed a bit. Coolly he slowed down as if to stop. And when the police moved to the side of his vehicle, he put his foot firmly on the pedal and gave gas full throttle and sped away in unusual speed. Immediately, alert information went to the police stations at Chavara, Neendakara, and Kollam as well as to the police superintendent at Kollam, who informed Mr Sukumaran of the incident. Sukumaran immediately knew who could be in the vehicle, and asked the superintendent to get hold of the vehicle at any cost and keep the passengers in safe custody. Several check posts were ready to catch the vehicle. Finally they were nabbed before the Neendakara Bridge.

The fall of Noorudeen into the hands of the police was a terrible shock to the whole organization. But up to now, Noorudeen had not given out any secrets, despite the third-degree methods of interrogations.

Baiju Kottar and Noorudeen were kept in separate locations. Neither of them knew what was happening to the other.

After three days of interrogation, Baiju Kottar began to open up. He told the police everything that had happened between him and Noorudeen. Police offered him pecuniary benefits and safe anonymous life. He did not want to be persecuted. He reached an agreement with the investigating officer—a quid pro quo. If he was not persecuted and set free after the interrogations, he would narrate all that he knew. Now that Noorudeen was in the custody of the police, Baiju did not have anything to fear from him in the near future! Baiju had always been a very pragmatic young man and cared little for keeping his word. His own life and luxury were important for him. For this he was always ready to cheat anybody and make compromises.

Once Baiju opened his mouth, it was easy for the investigating officers to get more and more details from Noorudeen as well. Noorudeen finally gave out the names of persons involved in the operations and the exact locations in Coimbatore, Chennai, Thiruchirappally, Trivandrum, Cochin, Calicut, Mangalore, Davangere, Belgaum, Kolkata, where some sort of action was planned. Sukumaran now knew even Noorudeen's contacts in Dubai and Afghanistan and Pakistan.

He had given strict instructions to his lieutenants not to say anything about the investigations to the media or even to any other police officials without his express instruction. He knew that he was on to something big and unimaginable. This was going to be the strike of the century. He was going to become known all over India. His fidelity to duty and love for the country had always spurred him to take up difficult and complicated assignments. Now he was going to have the catch of the century.

Sukumaran could trust the chief of RAW like a father. Sukumaran had the fortune to get three-month training under Alan Robeiro at New Delhi. When Robeiro was promoted as RAW chief, Sukukaran was summoned to Delhi for a special sensitive operation at Mumbai. Since then Sukumaran had direct access to Robeiro.

'Yes, Robeiro here.'

'Sir, this is Suku, Sukumaran from Trivandrum.'

'What is the matter, Suku? Are you in charge of Operation Island? If yes, you have always direct access to me. Give me information whenever you feel you are on to something important.'

'Now I have something very important.'

'That is?'

'It's regarding one Noorudeen. He has links to militant group Lashkar-e-Afghan. He is their co-ordinating operative here in South India.'

'You have booked him?'

'Yes, sir. He is in safe custody. They are into something big. The whole Lashkar group and their associates in India have an extensive plan to carry out something big on the 14th of August this year. Targets are Delhi, Agra, and/or other western cities. You will do well to notify the army and ask them to intensify their surveillance of the border areas.'

'Thank you, Suku. I understand the importance. I think what you said is important and useful. If you can, come over to New Delhi tomorrow itself. I need to know the full details from you personally.'

Robeiro had a good and cordial relationship with the army chief Gen. C. D. Chatterjee. Chatterjee asked Robeiro to meet him at his residence in the evening.

Robeiro spent thirty minutes with Chatterjee over a glass of Heineken beer, and impressed on him the importance of putting increased surveillance on the western border.

'You know, sir, the crucial agreement between India and Pakistan is going to be signed on the 14th of August. And the enemies will try to thwart it at any cost. The powers on the opposite side are big players.'

'I know the importance of it, Mr Robeiro. We shall do whatever is required.'

'Thank you, general.'

'Bye, Mr Robeiro.'

Chatterjee was a man of action. He grasped things fast, and an action plan would immediately materialize. He ordered immediate movement of additional troops along the Rajasthan border. He called up Air Marshal Virendra Patil and apprised him of the situation.

'Could you perhaps ask your boys to intensify the air surveillance along the sensitive border area?'

'Sure. We will call in the service of the Reconnaissance Squadron. The recently launched G-PicSat has a special transponder, which is devoted to our geographic information requirements. We can ask our people to go into more detailed reconnaissance of the area with the help of data supplied by G-PicSat.'

'That is fine, air marshal.'

'You know, general, the G-PicSat is an electronic and communicational superlative which will replace many of our old systems of information gathering.'

General Chatterjee asked his trusted communication specialist General S. B. Gupta to contact squadron leader Capt. Puneeth Sharma to learn more about the exact working of the G-PicSat.

Gupta arrived exactly at 3.45 p.m. at the communication network station of the air force at the Contonment. Capt. Puneeth Sharma was all sweet hospitality. But he was also correct in his manners.

Capt. Puneeth Sharma joined the army after a stint as professor of electronics and telecommunication at Lucknow University. He had a doctorate in electronics and telecommunication from Arlington University in Texas, USA. He liked to be addressed as Dr Sharma, which he told his unwitting guests.

'In fact, General Gupta, I am more an academician than a military man. I am happier when people address me as Dr Sharma.'

'Sure, Dr Sharma. I have heard of your immense knowledge of electronics and communication. You are an asset to the air force of our country.'

Capt. Sharma enjoyed the dose of praise. 'Thank you. I do my duty. I use my knowledge for the country and its safety. In the present age, my subject has become very important, because at present any war is fought on the strength of technology.'

'You are right, Dr Sharma.'

'For information gathering and information channelling, electronics and computers are of immense help. Without the costly and precious engagement of manpower, we can gather information with the help of gadgets like satellites. It should have the capability—that is all.'

The professor in him was awakening. He liked to teach; even when he was talking to his superiors, the persona of a lecturer got into his blood.

'General Gupta, I shall now show you a beautiful piece of satellite technology. Follow me.'

He took General Gupta to the model of the G-PicSat satellite, which was recently launched by India. He was most happy when someone was listening. He wanted to explain to the general even the minute intricacies and capabilities of the satellite.

Dr Sharma was lucky, because General Gupta was a good listener.

'The G-PicSat offers highly accurate, high-resolution images of the earth. Its lenses are very powerful; they are specially designed telescopes with a large field of view, high contrast, and high signal-to-noise ratio. It has a 12-bit dynamic range.'

General Gupta did not understand much. But he understood that this satellite could take very accurate pictures of the earth segments, and he knew that those pictures were of immense strategic value for the armed forces.

'Its high-resolution sensors can capture 2-feet panchromatic (black and white) and 8-feet multispectral (multicolour) images. It offers less-than-2-feet resolution imagery and provides geolocational accuracy. Its imaging footprint is five to fifteen times larger than any other high-resolution satellite. Its on-board data storage system is very large. And its transmission rate is high.'

Dr Sharma looked at General Gupta to make sure that he was listening.

'I'm all ears, Dr Sharma. Every word is interesting. Please carry on.'

'Besides, the satellite is designed for a lifespan of over ten years. It is robust and can withstand the vicissitudes of space. Its capacity to collect images of earth segments is enormous; in a day it captures imagery data of over eighty million square kilometres.

'Its normal swath width is 15 kilometres at nadir. In a single area the imaging is done on 15 × 15 kilometre area. As a strip its images are 15 × 150 kilometres.

'Its multispectral images have the following colour capabilities: blue is 450 to 520 nanometres, green is 520 to 600 nanometres, red is 630 to 690 nanometres, and near-IR is 760 to 960 nanometres.'

'The panchromatic images are black and white with 480 to 820 nanometres.

'With this satellite, we can comb every inch of the earth, and store the data in our huge data storage facility at the ground station, and can be recalled by any client who has access to this highly classified data. And our armed forces are a regular customer.'

'That is why I am here, Dr Sharma. Your knowledge of details is fantastic.' General Gupta broke his silence. But Dr Sharma continued unabated.

'In our modern technological warfare, accurate geographical information and digital imagery are of prime importance. Once you have this information, you can pinpoint your enemy target, and also recognize your own troop and hardware geographic positions, I mean geolocational information.

'With this type of highly accurate and high-resolution imagery, we can easily locate buildings, roads, bridges, vehicles, and other infrastructural installations with sensitive information with sub-metre precision.

'Within three days, the satellite revisits the geolocation again and collects and reassesses imagery data for further precision and accuracy.

'The G-PicSat has an added capability, namely its capacity to send magnetic resonance waves for collecting imagery data and to pinpoint the geolocational position of specified targets, like weapons-grade metal.'

The technological lecture of Dr Sharma was very interesting to General Gupta. He swallowed everything he said, hook, line, and sinker. Dr Sharma on his part enjoyed the role of a teacher. It was quite some time since he had been to a lecture hall. General Gupta had no questions. He was keeping his mind sharp to grasp as much information as possible. He was used to the verbal acrobatics of specialists like Capt. Dr Sharma.

'I hope I have not bored you with such a torrent of information.'

'No. Not at all. Every bit of information you gave was highly educative and useful, and I thank you so much for your patience and comprehensive approach to the matter.'

25

Saying farewell to Capt. Dr Sharma, General Gupta headed for the Air Force headquarters. He now knew all the possibilities there were in the G-PicSat for the air force to pinpoint the geolocational placement of hardware and manpower.

Once he had given all the information to his superiors and to his team, he typed in certain code words to ask the G-PicSat satellite to send magnetic resonance waves to locate metallic hardware and to activate the sensorial devices in the satellite, so as to get even the slightest explosive chemical signals. Magnetic resonance imaging and digital wave imaging were used to locate military hardware and chemical presence. Off went the directive to the reconnaissance satellite in space at about 450-km height in geostationary orbit.

The air corridor triangle between Delhi, Jaipur, and Agra, and the geographical space between the western border and these cities, had become supremely and strategically important now. There could not be any mishap, no lapse in the security of the highest personalities who would be visiting Agra and/or Jaipur and Delhi for the extraordinarily important functions there. This area had to be electronically combed for possible indications.

The images taken by the military transponder in the satellite G-PicSat had shown small but regular traffic along the Bahawalpur plateau. The images were handed over to the RAW. The strategic analysts of the RAW did not find anything harmful or dangerous in the pictures. Mostly ponies and trucks were going this route, often with hay and firewood, and hence were not given the attention they deserved.

Now that some suspicious indications were there, the intensive satellite surveillance was ordered with immediate effect. The G-PicSat continued its mission and regularly sent magnetic resonance waves to locate metallic hardware and activated its sensorial devices to get even the slightest explosive chemical signals.

A squadron of unmanned vehicles (UVs) too were deployed in order to conduct an intensive reconnaissance operation in addition to the service of G-PicSat along the marked sensitive border areas.

The drones were provided with a modified version of the LOROS (long-range observation system) which could clearly see targets up to 16 kilometres. The drones were supposed to fly at 10-km altitude along the border. Both of them were fitted with short-range surveillance radars (SRSR) and long-range thermal magnetic resonance imagers (LRMRI). The SRSR and LRMRI were originally imported from Israel and were now manufactured by Bharat Electronics at its Nagpur plant. The SRSR could pick up clear images from as far as 30 kilometres, whereas the LRMRIs could pick up images from as far away as 45 kilometres, that too with higher resolution and accuracy.

The unmanned vehicle (drone) XYD-14 was making its usual sortie on the evening of the 10th of August when it came across a hotspot near Nawaskot and Bukanpur area almost 45 kilometres from the Rajasthan border.

The three chiefs of staff were informed by the defence minister that the five days from the 10th of August to the 15th were of paramount importance to the nation, and that the air corridor triangle between Delhi, Jaipur, and Agra, and the geographical space between the western border and these cities, had become supremely and strategically important.

Air Marshal Patil ordered a squadron of Mirage 2000 jets to assist him in the operation, and they were in a standby red-alert position for the next five days. The army chief was asked to strengthen the ground patrolling units along the border area, and keep them on red alert.

As soon as XYD-14 spotted the sensitive information at the Nawaskot and Bukanpur area, the information was immediately passed on to the air force surveillance headquarters. Consequently, two additional drones, XYD-15 and XYD-16, were pressed into service in order to reconfirm the findings of XYD-14. Their mission was clear. They had to comb systematically the suspected area around Nawaskot and Bukanpur and report back immediately. Round-the-clock surveillance was ordered and the data collected had to be transmitted to the command centre so the data could be matched with those of the G-PicSat for reconfirmation.

All the three drones confirmed the suspicion of hard heavy and weapons-grade metal presence and presence of chemical signals. But the military analysts were puzzled and could not explain the presence of weapons-grade metal and chemical signals in this godforsaken village area, wheat fields only what you see for miles and miles. There was no precedent of military or terrorist presence there!

The old records of the RAW regarding the area were recalled from the computer; they were compared with the geolocational imagery data supplied by the G-PicSat; the study of all the sources confirmed without a speck of doubt that ponies and lorries were making regular trips to this area. Air Marshal Patil was informed of the finding. By 8.30 p.m., it was clear that some immediate action had to be initiated to contain any possible danger.

'We have to strike before the enemy does it,' Air Marshal Patil told the defence minister over the videoconferencing facility. Both of them arrived at an action plan.

The interrogation of Senthil Paramasivan at Coimbatore, Ahmed Afzal Noorudeen at Trivandrum, and Usalampatti Sundaranar at Chennai all indicated the large-scale involvement of the Lashkar-e-Afghan. It gave also a lot of information regarding the preparations along the LOC. RAW chief Robeiro relayed information to the air chief marshal and army chief intermittently.

At the insistence of the defence minister, an emergency command centre with three chiefs of staff and three generals from each segment of the army was immediately formed.

As a first step, it was decided to reconfirm the information about the hard metal presence and explosive chemical signals at Nawaskot and Bukanpur.

For this, ground reconnaissance was necessary. It would be foolish to send human reconnaissance agents. It was also dangerous. What to do then?

It was decided to seek the advice of General Prakash Malhotra of the Nanotech Detection System (NTDS).

The newly developed Nanotech Detection System was introduced in the military only recently. It was meant to make on-the-spot surveillance on ground. The beetle-shaped surveillance vehicle had the necessary detection system to find explosive devices in the vicinity of 15 metres. They achieve this through the nano-chips embedded in their microelectronic system. If any explosive device was detected, it sent a preprogrammed message to the Nanotech Detection Centre headed by General Malhotra.

Four NTDS were loaded onto the drone XYD-14 and sent to the critical locations. Two of them were meant to Nawaskot and the other two for Bukanpur area. They were guided to the exact location with the help of the GAGAN (GPS-aided geo-augmented navigation), the system which worked with the help of the G-PicSat satellite system.

The G-PicSat satellite would give the drones enough and accurate geographical and geolocational data regarding the target area. The drones equipped with the GAGAN guidance system and NTDSs can achieve 100 per cent accuracy in positioning and striking the target. The GAGAN was built with licence from a US radar and guidance electronics major; it lets the civil and military carriers to get an accurate positional fix anywhere on the earth with the help of special receivers, which accept the GPS signals from the said G-PicSat satellite as well.

From both the locations, explosive presence was detected. Gen. Malhotra communicated the details to the newly formed command centre and immediately an emergency meeting of all the members of the group was called.

General A. M. Raviraj of the Western Command suggested the deployment of the newly introduced BrahMos-III missile. BrahMos-I is a land-to-air version of the Indo-Russian cruise missile system. BrahMos-II is the sea-to-air version. BrahMos-III is the air-to-air and air-to-land version of the same cruise missile system. At this time, the Brahmos-III missile squadron was headquartered at Patiala under him. He said, 'The BrahMos-III with its Mach 3.1 speed and centimetre accuracy can do the job without any flaw. With one big bang, everything will be done within minutes. Before anyone comes to know of it, everything will be over.'

'But that would not be the correct option, taking into consideration the international political impact it would create,' interjected Air Marshal Patil. 'It could be interpreted as a provocative action. Response from Pakistan and the world community could adversely affect our image.'

'There is a point in that. Hence you must remember that the political leadership would not allow the deployment of BrahMos-III against such a target at this point in time. Given the present positive political climate in the Indo-Pak relationship, we should do something that would look innocuous, with less explosive bang, but would really do the job,' opined the army chief.

The head of the newly formed Lagnex Group, General Y. B. Reddy, dissuaded the group from deploying the Brahmos-III missile; instead he suggested deploying the newly introduced LAGNEX (laser-guided nanotube explosives).

He explained the advantages of the system for the current need. The LAGNEX had never been utilised in any warfare. It was too tiny and unobservable. Its impact had its own camouflage. Its impact would not be bigger than that of an artillery gun. But its precision and effectiveness corresponds to the task to be addressed.

The LAGNEX are guided missiles with explosive device. The explosive is built by incorporating the newly developed double-wall nanotubes, which have roughly 200 times the strength of high-carbon steel. Hence they can be as pernicious and devastating as a large traditional bomb. The explosives built with nanotubes have high strength but low weight. The nanochips built into the LAGNEX are capable of storing data that can guide it to its destination.

The explosive system in the LAGNEX developed at the DRDO at Kanjanjunga in Hyderabad has been tried and found reliable for pointed military targets. They are small in size and resemble beetles in shape and size. They can be guided to a particular target area and can be exploded at the command of the controlling station. The LAGNEX are equipped additionally with smell-sensing chips; it is based on the finding that every combination of materials has a particular smell. LAGNEX are enabled to sense weapons-grade steel and alloys. Hence they find their way additionally through the directive of the smell function embedded in their guidance chips.

The drone command was ordered to equip the three drones with the newly developed LAGNEX, and to seek the help of the GAGAN system. The exact positional fix of the target was fed into the nanochip of the twelve LAGNEX which were going to be used for the mission.

In sensitive moments of operation, the drones were directed to fly in formation so that when one of them undertakes the operation, the other two can record the actual operation and its effects at the target. While in flight, all the visual and magnetic information that is gathered by the drones are minutely watched by the command centre. As soon as the target is located, the command centre will release the LAGNEX from the drones to the target. The LAGNEX will follow the digital data fed into their nanochips. They will be guided to the destination with absolute precision.

The XYD-15 was flying above the Nawaskot area. It sensed the suspicious location and command centre could clearly see the image and understand the message. Gen. Y. B. Reddy was personally present at the command centre to monitor and execute the sensitive operation. The information about the presence of weapons-grade hard metal was confirmed at Nawaskot. The target too was clearly visible on the screen. Praying to God Almighty, he started the operation within a split second. First thing he did was to communicate to the unified command centre the critical situation and the course of action he was going to follow. The command centre was alert to the situation and released immediate permission to activate the release of the LAGNEX.

Now the real task started. Gen. Reddy ordered all the three drones into a formation. From 40,000-ft height, the XYD-15 flew down to 10,000 ft. It was nearing its target at Nawaskot. Gen. Reddy was watching the flight on his control radar screen, and as soon as it was exactly above the target area, he pressed the button to release the first of the six LAGNEX. The other five LAGNEX were released at a quarter-second interval.

The LAGNEX flew down like beetles and landed at the target with the help of nanopropulsion device built into them. As soon as all the nanobuster LAGNEX were in place, praying to all the gods once again, Gen. Reddy pressed the command button. All the six LAGNEX exploded simultaneously like a mega-firework.

Simultaneously the same operation was conducted also at the Bukanpur area by Gen. C. K. Nair, the deputy commandant of this operation. The LAGNEX at Bukanpur too functioned properly and exploded at the command and the fireworks started there too.

Ahmed Badun, the local Lashkar-e-Afghan commander, was stupefied. He did not know what was happening around him. There was no reason for him to believe that anybody in the world would know anything about his operation in the godforsaken village Nawaskot and about the Al-Samoud and Taepodong missiles. But all of a sudden from nowhere, this conflagration and hellfire! The simultaneous sky-rending explosions and inferno engulfed them.

The hutment in which Ahmed Badun and his men were resting was smashed and was consumed in the inferno. They could not escape from the wildly spreading fire. 'Quick. All of you get out and run for your life. Somebody has cheated us.' But before his voice could leave him, he was smashed to the ground and consumed by the all-purifying power of fire. His voice too was drowned in the raging fire of the wheat fields.

At Bukanpur, Badun's friend Faizal Toufiq was commanding the two SA-20 missiles and his ten freedom fighters. The 'beetles' and the fire did give them the purification in fire.

Gen. Y. B. Reddy was jubilant. Without much ado, he had done what the Bofors guns and Brahmos missiles would do with a loud bang. 'Now is going to be the era of nanotechnology,' he said jubilantly in his command centre.

TV stations in Pakistan reported a huge fire in the border villages of Nawaskot and Bukanpur. The fire consumed several hectares of wheat fields. Eighteen farmers of the area too lost their lives in the mishap. The TV station could not report of the massive missile build-up nor about the identities of the 'farmers'.

Epilogue

Hasina and Anand boarded the Lahore Express at New Delhi bus station in Darya Ganj. He took out his jacket, loosened his tie, and put it in the overhead locker. Hasina pulled the scarf from her head, folded it neatly, and gave it to Anand to be deposited in the overhead locker.

Their marriage was conducted in the most secret manner as they had always wished. The original plan was to conduct the marriage at the Taj Mahal in Agra. But for security reasons, the marriage was transferred to Jaipur, Rajasthan; the Rajasthani registrar was brought to the guest house, and in his presence, they exchanged the marital rings and flower garland, and put their signatures in the marriage register. There were two witnesses: on the side of Anand, it was Anwar Siddiqui, the son of the former Pakistan high commissioner in India, and from Hasina's side, the witness was Mr Datta, the producer of her music album.

They looked through the window and enjoyed the landscape as the bus started rolling. They chatted about the landscape, the people, their dress and children all along the road to Wagah.

The declaration of the Nepal Treaty on the 14th and 15th was big news. There was only jubilation in both countries. All of a sudden, the tension along the border was gone and people were crossing borders to greet each other.

At Wagah check post, everything went smoothly without the usual bureaucratic delays.

The scenes of the simple marriage ceremony rolled out in Hasina's imagination like a veritable movie in slow motion.

'I liked the dress of the registrar,' said Hasina. 'Do all the Rajasthanis dress up like this?'

'Sure. It is their traditional dress, and they take pride in it.'

'Anand? Can you get one for you? I would say, you should wear it for our wedding party at Islamabad.'

'Why not? I will tell Anwar Siddiqui to bring one for me. He and I are of the same height and size.'

All along, Anand and Hasina were wondering how history is made in such a silent and unobtrusive manner.

As the marriage of Anand and Hassina was taking place at Jaipur, India and Pakistan got married in a most secretive manner; no one knew about it until it was over. The treaty was signed at the Rastrapathi Bhavan, New Delhi.

---⋅⋉⋅---

The Chinese army was making heavy movement of man and machinery along the Indo-Chinese border in Arunachal Pradesh. India was making countermoves too.

After the signing ceremony, Abdul Lateef flew to Beijing to inform the Chinese leadership about the treaty, and also to help cool down the political temperature between India and China. The friendship between Pakistan and China was useful at this juncture!

Loknath Singh phoned Abdul Lateef and thanked him for the good service.

Cyriac Thomas

The author is a seasoned journalist and an experienced educationist. He has widely travelled all over the world. All these have given him detailed knowledge of the political spectrum of India and of the world at large.

Cyriac Thomas was born at Trivandrum, Kerala State, India. He holds a Licentiate degree from Louvain University, Belgium; a Master's degree in Mass Communication, Linguistics and Sociology from the Munster University, West Germany. He worked as News Editor in the daily newspaper "Deepika", a Malayalam language newspaper in Kerala, for a few years. As Chairman of the Institute of Communication and Development he was active in the TV field for over 15 years from 1985 to 2000. Since the year 2000 he turned to education field; was Principal of Carmel Public School, Kochi, of Carmel International School, Alleppey, and from 2013 at Trivandrum as the Principal of Christ Nagar International School, affiliated to Cambridge University, UK. (www.cnis.in). He is author of the book "The Hidden Agenda" (546pp), which was a widely read book, popular among educationists and legal fraternity.

He is a Catholic priest and lives at present at Enath (near Adoor, Kerala) as Principal of Mount Carmel Central School.

Years of experience in the media and in education combined with the power of imagination have given the author the right platform to launch such a beautiful novel.

Printed in the United States
By Bookmasters